Raconteur

Also by B. Kearns

Anicca (Alexander Holt)

And it's slowly burning, it was never cheap

If you seen what I seen, you wouldn't sleep

Take me out L.A.

This place will be the end of me

- Abel Tesfaye (The Weeknd) et al.

Raconteur

B. Kearns

A NOVEL

ISBN-13 978-0-9949375-2-0

Raconteur is a work of fiction. Names, characters, places and incidents are products of the author's imagination, or used fictitiously. Any resemblance to actual events, or locales or persons, living or dead, is entirely coincidental.

Cloudbreak Publishing

Raconteur

CHAPTER ONE

FADE IN

The opening act—when nerves are at an all-time high and the audience is on its toes, wondering if anyone is going to fuck up or vomit. In theater, as in life, everyone has an opening act. If you fuck it up, your real talent shines when you can pretend like you were never even there. And as it goes, some are tempted to "shatter the fourth wall," as we say in theater, while others are tempted to run off of the stage, never to return.

If I were to try to sound pretentious and smart, I would suggest that the Malcolm Gladwells of the world would surely want you to believe that there are socially-determined factors and predispositions that contribute to your ability to keep your composure and achieve a well-received opening act. All the while, the wealthy suits will want you to believe that they have gotten to where they are simply by persevering, regardless of Gladwell's progressive-liberal ideologies. I'm not a Malcolm Gladwell statistic, nor am I a corporate millionaire—I fucking nailed the entry; it's the curtain call that has me on life support.

Luckily for most of the people that I knew in Westfield, where I'm from, their opening acts were simple enough to perform—all they had to do was fight their way out of a vagina to attend to a life-long career as an oil rig worker, a parking enforcement officer, or a professional in the exotic global industry of telemarketing, perhaps. Unfortunately for me, my road was slightly more publicized and demanding.

Goffman once said that "all the world's a stage," and no one else in history has offered up a better description of my life. His theory, as applied to my existence growing up, was both exciting and age-draining, something that would become an eternal performance that involved my dancing on the edge of a sharp, serrated knife for all to see. There was no social escape and certainly no running away if someone like me ever botched up an act in life. This is why right now, from where I'm writing, I am so incredibly and utterly fucked.

Going back to the beginning, I was the result of a male nurse whose love affair with prescription pills and gin was more poignant than his love for his wife. I won't say that this affair was more important to him than his entire family, but that's only because his faith in me kept his dosages down.

My mother was the dean of a local community college, which meant that she had to be a fabulous actor to endure my father's addictive behaviors and the charm that he lavished on other women. As it turned out, her acting skills would one day pave the way for my own, while my father's skills in life remained a constant warning that I would diminish into a lifeless existence if I ever were to stick around Westfield after high school.

To give you a better idea of our family system (as the social workers called it), you could have sat next to my parents at a family dinner and thought that nothing was wrong. While they chatted about their days' work and the cold weather that we suffered through, we looked pretty average. Where you might find concern, however, is if you dropped in for a bowl of popcorn and to watch the weekly pissing matches between my father and me—you would most likely have called child and family services by the end of it.

I always told myself that every artist worth mentioning had a background that included some form of attachment issue built into their early lives—this just happened to be mine.

Yet from the viewpoint of most, everyone in town knew me as the kid who was going to die a happier, wealthier, and more successful person. They knew I would never be the one huddled around some water cooler, trying to convince those around me that my new quad or pickup truck was bigger and better than theirs. I was leaving that future to everyone else around me, simply because my talents in acting meant that I was never going to have to fight in the Westfield war for recognition.

My father had fought in that war for most of his adult life while my mother had spent some time on the east coast of the United States during her post-secondary school years, giving her a bit of insight into my drive to leave the fucking place. She was a woman of faith and my father pretended to be, mainly so she would ignore the benzodiazepine and opioid mixology recipes he would follow when preparing himself a gin and tonic at night. Their relationship was a perfect storm that influenced my progression through life and, most importantly, my sorting out of the meaning of intimacy.

It was July, and school had been out for a few weeks. My friend Joe and I had just re-discovered the novelty of my father's Swedish porno mag collection that he kept in an open trunk in the basement. We were flipping through the abnormally sticky pages on the front lawn next to a hummingbird feeder, passing the photos back and forth with smiles as wide as jesters.

"Hey, fuckin' rights, man, this one's crazy good. You think Mandy's pussy looks like this one?"

"It doesn't. It's better, dude, nice and subtle." I paused. "Pink."

"What the fuck are you talking about, Zach?" Joe laughed. He appeared unsettled, as if he was unsure whether he wanted a response. I knew he'd liked Mandy since grade school and that he desperately wanted to take her out to a movie, dinner, or some romantic shit like that. Joe was the definition of a fucking Simp.

"Don't worry about it, man—miles ahead of you on this shit. We should actually get you a real girl this summer, ya know? I can do that for you, dude; I got you."

Of course, I had never seen Mandy naked. In fact, I had this odd feeling that since we'd broken up years prior, she didn't like me anymore in any capacity. I always seemed to ignore that fact, though, which naturally kept Joe in sexual frustration and erectile purgatory, thinking that I still had a chance with the love of his life.

Joe was an average-looking guy that no one had a strong feeling or opinion about. He typically dressed like me on the weekends, save his affinity for wearing 90s Dock Marten "chunky" shoes and cargo shorts. During the school week, his parents always made sure that he attended to his hygiene and that his baggy, well-pressed khakis matched his private golf club polo shirts and perfect 1990s Johnathan Taylor Thomas haircut.

He wore too much of the cologne that he kept hidden in his locker and never did quite figure out his own style beyond those fucking Dock Marten's.

Joe was the guy to tell girls shit like, "you're just the flavor of the week for that guy, you really deserve better," the guy who never understood why that didn't get *anyone* any women. By contrast, I was the guy Joe usually warned those girls about, despite his ignorance of that fact.

We flipped through a few more sticky magazine pages before we became youthfully desensitized to the images that were imprinting themselves on our minds. We rolled them up and shoved them into the back pockets of our faded, dirty weekend jeans as we dragged our filth into the house.

We entered through the dark-trimmed, 1970s-style doorway, and Joe kicked his faded Doc Marten's into the closet that was filled with sporting gear, dog leashes, single-use tools, and all sorts of other shit that no one ever used. My father and I liked to collect that sort of stuff; my mother hated the clutter.

Our house was straight out of a 1970s home and garden magazine. Brass fixtures were everywhere, along with dark wood paneling and vinyl countertops that my parents always bitched about wanting to replace with marble, if only they had the money. The outside was painted dark brown, and every year, more and more paint was always threatening to peel itself off after the snow had melted come spring. My father was not a handyman, which was unfortunate because our house constantly demanded him to be one. If there was a reason he did so many prescription drugs and drank as much as he did, it was that house.

As we stumbled in, Joe acted polite as he always did and greeted my mother, who was in the kitchen, calmly cooking up some Mediterranean dish for dinner. She smiled meekly through her perfect teeth, pretending like she hadn't noticed the porn mag in my back pocket or Joe's stupid, half-erect dick that was making a lump in his pants. Her disappointment in knowing that the magazine was from my father's own collection and her inability to vocalize any of it was life-draining. For all of us to see, she wore it in the skin that covered her ever-thinning body. Despite her feminist approach to parenting, she never held her own husband to those same standards, something that was obvious to all of the neighbours and her friends. In her own way, I think that she thought that she could protect every girl that I ever showed an interest in, whether it be a one-night stand or a long-term girlfriend, by encouraging me to treat them well. It was an obvious consolation prize for someone who had endured a marriage that left her on the side of a busy freeway with no gaps to break through to the other side. Unfortunately for the women of my world, it was just another of the many battles fought by Dean Monte that was lost. I endured a fleeting moment of empathy after noticing the oppression on my mother's face, which was suddenly met with my own histrionics, my desire to once again take centre stage, and I laughed as I hit Joe in his half-erect dick.

We left my mother alone in the kitchen to finish cooking for us and headed down the short wooden staircase, skipping every second step along the way. The staircase led to a larger, more open room housing an old upright piano, a few music stands, and a big white bedsheet that was pinned to the wall with an old VHS video camera aimed at it. We used this setup to film my rehearsal scenes and any auditions that my parents had paid for while I was developing my fame. We had called this area of the house “the creative art space”—my mother had the idea that this worked to foster creativity in schools, and so she’d assumed that it would work well for her own son. There was some merit to it, I guess.

A big, blocky TV stood in the back corner of the room. My father had spent most of his adult life in front of the thing, half-baked on Valium and engulfed in his favorite *M.A.S.H.* reruns—he was productive enough when he wanted to be, which wasn’t often. His preferred seat was a large, old woven couch, which we now kicked our feet up on while he worked for a change in his back office. We flicked on an episode of *The O.C.* and I began to dream, as I did nearly every day, about my fame and living the life in California as those characters did. It was never a fantasy world to me, as close as I was to theater and the understanding that cameras hid reality in more ways than one. It was all real to me: the set was an actual house, and the palm trees swayed in the real warm air—there was nothing fabricated about the future I saw in front of me every time I watched that show.

My father shouted for us to turn it down from the back room, where he sat at his old Macintosh upright computer, typing up a storm. His irritability at our fucking around meant that he was drifting off his daily opioid and strong French-pressed coffee kick; he usually had the dosing down to a science.

Joe always seemed to like my father, but it was probably because he got to see someone pick on me for a change, though my father’s bullshit didn't always discriminate. Like Joe, he knew I was destined to be a bigger man than he ever was—but unlike Joe, he didn't want to give up the throne.

"Fuck's sake, guys, turn that pre-teen shit down, fuck!"

"Watch this, man." I flicked the TV to *M.A.S.H.*

"Nice try," my father laughed from in front of his computer before the laughter transgressed into irritability again. "Turn it the fuck down!"

Joe and I both began to laugh at my half-high father's anger. If only I knew how close my own trajectory in life was becoming to his, maybe, at least maybe, then I would have made a few different choices along the way.

While as a child my doctor used to put his hands over my heart to determine how full of life that I was, my current one now puts his hands over my liver to measure the amount of love and disappointment that I have endured at the mercy of my decisions. Would I change how things happened? Would I forget about the fame and all that I have accomplished and lost? Absolutely, fucking, not.

CHAPTER TWO

I was an actor, while Joe and my father shared the same full-time career of being my biggest fans. I was the lead in all of the local plays and was the first person in our middle school to kiss a girl on stage in front of all my peers—I was the envy of all of the guys in the locker room when I'd told them how many times I got to rehearse that scene. There was no one at Westfield High who didn't consider me "the kid who was going places." My parents often pretended that they were impartial to my local fame, but something told me that my getting praise from the community was equally as important to them as it was to me. *The famous always live better, more fulfilling lives,* I often thought—and at that age, I was sure as fuck happy to be me.

Despite my busy acting career, I was the captain of both the football and basketball teams and not because I was particularly the best, but because I was a big, tall, handsome motherfucker who recognized the opportunity of capitalizing off of an obese athletics coach who needed someone important in his life. I was also the only kid whose parents coughed up tens of thousands of dollars every summer to send their son to basketball skills camps in the States.

My parents always had a back-up plan for my fame—if it wasn't going to be acting, it was going to be athletics. The skills camps were typically hosted by universities that promised a sixty percent enrollment rate for those international athletes who aspired to move there and make a living out of their athleticism. My back-up plan was a lifelong dream for most of the underprivileged kids on my football team, but I never gave those kinds of thoughts much attention.

Everyone knew that a scholarship to a Canadian university meant that you were a student first, before an athlete—either that or you ended up in the CFL making 50k a year, working as an electrician on the side just to make ends meet. If you wanted your athletics to come first, if you showed any real talent, you went to the U.S. to be groomed. Realistically, this was the same for acting, which was why I hadn't even applied to any Canadian schools when the time came.

You could make an argument that those around me benefited vicariously because of my drive to leave the country and do something more than remain idle, at least for the first half of my life. There were times when I literally got our coach out of trouble after he'd hit a kid (who had lost us a game) by insisting that we needed him or else I wasn't going to play for the rest of the season. My status allowed me to provide these little favors for the people around me and as a result, I found myself the captain of more than just the football and basketball teams—I was the goddamn captain of the high school, principal included.

Before we began practice for the fall football season, Joe and I spent the last days of summer drinking Pabst beers by the small river that passed through town while I lied—a lot—about how many girls I was sleeping with. I had always regarded lying as an art form or skill-set; you just had to be selective as to when you employed it.

We went to the week-long Summer's End Festival and saw all of our favorite punk bands that included *Alexisonfire, My Chemical Romance,* and *The Used,* who played alongside other bands with similarly angsty names. On the last night of the festival, we drank 40-ounce bottles of Olde English and tried to jump the fence in an effort to meet our idols, only to find out that they had lost the spirit of punk rock somewhere on the road before Westfield. We were tossed out and that was the end of the summer for us.

As senior year grew nearer, Joe continued to feel like he was special on the frequent date nights I had scheduled for us with various girls. He was unaware, as per usual, that I only did these things out of necessity, as it needed to appear like I was hanging with friends and not banging my girlfriends.

Joe's compliance with attending those dates was one of the few strengths that he actually brought to our friendship. Exploiting this strength was one of my talents, and I acted on it like any good friend would. One of my more effective moves was having Joe sit upstairs with a girl to watch some shitty PG movie so that my parents wouldn't ask any questions while I was inside the hotter girl in the basement. While Joe was deep in Free Willy Three, I was trying my best to free my own willy under the neon stars and theatrical lighting that I had pinned up on the basement ceiling—some real 2000s romantic shit.

Joe and I continued to pretend like things were cool between us, even though I was getting increasingly annoyed at his lack of self-confidence and he was getting frustrated with my successes with women, especially with Mandy.

I had worked so hard to get her alone in my basement if only to send the message to Joe that I was capable of the things in life that he wasn't. It made Joe furious but he never had the balls to show it. No matter how hard I forced his hand to grow in that area, he remained silent.

As our discord grew stronger from spending too much time together, summer faded behind us without notice. We considered prom and who we would invite to go with us, what kind of limousine we would hire, and how we would prank our teachers on that last day of class when it came. More importantly, we thought about how to get into the girls' locker room as much as possible after football games without being detected—that was a goal that meant access to bribing rights for the entire senior year.

As the days grew colder and darker, Joe began to dream more about Mandy behind my back, and I began to think more about taking on the world in front of his face. Despite his being a pain in my ass, Joe really was the prop that held me up against a different canopy than the Westfield skyline of unimportance. I needed him, despite my frustration with his simplicity and low level of achievement, and he needed me to keep from feeling totally irrelevant. We stayed friends—for the time being.

CHAPTER THREE

With fall came the beginning of the end of high school, and I had made my summer sexual and acting accomplishments known to all of the students and staff at Westfield High before the first class bell rang. The only story of any real truth was that I had acted in a modestly publicized outdoor summer play in New York City, playing the role of a non-important jester. I had one line in the entire performance but had taken the not-for-profit gig as a means to improve upon my facial expressionism, or something like that. Decidedly, I had brought home those learned facial expressions, as they seemed to pair well with the circumstances of my everyday life. What you need to remember about Westfield is that playing the role of a dildo in one of my father's magazines would equate to fame —so the jester gig? Not bad.

Joc sat outside in front of the school before the bell rang, having driven up in his parents' Porsche convertible that he loved to cruise around town in. His parents had money, and that had always bothered me. His father was one of the few parents I knew who actually worked in the big city, some forty minutes away. Despite the community's admiration, I had always seen him as a pleb who worked a boring working-class job, a man who would never aspire to any fame, status, or importance like myself. It was that belief that kept Joe in his position below me, despite his family's wealth or that fucking Porsche.

I walked up to him, noticing that Mandy and a few of the other girls were watching as I approached his car.

"Taking daddy's car out for the first day, hey? World-class douche move, my man. Fuck's sake, everyone knows you rode a bicycle with training wheels until you were sixteen."

The put-downs, they kept me up; it was just how the world turned.

The girls gathered around the Porsche and I sat on the hood, leaving an indentation on the engine-warmed metal.

"Yeah, New York, pretty wild place. I ran into more celebs than Joe here knows about. I'm totally fuckin' going back; I mean, fuck, I'm meant to be there. It's like, the acting and the singing, it really speaks to me. Who knows, New York, L.A., Miami—I for sure will be moving out of this shit hole of a town right after high school. It's the stars and lights for me." I made a gesture toward the sun above us, pretending as if it were shining only on me. The other girls ate that shit up, but Mandy still looked at me with the knowledge that I had recently tried to finger-rush her under those neon stars in my basement, ending up with dry fingers.

"Eh, bud, off the hood. You're denting it, it's thin metal."

I ignored Joe's plea.

I also avoided eye contact with Mandy, trying to evade any display of insecurity, which worked for the time being.

The class bell rang for the first period and everyone rushed into the halls, filling up the school for what promised to be another lame, boring, relatively uneventful senior year.

The only thing interesting about Westfield was that everyone expected this boredom—the natural result being that everyone did everything they could to avoid it. This generally meant heavy drug use, big parties, and sexual deviance that we tricked ourselves into believing generations before us would shudder at. If they were from Westfield, they wouldn't—it was how ninety-nine percent of us were conceived.

CHAPTER FOUR

My mother and father immigrated to North America when they were in their twenties. They'd lived very marginal lives in Croatia but had been exposed to the benefits of a transatlantic transplant through friends who emigrated five years before they did. Even before their arrival, they had developed quite a grandiose idea about what their future child's life would hold. No way would any son of theirs go without the best education, the best acting courses, and the best performing arts teacher that money could import from the big(ger) city. They had told me at a young age that I was going to be a lonely empire, that this was how they were going to invest their time and energy as parents. This meant that I had better accept that I was *the* chosen sperm cell and that I should move on to greatness sooner rather than later. As a result of being first-generation immigrants, they were more star-struck by the idea of fame and fortune than I ever was—they were just too old to live that narrative out for themselves.

Every Monday night I had singing classes, every Thursday I had acting courses, and every Friday I worked on the upcoming plays being staged by the local municipality's poorly-funded drama collective. The only thing I had refused to do was fundraise, and I didn't think my parents wanted to see their son begging for money, either—this was one decision that wasn't debated.

I invested a lot of my childhood into acting and I often blamed my parents for the pressure that came with this commitment and eventual fame narrative, despite wanting it so badly myself. If I had to describe this narrative, it would be one where I was the shining star that was going to fall from above a shitty town and rise again like my man Jesus under the Hollywood lights. Truth be told, I fucking hated the classes, the time away from friends, and the hours spent learning the notes of songs that I despised. All I wanted to do was figure out how to fuck Mandy before everyone found out that I hadn't yet—and, more importantly, before Joe got his shot.

I sat in bed on a Tuesday night flipping through an SAT study guide, the posters of The Used, Kelly Slater, Tony Hawk, and Peter Line staring at me as I sat there, cursing at the material. I was relieved when my phone finally rang. It was Joe.

"Sup"

"Hey, buds, what's on it fer tonight?"

"Just studying for the SATs, man, I have to pass this. Why do I need to know this shit? I'm pretty sure most actors don't have to write these tests, or even know how to do… calculus."

"Well, SATs are for any American university, right? So if you're going into university there for acting, it kinda makes sense, eh?"

"Yeah, well, university is just the cover. And what the fuck do you know, pleb? I'll be in Hollywood or New York acting in no time, and it's just for the Visa. But it's a lot of work just for a goddamn Visa, man—a lot of bullshit."

“I wish I was goin’ with you, getting outta this place. Fuck, it would be super nice. There will be so many Mandys down there, you’ll forget all about this shit that’s being said about you, no doubt.” He said it with a hint of dick on his breath.

“What are you talking about, fucker?”

“Ya know, Mandy telling everyone that you tried to go down on ‘er and how she told you not to. Then how you, like, told her to just tell everyone you did, so that you wouldn’t ask her to do it again?”

“Fuck her, man. You know me, her regrets aren’t mine.”

“Yeah, I mean, fuckin’ that’s what I told everyone. So, what do ya say? Drop the books for bit and meet at The Den? The whole team is pretty fired up, could be fun.”

“Yeah, yeah,” I finally offered after cooling my temper. “I guess this shit can wait till tomorrow.”

The Den was a favorite spot that we frequented because they would let us in with the fake IDs I had made when I was in Miami on a family vacation. They had never cared that Joe wasn’t a 350-pound diabetic from Michigan and had never questioned my age since, even at sixteen, I had the features of a 25-year-old.

I had turned eighteen before anyone else in my grade, anyway, and in those parts, eighteen was your ticket to ride—there was a lot of booting going on and, given my legitimate age, I was always the star for bringing the beers for everyone.

“I'll catch you for a few drinks, just have to sneak out. Pick me up in the Porsche; I’ll drive.”

Joe picked me up and I drove us to The Den, doing a circle in the parking lot to make sure everyone saw me driving. I had even cranked up some punk music for added effect. We'd just played a big game against a rival team the day prior, so the stoke level was high among the cheerleaders we all loved to spend time in. Given the legal age, a high school rally at a bar was typical and it was packed that night—no bar owner in Westfield thought twice when a bunch of half-pissed high school kids showed up ready to fire things up at their bar. Fuck, the economy *relied* on it.

There was always some shitty classic rock cover band playing at The Den, or anywhere in Westfield, for that matter.

It was a cock-rock town with a bunch of dick-bag Dodge Ram Quad Cab drivers hanging their rubber ball sacks out from under their trailer hitches, shouting at chicks as they did burnouts in the parking lots. I loved being on the football team because it made me look well-rounded, but I hated the other fucktards who reminded me that I was from Westfield.

Joe and I grabbed a Pabst each and walked around chatting with some of the girls before I was interrupted by a hard slap on the shoulder.

"Zach, my man, shot of vodka for you, bud?"

Johnny fucking Ratkin, the rat face. I hate this Dodge-Ram-driving dickhead, I thought and almost said out loud. We called him Johnny Rat Face partially because of his pointed face, dark eyebrows, whiskery mustache, and bad acne, but mostly because no one really liked him. No one likes a guy whose greatest skill is cock-blocking at parties.

Rat Face was a bully from the first grade and likely hadn't stopped being one to this day—he was the model of insecurity in a man, and part of me pitied him for that. As per usual, he was wearing his Von Dutch leather jacket and Affliction bandana with a sweat-stained Yankees hat over top. Rat Face thought himself a real trendsetter because he had picked a bunch of that shit up while down in Vegas three years prior—he hadn't updated any of it since.

"You know I only drink the good shit, none of that Russian filth. Tequila, Ben, and thanks—for serving me and this idiot."

"Who you calling an idiot, max playa? Get on your knees and kiss my shoe, bud." That was his favorite move, getting people to kiss his shoe; he was the real-deal douchebag of the west.

"I'm calling *you* a fucking idiot. Now, drink for your captain," I replied after studying his body language for any real aggression. Despite my ego and reputation being bigger than his frame, he was a tiger that needed to be tamed and was not a person to turn your back on.

"Come play some pool when you get a chance, bud. The girls are asking for us, hey."

"I think what you mean is they're asking for *me* and will only play with you unless I come over—kids in a fuckin' sandbox." He didn't get the reference.

"You really are a dick, hey bud? I like it, I love it, I want some more —"

"Don't finish that," I interjected, throwing back my shitty tequila shot.

I walked over to the pool table and thanked the girls for their effort on the field before racking the balls. Without asking, I broke and then gave the cue and white ball to Rat Face.

"Your game. Enjoy, Rat Man."

It was the least I could do for old Rat Face. What a charity case.

I had a few more drinks with Joe, listened to a shitty cover of some Guns N' Roses song, and then found myself in the shitty washroom that only had one stall with a half-hinged door hanging from it. I pulled my dick out and started to drain some Pabst into the porcelain, avoiding the piss that was already on the floor that seemingly never got cleaned up by the staff.

"Well, look who it is—the old captain of kings, fuckin' guy himself." It was Adam, Rat Face's Rottweiler.

"How'd the pool game go for old Rat Face?" I replied, not even looking over my shoulder.

"You think you've got it all figured out, don't you, shit face? Well, let me tell you, son, you're going nowhere and I can't wait to see you fuckin' burn. I know what you and all your fairy-fuck drama guys say about me and Johnny in the locker room, that he's a cock-block and shit. Well, fuck you, Zach, your time is coming."

"Are you done? You fuckin' dumb shit," I replied calmly, zipping my pants up and turning around. I took the hand that was just holding my dick and gave him a slight slap on the side of the face. He lunged at me.

After about two minutes of exchanging punches, three 250-pound bouncers rushed into the small washroom—which was quite the comedic sight to see—and broke things up. They dragged Adam out back like the dog he was and gave me the benefit of the doubt, allowing me to leave through the front door.

"Take it easy, Zach. We'd hate to have to ban you, hey?"

"Thanks, gentlemen, for your service and protection! Fuck me, my jaw hurts."

Not everyone thought so highly of me, something that those pussies only ever verbalized when they got wasted enough to say something. *Fuckin' great left hook*, I thought as I massaged my jaw in the parking lot. *That pack-rat deserves a second round with me.*

Fights were typical at The Den, so no one really thought anything about it when they broke out. If it wasn't Adam and me, it was Rat Face and some kid who'd had enough of being bullied. The fights were good, they were ways to manage the stress of living in such a mundane hamster cage. Without them, there certainly would be more devastating violence of the kind that was broadcast by the shitty U.S. news channels that we got up north. That night it was just my turn to be the regulator.

I took my sore jaw and walked the two kilometers back to my house alone, feeling dizzy, then vomiting and calling it a night.

Shoulda stayed home and worked on those fuckin' SATs.

CHAPTER FIVE

To pass the SATs, I had managed to recruit my math teacher, my English teacher, and the vice principal to support my cause. I had them working overtime to teach me the basics of exam-time management, advanced methods for scoring, and U.S. fundamentals of test-taking. I had spent long hours studying in the library alone and even more hours working with teachers after class, having pulled out my hair in frustration on more than one occasion. Say what you will about the American education system, it was beating me down daily.

The only thing that kept me going was the constant reminder of how much I hated Westfield. I had to consider myself a bit lucky, though, since most people would be given a pamphlet for an SAT prep-course with a $1,200 price tag and made to suffer alone. Somehow, I always managed to get the teachers around me drunk on my purpose in life and the prospect of my potential. It helped that everyone in town wanted to touch fame, and fame was me—everyone with the exception of Mandy.

It was late May and the frost had begun to recede from the soil and rise back into the air. With the help of the academic team behind me, the one that I would never thank at the Oscars, I wrote my SATs and got a decent grade. I was setting up interviews with various universities throughout the States and enjoying some time away from the library.

Joe had lined up his enrollment into a top business school in Canada and was enjoying the prospect of having Mandy attend the same school without my being there to try and finger-rush her. When I began to inch closer to leaving, I figured he could have his chance in the end—I gave him that as a parting gift. After all, the only thing she was currently offering me was a lack of attention.

Mandy and I had formally dated back in middle school and, despite my best efforts to rekindle things, she just appeared uninterested now. I had broken up with her at the time to date her best friend, solely based on my attraction to someone with a different hair color—maybe that was it.

Regardless of my failures with Mandy, I had succeeded in setting up my admissions interviews with universities in Los Angeles, New York, and Miami. I planned to attend the Los Angeles interview in person but had to do the others via telephone, as my parents couldn't afford the flights. Telephone interviews were always discouraged by the universities, especially for a program like the dramatic arts and performance, but I had no choice.

I wanted to be in New York—everyone wanted to be in New York. I had preferred theater and had heard that *The American Academy of Dramatic Arts* routinely selected the best students from the second year to attend a prestigious third year—and prestigious was my favorite word. I had always banked on the fact that that third year, once I got in, would certainly guarantee the spotlight and monologues that I so deserved.

My parents, as per usual, were monumental in ensuring that I had the proper preparation for these interviews. My drama classes were ramped up to Mondays, Tuesdays, Thursdays, and Sundays, and I was grilled every night for two hours. Hell, my dad even stayed sober for a few weeks prior to help get the job done. They had invested all of their extra income in me—their lonely empire, well over $30k a year.

Meanwhile, they were still driving a shitty station wagon with beaver panels on the sides that had been fashionable in the eighties. At a young age, I had just guessed that I was worth this investment, and as time went on, the continued backing from my family and the community made me certain that I was.

L.A. was first on the list of interviews that I had to attend, but before I left, Joe and I decided to get the football and basketball teams together to have a raging party out on our friend Lyle's farm. I fucking hated cowboys, and although we didn't truly live in a rural town, it sometimes felt that way, given the lack of diversity and culture. The Dodge Ram dickheads like Rat Face didn't help, either. They would always be drinking shit beer behind the wheel, sucking on a mouth full of chew, singing shitty country music and bragging about their midget hockey stats —it made me sick for 364 days a year.

Despite this distaste, every year on that one day in May, we went out to Lyle's farm, threw jerry cans of gasoline on a massive fire, rode dirt bikes around, and got absolutely gunned on shitty beer like those fuckers in those trucks did on a daily basis. I'm talking some real honky-tonk bullshit, and I loved it—for one day.

My favorite part of this day was the mud pit. It was often mandatory that Joe and I beat the shit out of each other in the mud until neither of us could stand. Most years, I would end up going home soaked in mud from head to toe—with the exception of my dick, which always ended up squeaky clean after a run through some girl.

This year, that girl was an ex-girlfriend of Joe’s. He'd been pretty torn up over her a year prior, but as per usual I didn’t really give a shit; in fact, it added to her attractiveness. She had approached me to do a beer bong which resulted in her getting down on her knees and looking up at me with big, blue, doe eyes, and proceeding to display her open throat talents and techniques for the entire crowd to witness. We made jokes about it behind Joe’s back and when he took notice, I told him that he was too good for her and that I was there for him if he needed to have a drunken chat.

At the end of the weekend, Joe and I had that chat next to the dwindling fire that had been fueled by burning beer boxes and the now melted, smoldering jerry cans. As a solution to Joe’s sorrow, we got up and threw our half-empty bottles of rum and tequila into the nearby pond, declaring that it was our departure from the girls who wronged us during the high school years that had come to pass. Unbeknownst to Joe, I’d just had the girl his bottle was thrown for—six hours prior. This was to be the final year that I would get to do this, and it felt fitting that I’d had my way with his ex-girlfriend knowing that he was trying to have his way with Mandy.

Once the fire burned out, we all filled into those Dodge Ram trucks and blasted down the highway toward town—country music blasting, and my desire to leave the place increasing with every mile. I sat in the backseat with my hungover-head bouncing between my legs with the freezing-cold morning air blasting at me.

“Roll up the goddamn window, Rat Face,” I said quietly, somewhat ashamed for feeling cold.

“It’s my dad’s truck, bud, can’t have the smell of weed in it,” Rat Face said.

“Then don’t fucking smoke weed in it!” I yelled back.

Everybody laughed, and I shivered all the way home.

CHAPTER SIX

I had always enjoyed the airport but had begun to develop a distaste for coach class. The after-hours drama classes and brief stints in New York had me wanting a G-5 with personal blow jobs at the push of a button, not an overworked and underpaid stewardess who kept telling me that a full can of Coke would cost me five bucks.

I sat down in seat 20F and the smell of jet fuel burned its way into my nostrils. I looked over at my in-flight partner seated next to me. She was around twenty-five and had skin that was certainly browned by the Californian sun and not the black hole of some tanning bed from the city we were departing. In an effort to lubricate a conversation, I smoothed into the flight with a bourbon, straight, rather than sitting with my dick in my fingers, wondering what to say to the woman next to me.

I got the drink, took a sip, and then pounded it back.

"Heading on vacation?" my in-flight partner inquired, looking up from her *Vogue* magazine.

"I'm an actor, going to film," I replied, not making eye contact on purpose for added effect.

"Right, L.A. I'm from Texas, been on a trip to see my relatives, and then I'm connecting in L.A. back to Dallas. What are y'all auditioning for? That's excitin'."

And that moment was when it all became real.

Lights, camera, action.

There is always a tipping point when those who are prepared to fabricate their existence do so, reaping the rewards that others fear to accomplish. Remember what I said about old Goffman? This was my preparation for the opening act.

"I've got a gig set up, shooting in Agoura Hills, some western or something. I was just up in Canada doing something for an old actor friend, more of a passion project with the elderly to appease him." The acting classes had begun to pay dividends; I was doing fairly well at the game already.

"You were a child actor? You seem pretty young to be so accomplished, hun," she remarked.

"No, I'm not a child anything, I'm twenty-five."

"What have y'all been in?" she asked, too forcefully for my liking.

"I've written and directed more than I've been in front of the camera lately." I began to sound irritated, and she took the hint.

"Right, okay, great! Well, enjoy your next shoot, er, job, whatever you's call it." She was acting smitten now, or perhaps embarrassed.

I couldn't understand it, but she didn't speak to me for the rest of the flight. Deep down, this defeat was unsettling; my actual opening act would have to be much stronger than that.

As the flight droned on in silence, we approached the California border and I looked out of the airplane window to see a widespread view of the nighttime city lights that covered the land like wildfire, stretching as far as the eye could see. Los Angeles was intimidating from thirty-thousand feet, with its seemingly endless array of traffic and grids of concrete buildings. I tried to pick out Malibu pier from above as we approached the airport, but could barely see a thing past the overwhelming tightness in my chest.

I found myself picking up my bags with the coach passengers I had arrived with and took a taxi from LAX to my temporary shared accommodation. While the other kids my age were back home drinking at The Den and drunk driving their goddamn trucks in circles, I was finally in the city of dreams come true—if only for a weekend. The cab driver said nothing as we droned on in silence down the freeway. He opened his American-sounding mouth when he dropped me at the steps of my accommodation, requesting a hand full of American bills. I'd noticed how smooth the concrete on the freeway had been—it was such a stark contrast to the shitty, potholed roads that Westfield could afford. If the roads were any sign, I was already convinced that my childhood suffering was worth it.

The shared accommodation was moderately clean and excessively expensive for the short time I was there. I dropped my two duffle bags on the small kitchen table and cracked open a beer that had been left in the fridge by the tenant before me. I wandered over to the couch and pushed on the window's rusted hinges to open the room and let in the warm Californian air. The air was a massive reprieve to my frozen, dry, Westfield skin, and my bones welcomed the heat.

I flicked on the TV and fell asleep with the half-empty bottle of warm beer in my hand, listening to some news story of another gang shooting somewhere in that great city. I felt at home for the first time in my life, like a Muslim who had just made his pilgrimage to Mecca.

BANG!

A gunshot rang out in the streets outside of my window, and I dropped my half-empty bottle of beer on the faded carpet and crawled over to look. I peered up and out through the 1980s-style blinds and into the dark street, witnessing nothing. My heart raced with excitement as if I had already been cast in some movie; I pretended it. I saw no movement, so I ran across the room and walked out into the hallway where I was greeted by a thirty-something Latina who was half-clothed in a silk nightgown, carrying a small child.

"Shit, did you hear that? Everything all right? Fuck."

"*Estas loco, chinga tu madre,"* she said to me, which I later came to understand was a suggestion that I go fuck my mother—but I didn't know that at the time, so I smiled and waved at her child. She looked at me, puzzled, and then spoke in English:

"Stupid gringo, it was a car backfiring. Pasty white motherfucker, go back inside." Her child began to cry, which made her even more upset at me.

"Right, sorry, umm, chinga tu, er, whatever you said, to you as well. Night." I cowered back into my room and locked the door; both locks. Looking down at the now-empty beer bottle on the floor, I kicked it and cursed, stubbing my right big toe on it. I noticed that the floor looked like it was used to having beer spilled on it and stumbled back to the couch more upset at losing the alcohol than the cleaning fee I would now have to pay. I sat back down, exhausted from the adrenaline of it all, and fell back asleep.

In one single night, I had seen more of the real world than anyone I knew—even if it was just a car backfiring.

CHAPTER SEVEN

My first visit to Los Angeles was overwhelming. I used my fake ID and drank hard the second night at a shitty bar down the street, waking up unaware of how I had gotten home. I had practiced acting like I was an actor at every opportunity that had presented itself while I wandered around Santa Monica, trying to run into celebrities on the boardwalk. The interview was coming up, but I was getting deeper and deeper into the experience of having no limits or boundaries.

The problem with Los Angeles for a new-on-the-scene actor from outside of the area was that everyone who'd grown up there already had a lifetime playing the game that you were trying to learn—and that is a real fucking advantage. I had tried playing that game growing up, but now, I had no Joe to dangle out and take advantage of for my own benefit and progress. I just had me.

I drank to suppress the reality of it all, knowing that it was going to be tough to get accepted by the city. There was also the added immediacy—an urgency to my acceptance—and this made the experience of it all that much more visceral. As a Canadian actor, I had one shot at getting into the American industry, and that shot was as a young, attractive student with the benefit of still believing in dreams and ever-afters. If I fucked up, if I slipped on my interviews, I was as good as a Westfield layman.

Knowing these facts, I managed to stay relatively sober the next night by eating at In-N-Out Burger and only having a few beers at the apartment. As a result of that restraint, and a few of my father's benzos, the interview went fairly well the following morning. They were interested in my story and where I was from, and they thought that "I had a narrative that they could work with" when discussing my admission to the program with the other decision-makers. They felt that I added a "diversity" to the program since I had a background in theater. Really, they were excited at the prospect of collecting my international tuition fees that would earn them four times as much as those of a student native to California State.

I left the interview, still unsure about my fate, and wandered down to Venice, shaking out the nerves of it all. I crossed the canals and imagined myself sipping a cup of coffee with other actors, discussing how Venice had "gone to shit" and how all of the buskers and artists along the boardwalk had sold out when they stopped dropping acid and decided to attend AA meetings to improve their art and mindfulness skills.

I found myself wandering into a beachfront bar to act out my role as an L.A. someone worth something, and I ordered a tequila soda. I gulped it down and then ordered another.

I continued drinking until the sun began to set. When it had, I went out back, vomited all over my shoes, and then returned to my shared rental space and passed out again to yet another gang-related shooting on the news—great city, indeed. All it took was two days for the real sounds of gunshots to become part of the fabric that I so wanted to be a part of, and I vomited again at the idea of being a Westfield oil rig worker if it all fell through. I didn't lock my door that evening and the next day I woke up early, hungover, for my 6 a.m. flight back to purgatory.

In hindsight, my mind was made up somewhere between those tequila sodas and the resulting hangover—I was both hooked and terrified of losing out, all at the same time.

CHAPTER EIGHT

My first return from L.A. was a fucking spectacle. The energy behind my being anything but ordinary left me feeling euphoric. It was like I had already been accepted and was just home to pack my bags and head back out into that better future I had promised everyone that I was going to find. I called up Joe and we went down to The Den and got drunk—"L.A. drunk," as I now coined it, having had spent time in the home of filthy dark angels for a mere two days.

We met up with Mandy, who, for some fucked up reason, kissed Joe at the first opportunity she got. According to Joe, all it took was two days of my being away for Mandy to "feel comfortable" to let him know that she was "into him." If you'd asked me, she had finally realized that I was leaving for good and so she did what every other girl from a small town does—she grabbed onto whatever rock that she could, fearing the changing of the tide.

We spent time down by the river where we threw rocks at other stacked rocks, trying our best to waste the time in-between uncertainty and our final exams. I caught Mandy and Joe out of the corner of my eye engaged in what looked like happiness, but I also caught her eyes gazing into mine when they embraced. It was a natural romance to have occurred, but that didn't extinguish the anger I had with myself for not getting to her, again, before Joe had his opening. Truthfully, I had never been able to have sex with Mandy—she hadn't wanted that in middle school when we'd actually dated. At that time, I had to accept the bitter reality that my chances were all but lost to a second-rate, try-hard version of myself.

I began to rub in my "better future" by throwing quarters into the river and bragging about how I had no use for the Canadian currency, how I was now "on the American dollar" and didn't need "that shit" any longer. It made me feel marginally better about being around the two of them groping each other. Joe supported my enthusiasm, as predicted, and Mandy continued to push the issue of her newly professed love for Joe as we all got well-fucked-up on Pabst and Fireball whiskey by a fire on the riverbank.

I had two more interviews to attend to—two more chances to keep myself from a lifetime of shame for not being all that I was born to be. Unfortunately, the coming hangover was not part of the prep course materials that I had read on how to interview for prestigious universities.

CHAPTER NINE

I woke up with a bad hangover and ten missed text messages from my mother, which mainly read:

"Don't forget your phone interviews with NY and Miami today."

I sat up in bed, opened my flip-phone, and joined the first interview—mildly shaking and disheveled, with a thin heart rate of 140 bpm. It went awful. Miami was out before I even had the opportunity to be disappointed about it; my head was throbbing and demanded attention.

I got up, took a shit, decided to shave, and then showered. I made a cup of coffee, a French press, in preparation for my New York interview, and found myself on the phone with a panel of six professors. I felt like a doctor trying to interview for a job, secretly knowing that I actually didn't have a medical license. It was fucking difficult. By the end of it, I had sweat through my T-shirt and needed to take another shower. I was shaking at the thought of losing out on my future simply because I had decided to settle my nerves by drinking one too many bottles of cheap whiskey the night prior. That last bottle wasn't simple; it never is.

Within hours I had received word back from Miami that I hadn't made the cut, and within days I'd heard back from New York that I "wasn't quite what they were looking for." I was deflated, emasculated, and left to feel like a porn star who was told that no one wanted to see them fuck on screen anymore. There was no way out for me, no second chances—and I knew it.

I didn't tell anyone that I had been rejected, I couldn't; if I didn't get into the University of California, there was no bigger and bolder future. There was no Zach Monte. For the first time in my life, I thought about ending it all. Maybe jumping from the tallest building I could find in Westfield, which really wasn't all that tall, or overdosing on Pabst and weed, if that was even possible.

I wasn't going to go down as *that guy*, I wasn't going to remain idle with a smile on my face and a paycheck that barely covered the rent for some shitty basement suite in shitty Westfield. I began to consider my strengths outside of acting and came up short, resulting in a deepening depression. Then, after three more days, the phone finally rang.

"Zach Monte?" The voice punctured my eardrums through the long-distance phone line.

"This is he," I replied, more formally than I had ever spoken to anyone. My heart was in my throat and I was sweating through my T-shirt again. I felt like I was going to kill myself if the conversation didn't take a quick turn toward fame.

"We would like to offer you admission to the program. We think you would be a good fit down here; we like your experience and your ambition. What do you say, kid?" The informality of his tone immediately brought me back from the edge.

"Absolutely, I mean, yeah, I mean, I would be a great fit. Thank you, thank you guys, I look forward to it." I was really yelling *FUCK YES!* and *FUCK YOU, MANDY AND JOE!* in my head.

"Great, let's get your visa situation sorted out. I'll get you connected with our admissions clerk, Cass, she'll handle it and walk you through it all. Sound good?"

"Absolutely, yes, for sure. Thank you."

"Haha, of course, best part of the job. See you in a few short months, Zach, and hey, congrats, man. Welcome to the big leagues."

I wasn't sure if it was just a part of his pitch or if he was being genuine —and I didn't care. I was going to Hollywood.

Perhaps, in hindsight, California had picked me as much as the university did. In L.A., they had respected my bloodshot, hungover eyes as an indicator of artistic potential, while the other two likely would have scoffed at that sort of artistry. New York was for professionals with credentials while L.A. was for those contaminated with the artistic burden of wanting to be happy, but knowing that sadness and substance abuse was the only way to greatness.

I felt ecstatic after accepting the offer but still defeated at the idea of not becoming the next big thing on Broadway, of not making the cut for that prestigious third year in New York. I had to have a strong conversation with myself, and when I eventually considered what was available in L.A. and what was available in Westfield, everything seemed okay. I called Joe and my parents to tell them of my decision but left out the part that I had gone into two of the interviews hungover and scored extremely low on them as a result. My father was the only one who was upset about my choice, and that was more for him than it was for me—he loved Miami.

-

Later that week was the year-end school dance that posed as an opportunity for me to relax and take in the farewell-to-all-things-Westfield vibe that my acceptance had provided me. I hadn't even thought about the dance up until being accepted, I was so tangled up in the idea of ending my life—which now seemed like some shitty teenage coming-of-age television show drama. I ignored the notion of suicidality and moved on to discussing, with everyone that I ran into, how incredible my future was going to be.

I had always enjoyed school dances as a younger me, especially the butterflies that always showed up when I walked across the dark gymnasium toward the hot girls as soon as that slow, popular boy-band song came on. I also enjoyed fantasizing in class about what it would be like to grind up on those girls; closer than the chaperones pretended that they didn't like.

I had some intuition as a kid, and I did wonder about the sickness of those chaperones. They'd show up just to watch thirteen-year-olds grind up on each other—why else would some parent want to go to a shitty dance and be a shitty person telling kids to stop having too much fun? They all wanted to watch it in some state of pedophilic nostalgia. That was my theory, at least—probably because they always ruined it for me, which compounded my issues with authority.

Before the dances that had come to pass, Joe would always come over with a few of the other guys to fire up our teenage testosterone levels. We would play computer games and talk about immature shit to keep the butterflies at bay. Joe was obsessed with this military-style strategy game and always tried to make us sit there and watch him play the one-player game that it was. I wanted to play Tony Hawk's Pro Skater II and, generally speaking, I got my way because everyone else was tired of watching Joe be a loser, too.

Thirteen-year-old me was in rehearsal for acting as much as eighteen-year-old me was; in fact, so was five-year-old me. The nights of school dances were a nice exception from the midweek drama classes, but they were more of a stage for performance than a total reprieve.

Back in middle school, the dances were always held closer to the beginning of the year. It was always cold, mid-October cold, but it wasn't a Halloween theme or anything, that was just how the timing went. The leaves had always begun to fall already and everyone would be bracing for the cold snap of winter, which meant snow and shitty driving.

We would walk up to the front of the school together as a group of guys ready to live out our twisted, denim-rubbing fantasies, and we would pretend like it meant everything in the world to get to do so. The dances always seemed the same, almost as if they were a film in reverse, over and over. We would walk up the steps and gather around inside the musty-smelling, beige-tiled main hallway of the school and try to nervously eye out the girls who had already arrived. You could hear the latest Savage Garden or Ja Rule track in the gymnasium to the immediate left, right next to the music room where I practiced my vocals for the show tunes that I performed. There were always soft drinks, for a price, as well as chips, gum, and long-stemmed roses that the guys occasionally bought for the girls when the other guys weren't looking.

The hallways during the school dances were always so different—darker, almost filled with mystery and adventure. We would run in these hallways because we could, and we would spark joints that some Thai kid's older brother would sell to us, because we were told we couldn't. We never got caught, though the janitor did join us one time, which was a highlight for a stoned fourteen-year-old in a rundown locker room hanging out with his friends.

Now, some three years later, this dance felt different. It was all the same old music with the curse words bleeped out, with the girls on one side of the bleachers and the guys on the other—all still acting like thirteen-year-olds incapable of speaking with one another until that specific, trending song came on. The smoke machine still pumped smoke into the air and the bright lights cascaded across the bodies and sequins of the dressed-up teenage girls. It all looked the same on the surface, but the vibe was different—it was a vibe of change and transition.

We still had two weeks left of school and final exams to write, but everyone was already well on their way to their separate places in life. Naturally, everyone was thinking that their decisions at that age defined their final resting places in the world, but I knew that most of those kids would end up a world away from their intentions—not me, I wasn't allowed to be.

I stood in the dark behind the bleachers and watched Mandy making out with Joe; I watched Sam and Julie feel each other up; and I watched the DJ put his hand down a girl's pants, acting like he hadn't graduated the year prior and made DJ'ing his full-time gig. *Fucking Joe,* I thought, *fucking Joe, off to a perfect life with perfect Mandy*. I found comfort in the fact that their situation could change at any moment; it was volatile, everyone's lives were back then. I reminded myself that the only person in that room who had a destiny laid out before them was me.

“What are you doing under the bleachers, man?”

“Chillin’, what’s it to you?” I replied to the faceless voice in the dark —it was Cyril.

“Shit, these dances are your thing, captain famous.”

“Yeah, well, sometimes you gotta make a statement and sit in the back row at the Oscars when your real seat is up front. Just taking it all in, man”.

“Shit, I hear you, Zach. Times are changing, man, a—”

“Ha! Save it, Cy. Fuck’s sake, you sound like every coming-of-age movie script that has never seen the screen.”

He laughed. “Shit, must be this dank ass weed I've been smoking. You tried this new purple indica? It’s savage.”

“Give me that.”

“Bro, wait, not inside!” He laughed again, that raspy laugh of his, more amused than actually caring. He was the only kid in high school with a face tattoo—he was a bold motherfucker.

“Who is smoking marijuana cigarettes in this gymnasium?” a teacher shouted from atop the bleachers, looking at everyone who was sitting beside her and scouring the remaining seats.

“She doesn’t know smoke rises, bro!” We both burst out laughing, running out of the gym.

“Thanks for the maaarajuuuana, budday,” I said in a mocking tone.

"Take it easy, Zach Monte. Enjoy your life." He took the last drag of the joint and stomped it out on the tile floor in the center of the main lobby. I liked Cy—he dressed like he belonged in the movie *Grease*, but I liked him.

Outside I found Mandy, alone, sipping zero-cal canned soda water.

"Well, hey there, stranger," she said, grabbing my arm.

"You got some alcohol in that zero-cal bevvy or something?" I asked, somewhat surprised at her enthusiasm to see me.

"A bit." She smirked.

"Cheeky."

"You have no idea, Zach Monte."

"Well, whose fault is that, darlin'?" I exclaimed, grabbing the drink from her and taking a swig.

"Come on, Monte. You and me, we never would have worked."

"We did work."

"We worked in grade eight… and barely, at that."

"That was one hell of a kiss in front of the entire school, dancing to Boyz II Men." I glanced at her with a seductive look that I had practiced during those after-school rehearsals.

She grabbed me and held me close. "I'll miss you."

"Come with me."

"Fuuuck," she said. "That's the problem, Zach… that comment right there. You just… you don't get it, you know? Fuck!" She took her drink back, pushing me away from her body and sipped the spiked soda between her pink lips. I watched her in slow motion and noticed that her face glitter had transferred from her cheeks, to the can, to my hands.

“Get what? What’s there to get? You’re totally gorgeous and I'm going to be living in L.A.—you *deserve* that lifestyle, don’t *you* get it?”

“I don’t *want* that lifestyle. I want my own life, I don’t need anyone else to follow.”

“What about Joe?” I retorted.

“Joe is great. Maybe we’ll work out, maybe not, but I'm going to Toronto for me and not him.”

“Your dad always was a real pusher of religion, conservatism and shit.”

“What’s that supposed to mean? That doesn’t even make sense.”

“Come on, you used to tell me all the time in those notes during English class; your dad is a total fanatic and he’s controlled your entire childhood. Don’t pretend we didn’t share that shit. You’re making choices for him again.” I lit a cigarette and tried to suck in the red embers.

“I'm doing this for me. Smoking those too, now, hey? How classic Westfield of you.”

I ignored it. “You’re fucking beautiful.”

I reached over and kissed her, putting my hand on her face and holding my lit cigarette up in the air behind her head. She didn’t force me off.

“Zach,” she said after our lips parted for the last time in our lives, “take care of yourself. You’re a volatile guy with such great expectations in front of you. I do worry that it’ll get the best of you someday.” She let go of my hand slowly, kissed my cheek, and headed back into the school to find Joe. I was covered in her glitter.

“Why the fuck does everyone keep calling me *volatile*?” I yelled at her footsteps.

I sat on the front steps of the school, pulled out a steel flask, and threw the entire thing back, chasing it down with more tokes of red ember. The football team was across the street in the back of Rat Face's truck blasting metal music and protesting the shitty dance by not going inside, getting wasted in public instead. These were my all-American boys. I lifted my flask to salute them while Rat Face finished a beer bong and began to head bang along to the music.

I sat a little longer and looked up into the night sky. A thin layer of clouds passed overhead, sailing smoothly through the warm spring air. *It isn't always like this here,* I reflected, reminding myself that L.A. was going to hold more of this in one year than an entire lifetime in Westfield.

I left the dance and began the twenty-minute walk home that I had done for the past three years of my life. *Joe never did this walk; he always drove that fucking Porsche.*

CHAPTER TEN

Joe left for the University of Toronto before I departed for LAX again. All the while, he and Mandy had been groping at every opportunity. I had three days to tie up loose ends, and to try and hook up with as many girls as possible. There was no doubt that this would serve strictly as a means to bolster my competition factor before arriving in a city where I was currently way out of my league.

I met up with Marissa on the final night before I left town. She was used to the late-night callbacks from me, given that we had dated for a few months in high school and had always had reasonably good sex. She was mild-tempered, dressed expensive—like, Orange Country expensive—and was the offspring of two divorced parents, which was something I could relate to, despite my parents' legal relationship status.

Marissa and I met up and hiked the hill that Joe and I had used to climb on the outskirts of town when we were feeling angsty and bored. It was a place where we could share joints and build bonfires, a place where we would listen to Jimmy Eat World records about sundowns, fireworks, and a whole lot of other emotional bullshit. There was no Joe there this time and Jimmy had already spun the last song of my youth. If anything, tonight's soundtrack was brought to you by The Ataris to match the "So Long, Astoria"-type situation that we had on our hands.

Marissa always enjoyed giving blow jobs and I always enjoyed going down on girls, so naturally we wrapped ourselves up in flannel blankets and began a sixty-nine. Everything was quiet, save for the moaning in the midnight air, until I noticed some extra lube dripping down onto my stomach. *Was she crying?* I couldn't decide in the moment if I was turned on by the idea of her using her tears for lube or if I was disgusted at her emotional outburst.

"What the fuck, Riss?" I said.

"Sorry, I was just thinking of all the head we missed out on in senior year." She got off of me, looked at me, and we both began to laugh. She was a good chick and she knew what was up, that was why I had called her on that last night and not someone who might actually be honest with me.

"Do you think that we all end up where we're supposed to?" She sat back into me, putting her head in my arms.

"And just where is that?"

"I don't know, where we're supposed to be. Like, if we believe it, and want it, we'll get there, or something. I'm not making sense."

"Listen, I've spent my entire life since I was five years old acting, performing, and being subjected to hours of relentless negative and positive feedback on my abilities. Let's just put it this way: if *I* don't make it, some God's gonna pay."

"True, but I mean, for me. You're going places and we all know where that is, but me, I dunno." She was waiting for me to ask what she wanted from life; I didn't bite.

"Listen, you've got a lot going on for you, you're going to fuckin' Western, for fuck's sake, you're gonna meet a lot of dudes who are better for you than me, and you're gonna make it outta this fuckin' place for good. You won't get stuck here—you and I, we don't belong in a place like this. Look at Mandy, she'll end up back here, with fuckin' Joe, and we both know the outcome of that story. I dig you, Riss, you're the only chick in this town who I have no idea about in terms of where you'll end up—and that's a good thing."

"Thanks, baby." She kissed me in the way that she would kiss a boyfriend.

My speech, my acting, led us straight back into foreplay, evading any further existentialistic banter. After we had finished each other off, we lit a fire, sparked a joint, got really high, and passed out in each other's laps. We gave ourselves to the mercy of my final night in Westfield with "So Long, Astoria" now actually playing in the background on my mini-disc player.

I always was a bit of a sappy fuck.

CHAPTER ELEVEN

I sat in the airport lounge at 10 a.m., drinking a tequila and orange juice with my headphones on, listening to "Take offs and Landings"—a natural sequel to "So Long, Astoria." I had done the whole goodbye story with my parents and had packed light, knowing that I would surely benefit from buying into L.A.-fashion once I got there. Although I was fashionable in Westfield, I was likely a generation or two behind what was acceptable in L.A. I looked around the room as words of "California" by Phantom Planet now rung in my ears—more cliché guilty pleasures that I would be embarrassed about if anyone were stealing my Bluetooth connection.

Two, three, four more tequila OJ's had me thinking of a T-shirt that I had seen in my younger years while on vacation with my family on the beaches of Oregon. *One tequila, two tequila, three tequila, floor,* I think it had read. I was feeling close to it.

"Flight 656 to Los Angeles is now boarding through gate 54. We are asking that anyone with a disability or carrying small children to please check in."

I seriously considered trying to make a case that my current state of intoxication qualified as a disability but then noticed a familiar face across the bar from me. It was my high school math teacher, Mr. Jacks.

Phil Jacks had always liked me—who didn't—but it was obvious that he always wanted to be something bigger than what he became. He was a skinny, five-foot-seven geek who wore round hipster glasses, polo golf shirts, and corduroys. He sported a fashionable edge that brought him up a notch from 'math loser' to 'Silicon Valley influencer.'

"Phil, what's up? Where you headed?"

Phil looked happy to see me. "My friend! You must be off to greater things, it's great to see you!"

He was drinking a light beer and eating a hot dog smothered in relish that was dripping down his chin and getting caught in his black, straight goatee.

"Onwards and upwards, as they say!" I replied.

"I'm heading to see my mother on the island; I go every year before the school semester begins. I bet you'll be glad to be sitting in university classes instead of hearing me ramble on about algebra in a few weeks, hey?"

He was right.

"You know it. I should actually get running, it was good to see you. Enjoy your mother." I gave him an awkward eye and then laughed inside at what I had just said, knowing that he had no fucking clue what I had actually just said—that was the problem with Silicon Valley kids, as I would soon learn.

"Final boarding call for flight 656 to Los Angeles."

Okay, you bitch, I'm coming.

CHAPTER TWELVE

I had moved into my dormitory at the university and met a few of the dick-hats who were eager to get drunk and measure up the other wannabe actors. There was Jed, Jeff, and Jeremy—the three jerk-offs, as they later became known as. They all lived on my residence floor and we immediately hit it off over some drinks and drinking games.

We had begun to crush a few bottles of rye that I had brought down with me as a measure to show how Canadian I was, or something. We passed around the bottles in the common area, taking bigger and bigger swigs until they were nearly empty, marking the adequate levels of confidence that we needed to hit the strip. None of us were of legal age, but we had all come well-prepared with fake IDs—if you hadn't, you were fucked out of being important from the beginning.

We grabbed a taxi from the front of the dorm and stormed out into the L.A. night. From behind my lightly tinted *Fear and Loathing* sunglasses, the street lights of Sunset Boulevard cascaded across my corneas. I settled back into the seat, finding exhilaration in an experience that so many people lived every day, not thinking twice about it. We got out at a rooftop bar in the West Hollywood/Tri-West area and used our fake IDs to get upstairs. There was an Asian-themed restaurant on the middle floor, filled with smells that I had never experienced before. I noticed the seemingly happy conversations happening between seemingly wealthy locals and wondered at what point I would sink into their lifestyle—I felt anxious to get there as fast as possible.

The bar was packed and there were more hot women around than I had ever seen in one place. Every girl was dressed fashionably casual and sexy as fuck. My dick was a pit bull that had finally been let off of its leash in a field full of rabbits. Jeremy managed to find us a spot at a small table next to a gas fireplace that overlooked the hills, and he insisted that we all sit down. Jeremy, who had grown up in Huntington Beach, was familiar with the ins and outs of picking up "L.A. chicks." He had allegedly picked up two girls older than him the week prior, at that exact same table—given this fact, we all had to comply, so we sat down with our drinks and hoped for the same outcomes.

We ordered a few pitchers of cocktails and began to deepen our states of intoxication.

"Leave the bottle, darlin'," I found myself saying more than once.

Out back in the designated smoking area, next to the washrooms that all of the girls were coming and going from, Jed lit a hand-rolled cigarette that I took a pull from. I had smoked spliffs before but had never strictly smoked hand-rolled cigarettes. Still, there I stood, smoking darts in shorts and drinking my summer earnings away. I reflected on my *schadenfreude* concerning those back home gearing up for the cold Westfield weather and more of the mundane. I felt invincible.

"So, what's the plan, Zach? Actor? Writer? What's your deal?" Jed asked casually.

“Actor. Been in a few plays in NYC, I wanted to go there but I got too drunk and fucked up my admissions interview,” I replied.

“Shiiit, brutal, man. Lucky you got an interview there, which school?” he urged.

“The American Academy of Dramatic Arts.”

“Goddamn, bro, fuckin’ tried to get an interview there and I couldn’t even get that much. Good on you, that’s a step in itself. We’ll have a good time here. L.A. is fun, lots of hot chicks and opportunities.” He gave me the cigarette back, gesturing that I should take another drag.

“Hot bitches and opportunities, sounds like my kind of Hollywood,” I joked, staring at a girl’s ass as she hurried into the washroom.

“Speaking of this town, you ever heard the story about Hollywood?” Jed asked.

“Nah, man. Well, I mean—what you mean?”

“Like the name, how she got her name,” Jed inquired again.

“Nah, can’t say I do.” I took another drag and a sip from my now warm beer.

“Well, you oughta know, if you’re living here. See, there was this guy, Whitley, some wealthy fucker who bought some land—like a lot of fuckin’ land, like 500 acres of the Hollywood hills. He was already some big landowner. Anyway, back in, like, 1886, he was out for a walk up in the hills—you know, just minding his own business, taking in that goddamn view that we all know and love in this city. Well, this foreigner —I dunno where he was from, England or something, ha, maybe Canada —well, this guy walked by.” He took the cigarette back for a drag and passed it to me again before he continued.

"This guy walks by him and they chat, you know, shoot the shit and take in the view from the peak. The guy explains that he's just hauling wood, like some poor bugger, who knows, but actually, yeah, he was Chinese or somethin', said it like, 'haaauly wood.' Just imagine, man, this poor guy hauling wood next to this rich-ass guy. Ya know, it's like this town now, sorta, walking by millionaires every day even though we're broke!"

I laughed, somewhat amused by the punchline, somewhat amused by the girl who came back out of the washroom.

"But yeah, so, this guy has an accent, right? 'Cause he's a foreigner and all, and old Whitley thinks he says 'Hollywood' not 'hauling wood.' Whitley is a man of creativity, so he gets all excited and the name 'Hollywood' is born, because he decides that 'holly' represents England and 'wood' could represent his Scottish origins. So, anyway, he poses this name to a few friends over some drinks and it eventually makes it to this chick Daeida Wilcox, a friend or something, who tells her husband who then registers the land title."

"Crazy story," I replied, not sure if I was all too excited about it. Jed could tell.

"You're missing the point, bro. This city is all about what you do with everyone else's genius, it's a fucking cesspool of concepts and screenplays out there. Whitley heard what he needed to hear and old Wilcox stole the idea all the way to the land titles office. If you're a slippery fuck like Wilcox, you sign someone else's fuckin' idea into stone and you're a made man. What you don't want to be is that fuckin' foreigner 'hauling wood,' just fuckin' obliv' to what you're saying and doing, having someone else capitalize off of your words. For real, the Wilcox guy got Polio or some shit and died, but he's got the claim to the Hollywood name if you ask me. He stole it, fair and square—he's the one who registered it. Unfortunately, he also wanted to turn this place into a goddamn Christian sanctuary, so it's a good thing he was eaten alive. Whitley survived the fiasco and turned this place into the goddamn den of thieves, bootleggers, actors, and harlots that it is today—ha, Wilcox tried to steal the father of Hollywood's title and ended up with no legs, just like Lt. Dan." He looked very amused with himself and his depth of knowledge on the subject.

"Shit, did you come up with this lecture? All along I thought you were just another student, and now you tell me you're one of my professors?" We both laughed.

"Be aware of it, bro, keep it in mind." I didn't.

I put out our cigarette on the faded white railing and we headed back to the table. After we sat down, Jeff made a joke about Jed's story and told me that he had gotten most of it right, but again, no one really cared.

Meanwhile, Jeremy was sitting with a few girls that I would later learn he knew from Dana Point, and who I had more of an interest in than Jed's stories. I struck up a conversation with one of them. She was actually from Michigan and had just moved to southern California to study marine biology. I found her drive to leave Michigan intriguing and not so dissimilar to my own story of leaving Westfield.

After some banter involving the questions of "where did you grow up," "where are you going," "who else have you slept with," I decided that she was interesting enough to pursue for the night. We had a few more cocktails and proceeded to engage in some heavy petting under the table until we finally made plans to return to my dorm.

Just as we got up from the table, Jeff grabbed my shoulder and said: "Oh no, you don't, this night is for the boys. You take his number or you take hers, and if all else fails, you two fuck birds can call each other up when the night is old and tired."

Jeff wanted to be a screenwriter and he tried to speak as if he was one —all of the time.

"All right, man, all right. We get it. Let's do this," I conceded. She appeared disappointed, given that she wasn't from L.A. and likely needed a quick friend. She would soon learn to live with that disappointment, or she would end up having to move back to Michigan as a failure pretty quick.

We got into another taxi and found ourselves walking into a rock bar filled with girls pierced and tattooed in areas that I had never imagined was possible. This was not The Den, with its shitty cock-rock prairie bands, this was fucking death metal meets Springsteen. Within ten minutes, Jeremy was ordering more drinks and doing body shots with a chain wrapped around him that was strapped to a girl's choker necklace. After her tits came out, we all did body shots and sucked her nipples before Jed took a blow to the back of the head by her alleged boyfriend.

All hell broke loose as Jed and Jeff jumped on the guy, and his friends jumped on them. In a whirlwind of testosterone, I spun around and smoked a chick right in the face with a left hook. Then I took a kick in the balls, fell to the floor, and found myself smiling up at the ceiling as the lights and calamity danced above me; all the while, I sunk deeper into the sticky, hard floor. I could hear the music in perfect tune as the band broke into a grungy acoustic ballad, seemingly unfazed by the brawl that was going on above me. It was certainly not The Den that I was used to—I was glad to be lying on that floor covered in filth and blood. It was fucking amazing.

I got up from the floor and hurried off to the bar in a rampant stumble, hoping to get one last swig of liquor in me before being thrown out.

"Shit, looks wild. Gimme the bottle, babe, I'm-a finish this one off tonight."

The bartender reached over the bar and kissed me, biting my lip until it bled, almost putting her eye-tooth through it.

"Fuck!" I yelled in excitement.

"You can't handle another drink, lil' bitch," she said as she turned her back to me with more attitude than I'd ever seen in a woman.

I was suddenly grabbed by a man ten times the size of me, dragged out back, and then thrown into a pile with the three jerk-offs. As if we had just come out of a comedy film screening, we all began to laugh hysterically.

"Bro, you hit a chick in the face!" Jed laughed.

"Shit," I said.

"You are one crazy motherfucker, Zach Monte."

Score one for Zach.

CHAPTER THIRTEEN

When I first arrived in L.A. and had begun to accept myself as the unimportant, nobody actor that I never thought I would be, I started to spend a lot of time scouring social media platforms and following B-list actors in hopes of garnering some attention. I would send them direct messages, post comments on their photos, and straight-up inquire about going on dates with the better-looking ones, guys or girls. I never found success in that technique, but it offered up a much-needed connection to a part of the L.A. culture that felt untouchable. You might run into a famous someone getting their quad-shot latte one minute but they were untouchable the next—and for someone like me, that was infuriating. I wanted to be that person, sipping that latte and then disappearing into fame, not the person trying to hunt them down.

I spent the rest of my time during the first few months of classes dodging between performing, networking, binge-drinking, smoking too much, and incessantly trying to fuck that bartender chick from the rock bar who had bit my lip.

I would drop out of classes early to catch her before her shift started and continually do all of the things that I had learned to do to pick up girls in Westfield. Problem was, this wasn't Westfield. After five attempts, she eventually let me in on a little secret: I was being fucking pathetic, which was not admired in L.A., let alone a bar with whips involved. I ditched the effort and chalked it up to some good old education and time well spent inside of a real classroom.

I managed to legitimize myself in the classes that were made up of rich kids from New York and *actually* rich ones from China. It became known that their parents had set them up in the hills with unlimited amounts of money to spend as a means of sheltering their retirement savings from the Chinese government. I enjoyed these kids—rich and dumb-as-fuck was my jam after a long day of becoming more and more broke and desperate for work to subsidize my party-boy lifestyle. My parents put a lot of wealth into me, but I was spending like a Saudi Prince's son, and they were Canadian public servants.

I had met a lot of girls from class, as well. In particular, there was a girl named Asha, who was a fine arts major from Newport. She was a slim brunette with blue eyes, medium-tall, worked out, ate well, and made me work to lay her. We had met on a Monday morning over the last bagel at the local health food bar that I couldn't afford. I naturally got the bagel, and her number, after making some joke about chivalry and sexual harassment.

After a few more meet-ups at the health food bar, we began to spend our days and nights together. We would get up early, drink expensive espresso shots and run up the Santa Monica stairs in the morning sun, racing the whole way. In the afternoons, we would take road trips down to Laguna, Dana Point, or Swamis in the 1999 BMW Cabriolet that I had bought. I was obsessed with seeing all of the places from a childhood that

I hadn't lived, and we spent a lot of time on the PCH as a result of that—but Asha didn't mind, she was used to the traffic.

Our favorite pastime was having Asha strip down to a thong bikini while I took photos of her around L.A. and Newport. She was an influencer before influencers got paid for pulling their tits out to pose in photos with organic oatmeal and lip gloss products in exotic places. Asha simply did it for the attention, and I joined in so that I could see her almost naked, publicly exposed and looking perfect whenever I had wanted.

Asha loved to pose on open stretches of beach with the sand stuck to her ass cheeks after she got up from the ground—it added "texture," she would say. She also loved to lie down where the ocean met the land, topless with her bare tits pressing into the sand. She was the supermodel from my dad's soft-core magazines, the one that I had always wanted to ask if she had shown her tits to the photographer in the end. In most regards, it was more than I ever could have imagined when I considered the ball-locking word: *love.*

Concerning my own level of exposure, Asha got me auditions for commercials that aired up in Canada through a connection she had with a childhood friend. While visiting Westfield on breaks from classes, these commercials were my eventual tickets of affirmation that spoke to my developing fame. They proved I was remaining consistent with the trajectory of the success and stardom I had preached in high school and that yes, indeed, Riss was right: my future was certain. In reality, however, I was falling behind on my rent and I had barely enough money to afford two meals a day.

Something had to give, as I was facing the real possibility of having to return home when my tuition bill arrived, noting that my grades weren't high enough to maintain my scholarships. Something *would* give, and it wasn't going to be my giving in and giving up.

Despite the infection of poverty that kept growing and growing all around me, I continued to work those small commercials and earn enough to get by. I had started getting drunk before going on dates with Asha to save money and occasionally, I would let her pay for dinners or our health bar fixes. I felt useless but strategic for accepting the money; it was the only way that I could maintain our shared lifestyle and keep moving forward.

Asha was wealthy enough to maintain it; I think she had some funding from rich parents who I hadn't met at the time. They didn't follow her social-media thong photos, or maybe they did—that wouldn't have surprised me. I had always wondered up until moving to that city how porn stars managed to break it to their parents that they were making a living by shoving dildos inside themselves and getting fucked from behind by some dude with Polynesian tattoos (who likely wasn't Polynesian).

After meeting Asha, I had begun to understand that dynamic a bit more. As wholesome as those southern Californian babes pretended to be, fame and making a decent dollar seemed to surpass God's words of wisdom. It was as though there was some piece of scripture from an even newer "Californian Testament" that every motel from Eureka to Tijuana stocked for the weary traveler to discover in the drawer next to the bed with magic fingers. In this Testament, there was surely an extra writer besides John, Paul, Peter, and the gang. Perhaps they were reading the scripture of a guy named Billy Bones, Max Hammer, or John Boneher. I'd laughed to Asha about this once, and had insisted that every porn star's bible had a scripture at the end that read: "Though shalt not commit sexual promiscuity, unless thou are in the middle of a ganging-for-pay, then shit's cool." I was witty like that, that's what made it easy for people to fall prey to my well-crafted lies.

Asha came up to me one day after class and asked for a favor that I felt inclined to fulfill, given that she was partially subsidizing my life. It was the Newport Harbor Yacht Club's annual fall fundraiser for some African nation, and she wanted me to attend as her plus one. Normally, I would have been thrilled at the idea of schmoozing a bunch of rich assholes; it would be a great opportunity to get them to open up their checkbooks and support my dying acting career. But instead, the idea of attending this ball had me sweating since I knew that my $800 graduation suit wouldn't cut it; it was going to cost me more money to attend the thing than I would likely receive in donations.

"Yeah, I, uh, I could come, I guess, but how much are tickets?"

"Of course, we're covering the ticket—we're members there, babe", she said with a laugh in her voice. I had no idea how wealthy her family actually was until hearing that.

"Oh, yeah, sure. I'll just have to get a new suit."

"Oh, fun, we can go shopping together!" she offered.

"No! I mean, no, its all good, one of the jerk-offs wants to go shopping anyway, we'll grab one," I lied.

"All right, well, it's tomorrow night at six. Pick me up? It'll be fun, can't wait." She walked over to her white Range Rover and got in, rolling down the window to blow me a kiss. *I'm fucked*, I thought as she pulled out of the university parking lot.

In the end, I didn't go shopping and decided just to wear my shitty, juvenile grad suit, as it was all I could afford. I had also decided to just formally accept the narrative of being a poor student, if anyone asked.

I picked Asha up at six and we drove down to Newport, which consisted of sitting in traffic for two hours.

"Fuckin' SoCal traffic, we're gonna be late."

"I plan these things. It starts at 8:30, we're good," she replied as she changed the song on my outdated stereo system. The traffic dragged on longer as the local police sped by in the HOV lane to pull over another rich, single-passenger driver trying to get to Newport before us.

"Should we just absorb the ticket and skip the lines into the HOV?" she had asked.

"No, no, it's cool. We'll make it there on time. I've got you planning shit, remember?" I replied, considering the impact absorbing a ticket would have on my dwindling funds. My parents had transferred more money to my bank account and they certainly would not have been pleased to see that it all had gone to the Orange County Sheriff's Department. We sat in traffic longer until we finally pulled off of the freeway.

We drove up to the Yacht Club and I offered my keys to the valet, who was either from Chino or Crenshaw. He accepted my ten-dollar tip as if we were in the same club by nodding his head and recognizing that my suit was worth just as much as his. We were greeted by a glass of expensive champagne and some hors d'oeuvres that looked like shrimp on a rice cracker with a smear of cream on it. I loved the atmosphere—this is what I wanted, but I didn't belong yet and felt uncomfortable in my high-school suit.

Once inside, Asha and I parted ways and I avoided contact with her for fear of running into her parents and having to explain that I was from some small town in the middle of some boring, cold tundra. My story was old and tired to the Newport masses, despite its appeal to the admissions committee at the school for the performing arts that I attended. I was a proletariat on paper, and that was all that really mattered in a place like Newport.

"Hey, you, what's your deal? Who are you here with?" A girl, roughly my age, bumped my shoulder with hers as I was standing next to the bar alone, trying not to be seen. "You look like you're hiding from someone, or something. What's your deal? You seem interesting—well, I guess that isn't saying much in a crowd like this."

"It's Zach. And I'm trying to avoid this entire place, at this point. Some girl was following me around, some girl from university that I came here with. I just wanted to check it out for myself, Newport Harbor."

"A bit scandalous, if you ask me," she said. I looked over at her to take a good look for the first time. *Not bad, not great,* I thought.

Her name was Sara and she was slightly less attractive than Asha. Well, a lot less attractive, if I were to be honest about the situation—Asha was a goddamn supermodel. I wanted to remain unseen, so I continued to entertain the conversation while walking it over to the corner of the room. My intrigue in the dialogue deepened after she disclosed that her father was a wealthy studio executive involved in the film industry. She immediately became more attractive than Asha. Say what you will—I wasn't that shallow; looks aren't everything.

"Yeah, I've been studying theater, screenwriting, some introduction to entertainment law courses, the standards. I've managed a few commercials, it's coming along," I half-lied.

"Well, I already work in the industry, so we should chat sometime," she said in a flirtatious way.

"Yeah, I'd dig that," I replied, knowing that our conversation was why I had bothered to attend the event in the first place.

"So, you act, then?" I continued to question her.

"Oh god, no, I've luckily avoided that rat race my entire life. I work in admin for my father's studio—kinda boring work, but I get to meet some cool celebrities and attend some red carpet events. You're not from here, huh?"

"What makes you think that?"

"Well, for one, you seem impressed that I work in the industry; everyone here works in the industry in some capacity. Whether you're nip-tucking tits for actors or revising screenplays, this place is all interconnected. However, acting, anyone who goes near that shit is just asking for a life of poverty and disappointment."

"So I'm learning," I joked.

"Hey, that gorgeous student friend of yours is looking over at us," she said as she typed her phone number into my phone. "And you're trying to avoid *that*? She *must* be crazy. I'll see you around, stranger," she said as she walked toward her father, who was laughing with his friends over a single malt scotch.

I watched as she sat down next to her family and proceeded to laugh awkwardly about her father's mishaps last summer on his yacht trip down to the Baja Peninsula. I continued to drink and watch her father, studying him and trying to find an angle.

"There you are. Have you been hiding from me?" Asha asked, somewhat legitimately upset at my lack of attention to her.

"Yeah, no. I mean, you know, just got lost talking with some people."

"I saw you chatting up that girl over there, who is she?"

"Oh, her? Oh yeah, I recognized her, we met at a workout class in Santa Monica."

"Cheating on me with someone else at Santa Monica Fitness, are you?" she replied in a jealous, yet humorous tone.

"Yeah, yeah. Let's get out of here, it's a bit stiff," I responded.

"We have to stay, my parents are here. Let me go chat with them for a bit and then you can come over and meet them. Grab another drink, relax—it's all free."

She was onto my insecurities.

While Asha walked over to her parents, I wandered down to the docks with a triple tequila and soda. I sat down, threw it back, and lit a joint that I had tucked away in the inside breast pocket of my cheap suit.

"Hey, bra, bit too stuffy in there or what?" I heard out of the darkness behind me.

"What's it to you?"

"Nothing. Pass that joint if you're a kind dude, I need some fresh air from one of those." I handed the joint to a long-haired blonde teenager who looked like a rich-boy surfer.

"Fuckin' yacht club events, bro. Get sick of em', hey?"

"First one," I replied honestly.

"Shit, no doubt. Name's Richard, nice to meet you, bro."

"Yeah, you too. So, what's your deal, you live here?" I probed.

"Yeah, dude, Newport born and raised. Fuckin' town is a drag, dude. I get exclusive rights to surf the Wedge, but fuck, gotta get out to Hawai'i or Australia, man. Rich folk don't get me."

"Well, that's cause you're rich, and that's a goddamn privilege."

"Ha! Nah, bro, money ain't all it's cracked up to be. My folks are fucked, fighting their whole lives for the dollar bill. I'm good with a hammock and a cool buzz."

"That sounds like pretty pointless living to me—unnoticed and irrelevant living."

"Say, what do you do, bro?" he deviated.

"I'm an actor."

"Ah, yeah, that explains it. You're a Leo, hey? Gotta be in the center of shit, I get it, that's cool. I know a couple guys who moved up to the city to take it on. Some made it, some didn't. I dunno what they're up to now, actually, probably burned out, surfin' Malibu point. You ever get wet, dude?"

"Like surf?"

"Yeah, dude."

"Yeah, I mean, I'm not from the beach where I grew up, so not really. Once or twice on vacation in Oregon as a kid."

"Goddamn, Seaside Point, dude—best left in America, if you can get a wave there without getting a black eye. Savage fuckers up there, living in their flannel under wooden A-frames. Real hard motherfuckers in pickup trucks."

"Now that sounds familiar," I laughed.

"Gotta get up there someday. You're lucky, dude."

"Ha, trust me, brother—if you knew where I was from, you would not be calling me lucky." I took a big pull of weed into my lungs and held it.

"Hey, thanks for the fresh air, man. I gotta get back in there. Good luck with your career and shit, just don't get lost like all of these fucking clowns here. It's easy to get lost in this place. Aloha!"

His words were those of a stoned, privileged surf-kid from Southern California for sure, but there also seemed to be some wisdom hidden in there somewhere. I considered heeding his warning and tried to figure out why anyone would choose a life of being unrecognizable and unaccomplished. *Cool buzz and I'm fine*, I thought. *Stole that from a fucking movie.*

I flicked the roach of the joint into the harbor water and went out front of the Yacht Club to get the keys to my car. *I got what I came here for; that Sara girl could really come in handy,* I justified to myself.

I called Asha on my phone and asked if she wanted to catch a ride back to L.A. She insisted that I was too drunk to drive and I insisted that she hadn't even seen me all evening. Finally, she conceded and settled on staying at her parents' mansion up in the hills for the night while I ripped up the 605 in the HOV lane to pass out in my shitty dorm room bed like the lower-class citizen that I was.

CHAPTER FOURTEEN

The next week, I was sitting on the patio of a café in Calabasas after a casting call for a small feature as a voice actor on a new network special. It was about some animated action character who was apparently mildly popular overseas. They'd needed an actor with a Canadian accent for an episode and, apparently, I had fit the bill. I'd never considered Canadians to have accents when compared to Californians, but I was happy to get the paycheck—I needed it.

I drove up to Burbank for the call in the morning and then decided to swing into Calabasas to buy a used car that I had my eye on. I had planned to sell the more expensive Cabriolet, as I had decided that it was perhaps a bit impulsive, given my current financial situation. I was able to fuck Asha without it, so it seemed like a wise, grown-up decision.

I settled into the café, sipping on a tequila soda under a palm tree facing the Calabasas Library. The café was surrounded by a large, open square that was filled with king palm trees and waterfalls. There were about fifteen people in the café, some attractive, some already drunk at eleven a.m., and some who looked like they shouldn't have left their beds in Crenshaw that morning; perhaps I was looking more like the latter by the day.

I recognized a few other students from my class sitting across the bar from me; it wasn't uncommon to run into other actors and students in Calabasas. The area was a spill-out spot for many of us after auditions or meetings in and around North Hollywood. Showing up there had a way of making us feel like we were a part of the upper echelon, so we all did it.

I looked around at the suits sweating in their blazers in the middle of winter. Something happens when you spend too much time under the California sun—it has a way of making everyone a bit stir-crazy with how pleasant the temperature is, how easy it is to order a drink in a T-shirt and joggers year-round. Without seasons, it's as though the ideal weather patterns of the world are taken for granted and the notion of change all but forgotten. It creates an almost stale cycle of never-ending expectation, so that when the tide does change, everyone feels it that much more.

I focused in on the conversation the students I recognized were having. One frizzy-haired Jewish kid was bragging about meetings that he had set up in the afternoon with a few of the larger networks. I recognized him from our screenwriting and directing classes; he was good, really good. I listened as he droned on about the story idea he had and the impact it was going to have on his career. He wouldn't share the concept, but by his ability to capture the attention of the other four at the bar, I could tell that his inquiry letter would be worth opening up. *What did Chuck Palahniuk call it?* I asked myself. *Crowd seeding.* He was seeding people, and they were all over his story.

The five kids continued on, drinking more and more until they all began to take turns pissing their OJ and prosecco into the porcelain. For a guy with a big network meeting, he was sure getting fucked up, I thought.

I should probably digress to explain the attitude I had adopted after eating spam and rice for my meals while drinking fifteen-dollar cocktails and seven-dollar espressos for breakfast. I had begun to become ruthless. I had turned off the idea of finding love with Asha, and had turned on the idea that I had to cheat, fuck, and steal to get ahead.

I became a savage asshole at auditions, using all sorts of psychological fuckery to make people feel like shit and even throw up and bail at times. If Joe had groomed me for a certain level of competition, I was now well beyond it. I was taking my ruthless attitude to unprecedented levels, coming just shy of murder to land the role of Bystander #4.

I had pissed on dorm mates' clothing before audition days, left cigarette burns in their costumes, and slipped them laxatives to steal their roles while sitting in as their backups. I had become a total and utter dickhead, all in the name of stardom. So, on that day in February when the weather was a little warmer than it should have been for that time of year, when the alcohol was flowing just that much faster and the bartender pouring just that much more into that Jewish dude's cocktails, I made a decision to make it in the world of Hollywood. And someone else was going to have to suffer for me to get there.

They stood up from the table and casually dropped a bunch of Benjamins down for the entire room to see. The Jewish kid looked over at me and gave me a wave, likely recognizing me, which was a good thing for my confidence at that point.

I looked at the ice at the bottom of my now-empty glass of tequila soda and asked for the bill, because I couldn't afford another one. I saw the waiter slip a bill from their table into his apron; *fucking good tip,* I thought.

I didn't leave a tip. I walked out to my Cabriolet and jumped over the door like I always had. Fumbling around half-drunk, I found my phone and noticed that Sara had sent me a text message. It was filled with emojis —happy faces, high fives, and martini glasses. I ignored her childish insecurities and got to the bulk of the message—she was asking to see me again after our conversation in Newport. My heart jumped at the opportunity, having had just decided that I needed to find an opening to exploit in order to improve my fame situation. I wrote her back, with a few emojis, and indicated that I "couldn't wait" to see her again.

I was never much of a believer in general fate, but I had a strong belief in my own; I took her call as a sign. I followed up by telling her that I would love to take her for a walk on the beach with a glass of wine—*classic,* I told myself.

"You sure our friend from the Yacht Club won't mind?" her next text read, with more insecure emojis that followed.

"Absolutely not," I replied.

I put my phone away and smiled like an emoji myself as I felt the leather seat warm my back. It reminded me of how much I loved that car, and I promised myself that I would buy a newer, better version of it sometime soon.

I accelerated out of the parking lot, screeching my wheels just like old Rat Face in a rush to sit in two hours of traffic. First thing was first: I had to exchange my last piece of false-fame for a typical, middle-class Toyota in the same way that I was about to trade Asha for someone like Sara.

CHAPTER FIFTEEN

It took some time, but I strategically worked my way into Sara. It involved a few business expenses that included dates and trips to visit the skyline in my rusted 1992 Toyota, but she took to my tactics quite quickly. Asha and I had broken up after she found out about Sara, and I learned firsthand what the notion of sacrifice was all about. My relationship with Sara was about business, even though she was unaware of that.

Asha continued to post new photos, taken by some new photographer/boyfriend, which put me right back to the status of "high school jerk-off Zach." *It had better be worth the sacrifice*, I thought as I thumbed through her latest half-naked photos. Sara was in my life because she was strategic and because I didn't have the luxury of pursuing anything that resembled a silver-screen romance. I had several nude photos of Asha still on my phone, anyway, meaning that my all-access pass wasn't totally revoked.

The more time I spent with Sara, the more I thought about her father and what he could do for my career—I became obsessed with it. I drank to it, I ran and thought about it, I punched walls and pushed my school life out of mind because of it. I was on a more important trajectory than they were; I was working on becoming famous and my plan needed to be flawless.

I was tired of the classes that provided students the opportunity to work in the mailroom of a studio, and I was tired of hearing people talk about the shitty roles they were getting and the ones that I wasn't. I ruminated on that little frizzy-haired fuck's enthusiasm about his screenplay while trying to sleep in my dorm at night, until I eventually decided to take something from his playbook instead of my own.

My idea was simple enough and, although out of character for me, I got it in my head that I could write a screenplay with a little help from a few of the pros. In my classes, screenwriting was always talked about like it was an easier gig to get into than acting, and God knows I had read enough screenplays to know how to format one. Whether it was the university's attempt to boost its numbers of "successful graduates," or if it understood almost outright that our chances of becoming Satan were more likely than becoming actors, the program pushed it.

Given that I had written fuck-all up until then, I had to get into the good graces of Sara's father so that I could get into his office to read a few inquiry letters from bigger writers to see what was selling. I figured it might be an honest way to kick-start my own writing career, given that my most recent efforts in class had fallen short of total shit; I needed all the help that I could get.

I hadn't seriously considered the tactic illegal—perhaps slightly frowned-upon, but not illegal. I had always re-affirmed to myself that this was what people did to get ahead in entertainment, that success was a collaboration of the bold and the slightly talented.

I had to face it: my acting was good, but all those years of rehearsal didn't mean shit in a city where talent only went so far. In Hollywood, you can be the next goddamn Brad Pitt, but, just like Brad, you'll be living in a fucking van for years before anyone notices you—and, most likely, they *won't* notice you, resulting in your timely move to a place like Nebraska or Idaho.

I wasn't going to settle for Nebraska.

Sara and I had just gotten a coffee in Malibu when I brought up the idea of meeting her father and seeing his office. She wasn't overly enthusiastic about seeing her father on her day off from promoting events for the studio—she enjoyed her job, but it wasn't her life. We took our coffees for a walk down to the private beach that her father had shares in, and I continued to rationalize and appeal to her sympathy. The sand along the beach's shoreline felt cool on our feet as we danced around the topics of entertainment and business. We bantered on about how Sara had gotten into the business and I tested the waters of what she thought about myself as a screenwriter.

"I thought you were an actor?" she questioned.

"Yeah, but I think if I really want to make it, I mean, writing might be something that has to come first." I was lying, even to myself.

"You think you can write? Have you even ever written anything? I mean, besides something in one of your classes—we both know that that doesn't count."

"Yeah, I've written lots. It was my main interest before I got into acting," I lied again.

Sara didn't fully buy it, but she eventually obliged to let me meet her father after I had explained how much it would mean to my career to meet a guy with his portfolio of films. She was rightfully cautious about introducing people to him; she'd been burned once by some douchebag who had ended up getting a role as an extra in one of his films—what a waste.

We walked up the beach to the parking lot where I opened the door to my Toyota for her, something that I rarely did, even for Asha. The lot was beginning to fill up with exhausted surfers who had made it out for a first-light surf session, and I turned the car over only to have it stall. After three attempts, it eventually kicked on—embarrassed, I drove out of the lot and onto the hot, humid freeway.

"Thanks so much for doing this, darlin'," I said.

"This means so much to me, it will be so cool," I said.

"You're the best girlfriend I've ever had," I lied.

We rattled along the highway in my white and rusted Toyota, eventually making it to the studio's head office. Getting past the front desk at a place like that was near impossible, unless you were fucking an executive's daughter—I was all smiles hanging from Sara's slightly fatty arm. Sara didn't work out at Santa Monica Fitness like Asha and I had, and I always noticed the areas of fat on her body because of that. I more often than not would casually try to pull away from her in public when other, fitter girls would walk by, but not that day. On that day, I was all-out husband material.

"Mr. Bellcheck isn't in right now, but he got your call and is expecting you two. You can go on up and make yourself comfortable, dear, he shouldn't take long. Thirty minutes, perhaps."

Thirty minutes, I calculated in my head. *Plenty of time.*

"Thanks, Tammy," Sara said with casual familiarity.

We made our way behind the desk and approached the stainless steel elevator as we were buzzed up to his office. There wasn't a fingerprint to be found on any of the surfaces, and the bright glow of the LEDs from the elevator floor-selection panel shone with an advanced level of arrogance. The elevator was fast—before I could count to ten, we had arrived on the fortieth floor. We walked down a long marble hallway that smelled like brand-new luxury cars. At the end of the hall, Sara pushed open a massive glass door that swung backwards into the largest office I had ever seen.

It had the presence of a cloud, overlooking the entire skyline of Los Angeles. A large Italian sculpture of a naked boy in the middle of the room matched the pearl-gray hue of the marble floor. It smelled like leather, clean, purified air, and sweet foreign cologne. The entire office had been structured so that everywhere you looked, you could see the skyline; it was an infinity pool filled with office furniture, hundreds of feet up in the sky.

"It's easy to dream up film concepts when you're above the clouds like this," I said. Sara rolled her eyes and began to play with a few of the awards that were on his desk, showing an almost disrespect for the level of status that her father had in the industry. You could tell she was his daughter; it was as if she was two years old, playing with the shit in his home office, about to break his Oscar's head off and get away with it.

I sat at his desk, and Sara excused herself to finish some work in her office before her father arrived. I began to snoop around and eventually found a pile of unopened letters from agencies—there were scores of them to read.

I'm not sure what exactly had gone through my mind at that point, but I found myself looking at the return addresses on the letterheads rather than actually reading the content. Then it dawned on me from the addresses that studios didn't receive inquiry letters—those were reserved for agents who then pitched entire scripts, a synopsis, or a writing sample to the studio for consideration.

I considered just taking an entire manuscript. *Fuck, that's too risky,* I told myself as I began to shuffle through the stack of thick mail, looking for a thin package that might contain just a sample of writing from which I could borrow an idea or two. I began to sweat at the idea of Sara—or worse, her father—coming in at any moment. I fumbled around faster, staining the pages with my sweaty palms. I needed a break more than anything and my pulse beating into my head was a reminder of that.

I found a standard-sized envelope and hastily ripped it open at the seam. Inside was a brief three-page synopsis and a fifteen-page sample of a story, addressed from the Russian Federation. I began to flip through it. It read like a social justice literary fiction piece, adapted into a screenplay for film.

The one writing talent that I had gained as a studied child actor was the result of reading hundreds of screenplays—I was able to recognize shit from fortune pretty easily. I considered making a run at Mr. Bellcheck's job as I read through the first few pages. I could tell that the story had an emotive opening and a good plot twist; it was dark, deep, and had the makings of a strong and incredibly marketable theme. It was about a marginalized homosexual kid from Russia who had been locked away in a prison cell for writing and submitting a screenplay to the west—based on a true story, it stated. There was a good chance that it was actually written from the inside of a Russian prison cell.

I pulled out my smartphone and Googled the address on the top of the opening letter. The map pulled up an apartment complex in Tolyatti, so I looked up Tolyatti. It appeared to be a city with a very high unemployment rate, the potential for social upheaval at any moment (hence the amazing content of the screenplay, perhaps), and, more importantly, a place where most people couldn't afford to pay a lawyer to deal with an international copyright lawsuit.

It was the Hollywood break that I had been looking for, and my intent of pulling a few cheeky ideas from a bunch of different pieces of work soon transpired into all-out theft.

Before I'd read much beyond the first few paragraphs, Sara came back into the room in a jovial way and I slipped the synopsis and manuscript sample into my bag. She began to ramble on about what she wanted to do for the rest of the day, and I nodded through my internally preoccupied state.

I had to find a way to change the contact information and letterhead without being noticed. I considered creating my own fake agency and requesting the entire manuscript, but then realized that this would be both time-consuming and risky. I told Sara that I also had to use the washroom and took the elevator down to the front desk.

I approached the clerk with my heart in my throat and asked if I could have access to a computer and a printer to print something off for Mr. Bellcheck; his computer was locked, naturally, and he had called to request that Sara do him this favor given his busy schedule.

She directed me to a small office with a laptop computer and digital printer. The font was easy enough to replicate, Times New Roman. I typed out a request for the entire manuscript and instead of putting the address for the studio, I put my dorm address. I would deal with the author's Russian agent if I had to, but I assumed that since his address was also from that same impoverished area, that he as well had little means to pursue international litigation. I sealed the request for the manuscript in a blank folder and approached the front desk again.

"Hi, Tammy, looking fantastic today. Sara and I were both commenting on that dress of yours, where did you get it?"

"Oh, this ol' thing?" she said with a Westfield drawl. "I got this just down the street at that consignment store."

"Well, you look fantastic in it, sweetheart. Oh, by the way, Mr. Bellcheck wanted you to stamp this with his seal of approval for request; he asked Sara to pass it along to be mailed—busy guy."

"No worries. You're such a doll, I hope to see you around more."

I winked in response and headed back up into the clouds to find Sara.

Once I arrived, Mr. Bellcheck—or Benjamin, as he asked to be called —was chatting lively with Sara from behind his desk, where I had just been sitting. He didn't appear half as scary as I had presumed someone of his status would be—if anything, he looked a bit feminine and meek. I shook his soft, exfoliated hand, noticed his gold Rolex, and said it was nice to meet him. With haste, my anxiety got the best of me and I launched directly into pitching Boris Somebody's Hollywood film idea.

Sara was taken aback and noticeably angry with me when I began my proposition for Mr. Bellcheck to consider reading my screenplay. He seemed amused, and inquired first about my background, which I was happy to provide. A poor kid from the northern tundra looking for his big break, who had often imagined what it was like to live in the Russian Federation as a homosexual artist, and so decided to research and write about it over a family vacation in the country—it was believable, I hoped.

Benjamin got up from his desk, sat down on his leather couch, and silenced Sara—mimicking, I'm sure, what he used to do when she asked him for more In-N-Out burgers as a child. He should have been more forceful back then.

I sat in silence on the other leather couch in the room as my heart rate began to regulate itself. What I didn't know, and soon found out from Sara, was that Benjamin himself had been a closet homosexual for some years until finally getting a divorce ten years prior after declaring his love for men. I took this as a sign from the stars above somewhere more forgiving than that city—it certainly made an impact, and it certainly explained the statue in the middle of the room.

After reading the manuscript sample taken from the full script, he began to cry. I was astonished that a man of his title and position would cry, ever, let alone while at the office.

"I don't think I've ever gotten teary over a sample of writing before, but this really hits home for me," he said while wiping his eyes with a red silk handkerchief. I began to notice his full flamboyance, with his tight blue pants and equally-as-tight high-collared melton wool sweater. He seemed almost to be acting, his reaction was so strong, and I didn't quite know what to make of it.

“So, you like it?” I inquired, with Sara scowling at me in the background.

“Like it? I love it, and I want some more”—I let him finish—“of it. This is a fantastic interpretation of a gay man’s struggle, especially as written by a straight man, Zachary! A real diamond in the rough of shit that I’ve been getting recently. I was told that I had to read something from Russia last week, you know.” He winked at me. “I like taking international requests every now and again, but this—I highly doubt that this will come close to anything else in this stack of stale writing.” He reached over to the stack of manuscripts on his desk, picked them up, and threw them dramatically into the trash bin.

“I’ll get others!” he yelled. “But this, this, I want it all! You can re-draft this, right, Zachary?” He winked, again, as if telling me something in a language that I didn’t speak. His excitement, or whatever it was, was contagious; even Sara became increasingly curious about what I had given him. He poured me a glass of scotch and we talked a bit more about the logistics of submitting a full manuscript without an agent, and then the phone rang.

It was Tammy. My heart rate shot through the roof again in fear that she was going to request his personal approval for the manuscript. *Fuck, fuck fuck, fuck!* I shouted in my head. I looked over at the door and considered making a run for it.

“Benjamin, your one-thirty is here,” she said, instead of mentioning that I had asked her to submit a request to Russia on behalf of Benjamin.

“Thank you, Tammy.” He hung up the phone.

"Babe, you look like you're about to jump from a building. Everything okay?" Sara asked.

"Fine, just overwhelming. I mean, I knew it was good, but this is all just so surreal. Thank you, Benjamin," I lied.

"Well, thank you, Zachary, and of course you too, my lovely daughter. Thank you both for bringing me this, this is making my week. It has been a shit show of a long one, at that." I shook his soft hand again and exited the room.

Well, that was the weirdest fucking experience of my life, I considered as the heavy glass door shut behind us. My heart rate remained high and I began to feel a bit dizzy.

"Better start getting friendly with the gay community, with a reaction like that," Sara said.

The fact of the matter was, I had successfully managed to get my name in the door by only sacrificing my integrity as an artist and a mediocre lay; most actors sacrificed more than that and came out on the other end with an STI and a lifetime of regrets. My future had awoken again, yet was still to be determined.

Worst case, I'll write a story about stealing the fucking thing, I thought as I exited the elevator with that jester smile I had learned in New York on my face. I walked out of the shining-silver building alone—Sara had stayed behind to catch up on work because she didn't want much to do with me at that point. I ran down the steps, feeling the Californian sun run through my soul once again after its seemingly long vacancy.

I turned the Toyota over, then again, and again, and again, until the engine finally kicked on. "Fucking piece of shit!" I yelled as I hit the steering wheel with my fist. I looked out of the rearview and noticed several suits looking at the poor kid in the shitty car cursing at the world. I clicked the transmission into gear and drove straight to my favorite beachside bar to get raging drunk on tequila.

-

For the next few weeks, I checked the mail daily and anxiously awaited a reply from my Russian ghostwriter, as I later came to refer to him. *The guy has no chance without someone like me, someone who has the artistic background and social connections to pitch it the way I can*, I rationalized.

On the third week, I received a large package in the mail from the Russian Federation—*this is it,* I thought. I walked out of my dorm's mailroom and sat in the quad to open the package with frantic, shaking hands. Inside, there was a letter thanking Benjamin and the studio for their consideration in reviewing the entire manuscript. I sparked my lighter and lit it on fire, dropping it to the concrete.

Without even reading the entire manuscript, I rushed to the campus library and made a forged copy with my name on it. I called up Sara, who was less than thrilled that I had "finished" it but was curious enough to read it. She obliged, again, and went with me to drop it off at the studio's office. I had been vetted by Benjamin at that point, and Sara had further vouched for me, so the full manuscript made its way to the creative acquisitions and production department for green-light review without question. Next, I waited to either be arrested or rewarded—there was a chance that someone had heard of the idea before.

CHAPTER SIXTEEN

It took several weeks to hear back from the studio. I had never been involved with that side of the industry and had largely been hungover during the lectures put on by pseudo-famous writers. I had always considered writers to be the mules of the entertainment industry, so a pseudo-famous writer's lecture to me was about as useful as a Barbie doll's vagina. The only writers that I did have respect for were the guys who came up with the actual concepts, but most of the writers I had met were involved in on-set rewriting and didn't have an ounce of creativity in them. On-set rewriting was generally the role of the person who provided shit filler during production—it was a high-paying job that kept the original writers at the bottom of a bottle after the film was released. I was already at the bottom of a bottle most days, given my anxiety level, so I really didn't give a shit what someone did to "my" dialogue in the end; I just wanted to get paid.

It was midday, and I had driven up the PCH to a small bar that overlooked the water. I was four tequila sodas deep when my phone rang.

"Hi, is this Mr. Monte?"

"Speaking."

"We loved the script—pretty impressive for someone with no fucking history, but isn't that how it goes in this town."

“Yeah, thanks. I've been working on it my whole goddamn life, it seems.”

“Let’s chat. Come back to our office, and maybe we can get this thing green-lit and in motion. No guarantees, Zach, but the people who have had eyes on this thing are excited, that’s all I’ll say. Who is your agent, anyway? Is this actually unsolicited? I don’t believe for a second that a spec script made it across Benjamin’s desk without ten other people having had eyes on it first. No one accepts spec scripts these days.”

“Who is this again?”

“Call me Benz.”

“His daughter.”

“What about her?” asked Benz.

“I’m seeing her, so I met him that way.”

“True shark in the murky waters, aren’t you, Zachary? I respect that, but I still don’t believe this shit was unsolicited and that no one's ever heard of you. I’m a skeptic, Mr. Monte, and I do my due diligence, background as a lawyer and all.”

“Well, I’ll come and convince you that I’m worthy of a green light,” I stated.

“Indeed, the salty, murky, shark of a writer that you are. I look forward to meeting you.”

Click

So far, no mention of fraud, which was an encouraging start to things after speaking with a “skeptical” lawyer. I took another sip of my tequila soda and wandered down to Sara’s dad’s private piece of beach. I was seeing less of Sara at the time, but was still enjoying the perks of dating her. I pulled out a cigarette and my flask and took them both into my system to help me digest the news.

I had continued to remain poor for many months until I got word of a real figure and indication that they actually wanted to produce the goddamn thing. I didn't need the press of a negotiation over price and I had no idea what writers actually got paid so I didn't haggle; I was just trying to make rent, after all.

I was assured that for a first-time writer, I might get an absolute fortune. Apparently, my potentially generous payout was a result of a famous director and cast who had agreed to sign on for the project—that meant a big budget. It was all too surreal; I just wanted to stay in California for another year before having to fold my cards and return home. Yet there I was, being told that I was going to be the creator of the goddamn blockbuster of the year.

I didn't argue about pay, but I had insisted that we change the title and requested that I be credited for it under the pen name "M. G." They didn't give a shit.

When the final numbers came in, I was promised at least $750,000—*that'll fuckin' cover the rent,* I laughed to myself when I got the call from Benz.

For all I was worth, I was clever but not a genius—but clever people always end up rich between three stage walls, while the geniuses end up on lithium between four padded ones.

CHAPTER SEVENTEEN

Sara and I had broken up after she'd figured out my intentions and after I had decided that subjecting myself to her cellulite was no longer necessary. She wasn't surprised—she was from L.A., after all—and her father understood because he had to at that point.

Despite the movement on the film, I was still living like a broke-ass actor destined for an early death by overdose. Without the funding of Sara as my girlfriend, things really began to shrink in terms of my leisure and social life, as well. I rented in Van Nuys after I could no longer afford residence and I fucking hated Van Nuys. I hated the commute, and I hated the fact that I was surrounded by relative poverty when I returned home from meetings with rich people.

I had to trade my expensive dorm room for a shitty one-bedroom apartment after I had spent almost all of my savings on booze and racked up over 15 grand in debt on my credit card trying to stay relevant.

I had found work to support my single-bedroom shit hole after disclosing to Jeff that I was struggling to make ends meet. Jeff was a very unthreatening guy; he was on student loans and didn't come from money. He was a theater actor, like myself, from Vermont—and having grown up with a few sisters, he had an empathic soft side that landed him an intern job in HR at a film studio. The only kicker for Jeff was that the studio produced porn films—I appreciated this, while Jeff was ashamed of it.

Jeff 's job was to make sure that all of the actors were well represented in processing their medical claims for various STIs and bouts of conjunctivitis that they had obtained on-set. My job was working as a stand-in actor in the films themselves. Anyone who has ever watched porn knows what my role was. I was the unlucky guy who walked in on his girlfriend getting slammed by the neighbor in the kitchen or the pool house. On the really spicy sets, I was the best friend who was peeping through the crack of a bedroom door, filming it all on an iPhone. While I never got naked on film, I had wanted to practice my improvisation skills on more than one occasion.

I think the only saving grace for Jeff was the studio's affirmative action policy to curb misogyny. Instead of:

"Oh my God, Daddy!"

"Jade! You slut!"

My lines were more like:

"Oh my God, Dad!"

"Tristan, you should be ashamed of the position that you're fucking your girlfriend in—very demeanin', get off of her right this instant, son, and show some respect for women!"

Fade to black.

There was a market for it; there were a few Jeffs out there who got off on that sort of thing. It was a fun gig and it paid for my tuition and cocaine use, but it wasn't a long-term solution. I worked every weekend and was assured by Jeff, who knew HR, that my videos would only be streamed on sites with IP addresses outside of North America—it was a nice way to guarantee that you'd still have a career if you ever made it big someday.

My part-time porn efforts had subsidized a much lower-class life than I was used to, and I began to enjoy the air in the flat that was permanently filled with a slight haze of weed, tobacco, and sex sweat. Out of necessity, I had kept a favorite couch that I had picked up off of the side of the road during my inaugural frosh run through Compton; it had become the main fixture in the small living room.

"It's more than a centerpiece of poverty," I would say, "it's a piece of hip-hop music history." Whichever way you looked at it, it was a slightly torn black leather sofa that had endured one too many pull-outs.

After a long day of sex-acting, I sat down on my piece of musical history and put on a vinyl record of my favorite band that I had been listening to at the time. I lit a joint and cracked a fresh bottle of tequila and waited for the phone or the doorbell to ring. Within twenty minutes, there was no ring but a knock on the door. I got up and opened the door to find Jed with two girls from class.

"Door bell's broken, dude," Jed said as he walked into the room, looking around—judging.

Jed and Jeremy liked to come by my place because of the privacy it provided. Back in the dorm, there were residence coordinators and a whole dorm of guys eager to ram something up your butthole when you thought you were alone with the girl you'd brought home from the bar. It was a zoo of children on Viagra resulting in constant hard-ons for anything that remotely looked like pussy. I had had enough for one lifetime.

“This is Jen and Stacey,” Jed praised himself.

“Drinks? Smoke?”

“Both.” Stacey smiled.

“This is the guy I was telling you about, the Canadian, eh, who apparently is debuting as a screenwriter but who is really a poorly-trained stage actor; how the fuck that happened, no one knows.”

“I've got tequila, who wants soda and who just wants to have a good time?” I asked, ignoring his comment.

“I don’t care what you say, those are writer’s words to me, Jed!” Stacey chirped.

She sat down on the couch, practically on my lap. We chatted and I talked myself up a bit, telling her about the advancement that was coming my way shortly. We flirted, drank, and smoked until the final track on the first side of the vinyl skipped to an end. As I got up to flip the record, Stacey followed, holding my hand and leading me into the bedroom.

My bedroom was in decent shape for an underage alcoholic with no limits. I couldn’t wait for that cheque to come in so that I could buy a bed frame and get myself up, and off of the ground—literally.

Stacey was a hot blonde with a tight, young, round ass that snapped back into perfect shape when you slapped it, no cellulite Jabberwocky bullshit there. Her tits were smaller, but perfectly youthful, and her nipples were pink and small. I knew this immediately because of the lack of a bra under her tight white shirt, and I knew it for sure when she pressed them into my face within two seconds of getting me alone.

She got me on the ground, beside the mattress, and straddled my head, crushing it between her tight thighs. We fucked around for a while before I had had enough and penetrated her. There was no romance in it, there was no nostalgia, and there really, truly was no purpose—and that was absolute perfection.

Apparently, word had spread fast in L.A.—I was about to be a rich-ass someone, and Stacey was the first to recognize it. We lay on our backs after I finished and I lit a joint as she smiled into the darkness above us while I smiled into the darkness that awaited me on the road ahead. I blew a ring of smoke softly up and above our heads, its tail getting caught by the ceiling fan, which dissipated the smoke, swishing it all around the room.

"So, when are you moving out of this dump, and when can I move in?"

"Ha, sweetheart, I hate to break the atmosphere and expectation here, but its already move-out day for you."

-

The next day, I walked across the street to a dive-bar called *So-Cali*—you couldn't miss the 1980s glow of its neon signage. I sat down for a cold beer to combat the hot weather and smog that was rolling in that day.

"What can I get you?"

"Blue Ribbon."

The guy in a leather biker's vest poured me a pint from the silver tap.

"Here you go, bud."

"Say, how long you lived in Van Nuys, brother?" I asked.

"Whole life, my man, fuckin' whole life. Why?"

"You like living here?"

"There's worse places to live in this world, that's for sure. It's America, ain't it?"

"Yeah, truth."

"Fuckin' oath, it's truth. Where you from, man?"

"I live across the street now, but I'm from Canada."

"Shits, Canada, eh. Far from home, aren't you, brother?"

"Nah, man, this has been home all along. I've finally managed to find my way—"

"You've found your way to the bottom of a pint of shitty beer in Van Nuys, my brother." He laughed a deep, dark laugh.

"Good on you, my man—finding where you ought to be can be a lifelong journey. But, hey, you signed up for a cheap beer, not a psychiatrist. I'll let you enjoy."

I appreciated his sensitivity to the situation. Looking around the room, I noticed ten people who appeared as though they had been trying to escape that bar for the past twenty years of their lives. For me, it was the place I had wanted to be for the past twenty years. I wondered what I would be thinking if I didn't have fame and fortune coming my way. I certainly wouldn't have been enjoying that beer in a place like that.

There was something special about that moment, something that sticks out as a turning point in my life; being so close to poverty yet so close to fame. I'd felt emotional inside, knowing that was what I had trained for my entire life, sacrificed my entire childhood for.

"Fuck it, brother, pour me another one. I got all day."

I was feeling fine, feeling poor, for one last time.

CHAPTER EIGHTEEN

Forget what anyone says, having *real* money is like drowning in wine made from water—it made my life worth living again. The movie I had been promised was finally produced after I had suffered through a full year of poverty in Van Nuys. Despite the suffering, my risky accounting decision and contract had paid off, and I was well on my way to the better life that I had always promised myself.

I wasn't offered a "20 against 20" deal like the old boys got, but I took what we called a "cash break" deal in Hollywood. I was raking in the Benjamins from a mix of net points and a reduced amount of profits from the first dollar earned at the box office; what we called gross points. They knew that they were dealing with an unsolicited, nobody writer and had covered their asses by guaranteeing that I would be fucked if it flopped, instead of the other way around. They knew it was a masterpiece, but if history had shown Hollywood anything, it was that good art doesn't always translate to dividends.

In my law and entertainment class, I had learned that most screenwriters got paid up front, making their line of work more stable than that of an actor. Typically, the good writers would see between two to three percent of the studio's budget even before production started—the really good ones made their fortunes doing rewrites for $400,000 a week.

I ended up in neither situation simply because I hadn't taken the course before I signed on the dotted line; I was clueless.

I had no idea that studios often expensed everything they could to make a film look like a loss even when it was a total success. The net points-type situation was often a joke for this reason, so I had gotten lucky, real lucky. The studio recouped their costs early and paid me out handsomely. Unfortunately for me, if it had flopped, I was the equivalent of an equity investor without even knowing it. Still, the $750,000 up front wouldn't have been a bad break, either. It just would have meant that I would be looking at property in El Segundo instead of Malibu and Manhattan Beach.

I was up into the millions before it was all said and done, despite the massive risk that I hadn't realized I'd taken.

"It's a rare occurrence for a first-time writer to be a part of such a successful project," they told me on the red carpet.

Whatever, I thought.

"How is it possible that we have never heard of you?" I got asked on talk shows.

Because I stole the manuscript.

"How do your childhood friends look at you now that you've written something that is nominated for four Academy Awards?"

Fuck Joe, he's an asshole.

"That was a really risky deal you made as a first-time anyone," I was told by the accountant that I could finally afford.

Yeah, well...

I ignored the static around the deal because I was just happy to still call L.A. home. After confirming that I had been paid, I walked out of the bank and got into my Toyota, which, once again, refused to turn over. Instead of punching the wheel, I smiled, put on my sunglasses, got it to start, and lit a smoke. I put the car into gear and drove the freeway up to Burbank, enjoying every rattle and jerk of the steering column as the sun set to black.

Once up in the hills, I pulled over with the dust from the roadside flying over the hood of the car as I rolled it close to the edge of the cliffs. I got out, put the shifter into neutral, and pushed it off and into the dark blanket of night below.

From above on the cliffs, I thought of those bottles of empty liquor that we had thrown into the pond back on Lyle’s farm and how they were just like my car. I watched the car's headlights diminish with a crash, but no explosion. I thought of the girls we had thrown those bottles of liquor for and the feeling of relief that came with extinguishing my past from my future.

I lit another cigarette and sat down on the side of the road in the glow of the half-moon, watching as the city lights below flickered like sparks through bonfire smoke. I could see the growing flames of my burning car below and decided that it would be wise to call a taxi before I ended up in jail for causing the next great southern California bush fire.

I called for a cab and paid the $150 to get back to the city, ignoring his questions about what I was doing out in the middle of nowhere. I could have paid five dollars and taken the bus, but I didn’t take public transit anymore, although I had always tried to avoid that sort of thing anyway. I didn't have to do anything that I didn't want to anymore—not only was my piece of shit car on fire, *I* was on fire.

The next day, I bought myself a Porsche for obvious Freudian reasons. It was a convertible 911 Turbo, which meant that I could once again jump into a car without having to open the door. I drove the highway from Santa Monica to Ventura at sunset, aggressively racing past all of the shitty cars that slowly putted along the concrete in my rearview. It was a goddamn scene from a movie, except for the lack of cameras. I wasn't an actor yet, but the highway of fame was finally open for business—and I wasn't pulling over anytime soon.

-

After the money had arrived, I made the difficult decision to pull the three jerk-offs along with me, to some extent, despite Jed becoming increasingly aware that something was amiss.

"When you writing another screenplay, Mr. Ink and Paper? Who knew a lowlife like you could write that shit? You holding back anything else?"

I wanted to punch the guy in the dick constantly. I needed Jed around like I had needed Joe, but something told me that Jed's writing skills might come in handy one day, giving our friendship the longevity Joe's and mine had never had.

It was February when an opportunity to satiate Jed's skepticism finally found me on the pier of Manhattan Beach. I was chatting casually over a cigarette with a brunette actor because she apparently had a way to get me into the acting game. I'd gotten an actual agent at that point who had offered up my number to the Manhattan Beach Pier brunette, thinking that it would be an easy sell. This particular brunette was in her thirties and she was extremely enthusiastic about discussing my getting involved in her latest project. I was recognized as a screenwriter at that point and it was proving difficult to break that mold. I had become known as the enigmatic writer who would turn down all other writing opportunities, no matter how big the price tag—I needed a project to make me look occupied.

The brunette got close to me to keep warm from the ocean's chill, showing me what she really wanted as she began to ramble on about her life in the spotlight as a real housewife of some county and her upcoming movie. She spoke of her dreams, her hopes, and her desire to get to the top again. She promised she could get me a role opposite her because she liked my work, yet it became more apparent with every sentence that she just wanted to take advantage of my cock in her trailer between scenes. Naturally, I had no issues with this form of payment, given the opportunity, so we had a deal.

After my verbal contract was signed with the brunette on the pier, my agent filled in the blanks for me and we discussed the details of the film *Mexicali.* My portion was for fifteen percent of the gross profits, which was much less risky than my first deal had been. Obviously, my agent knew that I wanted to get back into the game of acting, so she had recommended that I get involved as an actor instead of an on-set rewriter. I was excited by the idea of getting paid, but more excited by the idea of finally having my face on the big screen after all those years.

Without much effort, I forced my way into the career of a Hollywood actor by meeting with the casting crew of *Mexicali* and by spending a lot of trailer time with the brunette during rehearsal hours. It wasn't so bad, the sex—it was worth it for the gig and the movie sounded cool enough.

Despite the handout, I always was a good actor, so the filming of *Mexicali* in the Californian desert—which posed as Mexico—was no struggle for me. I'd just needed a bit of luck to get me in front of the cameras, and once I had made that luck for myself, everything came as naturally as if destiny had ordained it.

Shit happens fast when you're suddenly thrust into the spotlight, and it's easy to ignore the facts and warnings from a guy like Jed who tells you that staying relevant is what eventually kills many a great actor or writer.

Most exiled actors will tell you that the death of an actor is not a fast death—it is a slow and painful one, shitting in your espresso shots and dumping black, cancerous tar on your future plans and self-esteem. And, minute by minute, day by day, the actor's ignorance makes it worse, like a disease being fed a contraindicated cure.

In a rare way, I had experienced this phenomenon in reverse. I grew up as the star who was then snuffed out by a lack of relevance, only to rise again from my former death on the holy cross of small-town fame. I felt immune to the irrelevance factor because of this.

My wealth and success had allowed me to drop out of university and trade my 450-square-foot cell in Van Nuys for a 2,800-square-foot luxury home on Manhattan Beach. As far as I was concerned, I had found a credible way out of the rat race that was the formal education system, and it was now time to focus on my real education—diving headfirst into life as a celebrity.

I hadn't spoken with anyone back home in a year and didn't really care for thinking about that place. I had continuously wished as a child that Westfield wasn't my "back home," and the last thing I needed was someone to remind me—like an infection on the tip of my dick—that the place still existed. I really, truly believed that my *ET Daily* scandal would never surface. I also believed that the place I had so longed to leave, that "back home," would simply disappear from the map, like some marginalized writer from some small town in Russia.

CHAPTER NINETEEN

Six months after the production for *Mexicali* had wrapped up, I was partying with the cast and a few other B-list actors (who now paid attention to my social media messages) in West Hollywood at that same bar I had visited on my first night in L.A. Being where I was professionally, sitting back at that bar where it all began, it was a fairytale.

After finishing some drinks with the cast, I had managed to link up with a local alternative-rock band that went by the name Pistola; they were a branded mix between early Springsteen and a post-grunge-punk fuck-my-country type arrangement. They were celebrating an upcoming global album release at the bar and I was in the roped-off VIP area that was segregated for our film cast. It was a natural introduction when I had met some of the girls they were partying with while grabbing my next tequila soda at the bar.

I invited them behind the rope and we partied until close that night. I seemingly hadn't wanted the party to end at all, as I began to follow them around for the next few weeks from Encinitas to Ventura, attending their rehearsals and acoustic sets. I was enticed by their ability to party as hard as me and their capacity as a group of musicians to afford their own illicit substances. That was a change from the usual for me; most of my current friends were still struggling to pay their tuition and trying to bleed me dry for narcotics that weren't meth. Pistola was my first encounter with what I liked to call "fame-friends"—those who were worthy enough to party with other celebrities and those who closely understood the trials and tribulations of being in the spotlight. We bonded over the need to use narcotics and we became friends over our desires to move past the starting line of living life to its fullest.

My "fame-friends" came over a few weeks later to screen *Mexicali* on my home theater over a few joints and Coronas. It resulted in a good laugh about my character's tragic ending and some accolades that I wasn't fully expecting from a group of guys who lived life on the sharp edge of anarchy.

To give you an idea of what the film *Mexicali* was all about, I had played the role of a high school kid from San Onofre who had gotten in with the wrong crowd driving drugs across the Tijuana border to pay for his mother's heart transplant. In the end, my character's mother died, and my character was found overdosed with a quarter-pound of heroin up his ass. The scene of me sprawled out naked in the desert, ass-up, getting found by some Mexican cartel jefe with a huge smile on his face—well, I'm sure it made my parents proud and happy for spending all of that money over the years on my classical theater training.

Jake, the lead singer of Pistola, loved the ending of *Mexicali* so much that he tattooed my character's name across his chest—real rock stars did that kind of stupid shit. Yet, despite Jake's enthusiasm and his dumb tattoo, the film didn't screen too well in L.A. Maybe it was the joints and Coronas, but my confidence was clearly misplaced.

When Jake and the guys began to rehearse more seriously, the meetings with the studio began to fill up my schedule. Despite the bad reviews that were released, the studio had decided that I was still scheduled to be sent around the world to promote the other premieres—they were paid gigs, so I had signed on to do them despite how poorly the film was received once it debuted.

Before I left on my own world tour, I linked up with the band one last time in West Hollywood on the opening night of theirs. There were hundreds of people at the entrance when I casually walked by them all with my VIP badge, and I threw a wink at a girl who was caught up in line because she looked remarkably identical to the bartender who had bit my face off and taught me my first lesson about Hollywood women. I felt good, satisfied. With adrenaline in my blood, I went inside, threw back a shot of tequila, did a line of blow, and embraced the feeling of an empty room being filled with fans.

When things began to really fill up, I did another shot and went outside of the club for a smoke. I lit the spliff and leaned myself against the faded black paint on the side of the building, below a neon sign that read "talent and worthy goddesses only." Looking through the smoke, I recognized an old friend that I would never have expected to see through a drug-infused gaze across a California night.

"Zach? Is that you?" I heard yelled from across the street. "Holy shit, wait up Rach," I heard her say through the buzzing noise of the fans and traffic, "won't be a minute."

The girl ran across the busy street with lights and horns coming at her from all directions.

Mandy looked amazing, dressed to perfection; well, as perfect as someone from Westfield could dress in a city that ate the unfashionable alive. Her ass was pulled in tight by a small-town, short red skirt, and her tits were pushed high, as perfect as tits could be without being touched by an L.A. surgeon. She was so natural, so real.

"What's up, Mandy, what are you doing here?" I asked, trying to hide my excitement by taking a casual pull on my spliff.

"I'm here for a bachelorette party, you remember Rachel? She's getting married to this guy she met out east in college."

At that moment, it occurred to me that four years had passed and I hadn't called my parents once to wish them a happy birthday.

"Was that—" She pointed with her bright green eyes across the street at the guys from the band.

"Yeah, that's them. Good dudes, you want to meet them?"

Briefly, she looked conflicted between running off with me into the sunset of fame or remaining committed to the mundane and predictable, and then she re-directed.

"So, where's a girl have to go to get into some trouble in this city?"

"I'd say either Julian's on Sunset or Moderno would be good bets, but really, you guys should come see the show. I can get you backstage, no problem. We should catch up." I reached for her arm with the support of the blow in my blood as she politely attempted to pull away.

"I had better go, the girls are waiting, it was great to see you. Joe will be happy to hear that you are doing well, you should call him sometime!"

Despite my second attempt to brush her hair from her face, she and her perfect sexuality danced away from me through the night's lights without so much as a kiss. The evening was her stage, and she was performing beautifully.

She had once been so open with me back in middle school, giving me as many kisses as I wanted during play recitals. Not any more. I looked up into the variable darkness above me and promised myself that I would find a way back to her at some point in life, even if that wedding invitation of her and Joe's that I had thrown out was real.

I turned around to join up with the band, but out of the corner of my eye, I caught a glimpse of Mandy chatting with her friends, pointing over at me in the same admiring way that a tourist would point at a famous actor while on vacation. I *was* famous, and I finally understood. There was now a divide between myself and people like her—she hadn't walked away from me because she didn't want me, she'd walked away because of the expectation that would have been there if she had stayed.

Me being a famous someone meant something; I was learning that man-in-the-high-tower syndrome was a real thing—untouchable in the mind meant untouchable in reality now. *That can be a lonely place to live,* I considered in silence.

I threw my half-smoked cigarette on the ground at the bouncer's feet and turned back inside the club to continue to party backstage with the band. I was enjoying one last night with a famous group of people that I wouldn't have had access to six months prior. What I wasn't enjoying were the constant thoughts about Mandy. I drank more than usual to keep them steady and locked away in my unconscious mind.

The band went on stage and was greeted by the roaring screams of 2,500 fans. I stood in the audience now for full effect. Jake had told me that the music heard through the stage monitors was nothing compared to the thump in the chest that I would get from standing in the middle of the crowd—he was right. They opened with a cascade of jangling, slightly distorted and delayed guitars echoing over the entire theater, reverberating out into the night and colliding with the voice of the Pacific Ocean's crashing waves some fifteen miles away.

Jake entered last through stage right and began to sing with his foot up on the monitor, arms outstretched embracing the crowd's energy—the energy that would carry him through the full one-hundred hours of set time that he had in front of him on the road. I listened and watched as they commanded the attention of the entire audience with every string struck and every vocal cord strained. It was pure, raw power, being able to control the emotions of so many people in a living moment. I knew film was capable of that same power, but I was envious of their ability to impact those emotions live.

Jake announced that they were going to slow things down for a few songs, and they brought out the acoustic guitars to play in sync with the flickering flames of lighters. I could have sworn that I saw Mandy's face shine through the flaming, dark room, but the image was lost to the thousands of other faces. I wandered to the bar for a breath of air and to see if I could find her. My gaze scanned around the room, but all I could find was myself—alone.

CHAPTER TWENTY

After the show, I brought a few people back to my new Manhattan Beach home, totally fucked up on drugs and tequila. For that reason, I had elected to jump the back fence from the beach entrance to get in, falling flat on my face on the back lawn. I had a bunch of groupies with me from Portland—some were strippers, I figured, and some were going on tour with the band. Mike, the guitarist, tagged along, acting like he was one line of cocaine away from full-blown mania. They all jumped the fence, fell on their faces, laughed, and came inside.

I opened my smartphone screen and pushed a few buttons, and the fire pit, heat lamps, and patio lanterns lit up the backyard. When I pressed a button on the wall, a glass hot tub with fish swimming between panes of glass rose out from the patio. I pretended like these were luxuries that I had been used to all my life as I got everyone drinks.

I manually put on a vinyl record and we all continued to drink, grope, and fondle each other. At most points in the evening, I had no idea who my left hand was in and no idea who my right hand was in at the same time. It didn't matter; we were all groovy, passing joints and living the good life. It was 1960s Haight-Ashbury and I was their Oregon cult leader of sexual discovery and innovation.

When the night began to wind down, Mike headed for the lounger out back with his favorite of the Portland strippers and they passed out on top of each other, still soaking wet from the hot tub. I left the fire, music, and lights on and found my way to the bedroom, stumbling down the hallway leaving water prints of my hands on the walls and chlorine marks on the Persian rugs with my feet. I grabbed the other girl's arm and we got into my bed and under the warm covers, chilled from our exit from the hot tub. I never did end up getting to orgasm that night, but I did sleep like a child and woke up to waffles in the morning—Portland strippers really are a rare breed.

CHAPTER TWENTY-ONE

The parties at my place grew progressively wilder after the band left town and I slowly began to realize that I was becoming the owner of a frat house. I was also becoming increasingly overstimulated by stimulants and the multitude of various sex partners that I welcomed into my bed—an incurable STI was becoming inevitable.

I decided to take a vacation away from it all, somewhere secluded. I took to the airport with Lucy, a webcam girl from South Padre Island that I had met while my amygdala and testosterone were firing during a period of depressive isolation back in Van Nuys. Lucy had been in L.A. for a photoshoot and we had stayed in touch over the previous months—at first, it was because I was paying a premium for the connection. After my name had become a thing in the entertainment industry, I reinforced the need for a privacy policy and Lucy began to have webcam sex with me for free. She was a real upgrade from Asha, in terms of promiscuity and openness to deviant sexual performance in front of the camera.

We sat at a wine bar in the airport, drinking in some red California nectar—not my first choice, but my healthy bank account had spurred an interest in the finer selections of ways to get drunk.

"So, where are we going, Zach?"

"You'll see, sweetheart—a place where no one can find us and where we can fornicate and forget the day before today and the day after."

Lucy giggled that sexy cam-girl giggle that had made me formally reach out to her to begin with.

"Sounds good, baby, let's get first class," she insisted.

"Is there any other way?" I felt ashamed that I couldn't afford my own G-5.

My solution to an out-of-control lifestyle was two first-class tickets to Central America. We arrived in Liberia and booked a private yacht to take us over to the Alcatraz of Costa Rica on San Lucas Island. The air was even fresher than in California, and the heat and humidity made Lucy drop a few layers almost immediately. She was standing next to me waiting for the yacht in a thong bikini, her bottom half covered by a Hawaiian sarong that fluttered up in the tropical breeze, giving the staff a quick glimpse of her perfect webcam-girl self.

I had chosen San Lucas Island because it was a place allegedly riddled with haunted, bat-infested churches and ghosts of prisoners come to pass. It was a place where salt harvesting and bleeding chained ankles was a way of life in the late 1800s; a place just dark enough to make our sex that much more intense. I didn't know much about Lucy, but from what I had seen in her videos, she liked to take things to a dark level once in a while, and I dug that.

Lucy was excited by the rumor that many of the prison cells on the island were littered with hand-drawn porn figures, including images of naked women plastered with a prisoner's blood, giving a whole new meaning to the idea of a menstrual cycle.

The yacht arrived and we departed Puntarenas for the island, drinking prosecco and fresh fruit juice while gazing off into the peaceful star-encrusted blanket that was the waves of the ocean before us.

On San Lucas, there existed only one privately-owned house, generally reserved for celebrities and political sex parties when not occupied by the President himself. It stood alone on the top of a cliff with nothing else around it—money couldn't buy that form of solitude and perfection in North America. There was a small quaint dock, and on it there was no welcoming party, lights, cameras, or bullshit. We finished our drinks slowly, out of L.A. fashion, and stepped off of the yacht and into our private paradise. I was sure the prisoners that had come to pass had endured a very different welcoming party when they had arrived—and I was sure that it was some hell.

While there was still light, we did a tour of the cell blocks so that Lucy could orgasm over the blood porn. I had picked up a copy of *La Isla de los Hombres Solo* from a local Tico that I carried along with me while she checked out the cells. The book was known by *God Was Looking the Other Way* in English—it was an edition that was quite hard to come by, I was told, but then again, maybe I was just being another naive tourist.

While Lucy walked around, I read the book's back cover, which stated that it was written by one prisoner, '1713,' who had entered the prison we were currently touring as a barely-literate man. It told that while he was incarcerated, he had published several books about his time in chains and that by merely studying magazines on how to write and read, he had become an accomplished man of literacy. As an illiterate prisoner, the fucking guy wrote more than 24 books in the end; I couldn't even think of a goddam idea for one.

Once Lucy had had her fill of her blood porn, we went back to the private beach, where I began to read the book from the comfort of the warm sand that stretched along Playa El Coco. In the background, there was nothing but the sound of howler monkeys and exotic birds, seemingly singing with the breeze in the trees below the hot sun.

While I read, Lucy went for a walk to post photos on her social media in an attempt to connect with her fans—I knew this because I was getting the notifications on my phone. I laughed at the photos of her holding her tits up and teasing the world with her spread legs covered in wet sand. I then got horny, dropped the book, and ran down the beach with a hard-on to look for her.

As we had the entire island for the weekend, Lucy was naked the entire time; not like she was uncomfortable being naked in front of large crowds, but she appeared to enjoy the lack of eyes on her for a change. We had sex almost six times a day all over the island, drank body-rejuvenating fruit smoothies, and ate local food prepared for us by a very discreet local Tica. We were drinking and eating the same fruit and greens-infused superfoods that I had access to back in L.A., but these seemed to make me feel stronger, healthier. In reality, it was more likely the lack of narcotics in my system that was causing me to feel better, not the blue-green algae, but it was a nice thought that I found comforting. Narcotics had been too risky to smuggle in and, standing army or not, my illegal fuckery and promiscuity had a limit.

Lucy and I pretended like we were in love for the weekend, and I put on the best performance in history of *Zach on a honeymoon*. Our sex became more and more dangerously passionate as the weekend expired and I had almost convinced myself that staying in prison with a cam-girl from Texas was the best thing that I could ever do for the charred, black and suffocated veins that wrapped around my heart. If this place was a prison, I wanted to spend the rest of my years trying unsuccessfully to escape from it.

That night, we wandered down to the dock with a bottle of Dom and poured ourselves a couple of glasses. Lucy began to open up and tell me more about her dog, her father who died of cancer when she was a young kid, and her mother who took to the bottle shortly thereafter. The thing that always struck me about strippers, cam-girls, and porn stars was that they all were usually such genuine, interesting and better-lived people than anyone gave them credit for. While I was enduring the sensations of a beating heart at middle school dances, this chick's heart was literally being resuscitated back to life during an overdose following her father's death.

A lot of people, including the three jerk-offs who I still talked to once every few months, would never understand why I would take a web-cam girl that I hardly knew to an exclusive island like that. I hated the mundane, the usual business and the newsstand bullshit they depended on. Out there, on that island with that girl and her sad, sorrowful history of pain, I was truly free.

Now, I'm sure that Freud would have had something to say about that but from what my therapist told me, I was going to be all right, simply because no one used psychoanalysis anymore.

We finished the bottle of Dom and, naked, both jumped into the warm ocean, swimming in circles around each other, kissing like star-crossed lovers in some movie about traveling and falling for the most unlikely of people. The water was shallow enough that we could stand on the sand, and as our toes sunk partially into the submerged ground-up rocks, we understood each other for what we were and what we wanted in life. That was the moment that I had been waiting on for so long, and I never wanted it to end.

We woke up the next morning to a phone call, Lucy's hair still damp, curly, and salty from the ocean the night before.

"Shit, I've gotta be back in South Padre for that film I was telling you about."

"The porno? Fuck, what are they paying you? I'll double it."

"You know me better than that, Zach. I'm a strong woman and I don't care about the money—I care about my career."

She reminded me of Mandy.

"Yeah, yeah, I know. Fuck."

"Thanks, baby. You know, this weekend was incredible, I don't think that I've ever spent such a meaningful weekend like that with anyone before."

"Yeah, would have been better if we could have stuck with the actual plan, though."

I had a low level of distress tolerance at that point, largely because I could afford it without driving too many people away. I threw my belongings into my Louis Vuitton bags, and tossed hers in her less-expensive Coach bags with haste.

She began to become frustrated with how I was treating her belongings. “Hey, take it easy, babe, I know you’re upset but—”

“I’m not upset. It’s fine, just a bit of bullshit.” We were beginning to argue like a couple and it was turning the sweet taste of Costa Rica in my mouth to the taste of Chinese air pollution.

“What’s the problem? Did you think that we could honestly stay living like this forever? This is a break from reality, you should know that,” she said, patronizing me.

“I’m always on vacation, sweetheart,” I responded, trying to remain calm in my tone of voice but continuing to throw my things into the bags angrily.

“Well, some of us have to hustle to make a living. Some of us can’t just live off of royalties and endorsements.”

“And there it is—there’s the broken porn star that I knew was in there. You should really speak with your agent about getting endorsements for those dildos that you shove inside yourself every day,” I replied, expecting a yelling match.

“Oh, I get paid for those,” she said, as if unable to understand why that might be offensive to someone.

I laughed, I couldn’t help it.

“You are a goddamn professional,” I replied.

“What? What do you mean?”

“You know how to mitigate horny, angry men very well—now, if more women had that personality trait, there would be more women CEOs in this world”.

“You’re hilarious. Okay, we really have to go, I found a flight out, and first class again. Leaves in six hours—think we can make it?”

“Yeah, unfortunately.”

CHAPTER TWENTY-TWO

I fell into a trance on the flight back from our island in the middle of some universe. As the clouds passed beside, below, and above us, I drifted into a deep sleep, shedding the frustrations of our early departure.

My mind opened up in a field with green grass all around me. There was a mountain range high above in the distance with snowcaps melting into small steams that rushed down the mountainside, terminating in ponds scattered throughout the perfectly groomed grass. At the top of the mountain, I could see the remnants of an icy winter that had come and tried to pass, the ice still clinging to rock like a demented mind grasping at memories.

I was looking around in an empty field—initially, there was no one to be seen until I recognized the outline of Joe and Mandy, holding hands and walking away from me toward a small, white chapel that stood against the backdrop of the mountains like an image that a child might find in a 3D picture book. I rubbed my eyes, trying to focus; they felt dry and old.

Mandy looked back at me with a smile that only a wedding day could bring out in a woman. Joe was walking silently, chin held high, and not giving my presence a glimmer of attention. Mandy and Joe continued to walk toward the chapel as I began to notice that my legs were weighed down by something sharp and heavy around my ankles.

Joe turned to hold Mandy's hands and as they began to place rings on each other's fingers, he remained fixated on Mandy's eyes—and Mandy began to stare deep into mine, breaking the fourth wall of their performance. As she continued to gaze deeper into my soul, the white chapel exploded into the most extravagant display of flames that any human mind could dream up.

Joe turned to look at me right before he burst into a million blue and white birds that flew directly into the flames, catching fire and screeching for their lives as I watched on in absolute horror. The chapel began to fall to ashes and the mountaintops began to melt with a sudden flash flood of fire and lava, teeming down their sides and engulfing the inflamed chapel and all of the greenery in sight.

Mandy's once white and flowing wedding dress was now in flames as she stood there with her arms outstretched, reaching for the ashes of Joe. Her veil began to melt to her face, her skin beginning to blister and bubble, becoming one with the extravagant material. I could feel the heat of her burning flesh and heart on mine as the fire circled me, creating a moat that I could not stave off.

As this new universe engulfed me, I began to feel a pulsing burn around my ankles and wrists. I was in chains, much like those ancient souls who had died on the island I had just departed—a criminal.

I jerked awake to a warm towel on my face and that same intercom voice that always reminded me, first class or not, that I had to wake up and face the destination I had arrived at. I blinked hard, rubbed my face with the towel, and tried to remember what my therapist had said about dreams: "They are what you re-construct them to be." All of her education and wisdom never helped when I needed it to.

Lucy got off in Houston and I took the next connecting flight back to L.A. I couldn't rub the dream from my conscience so I took back three tequilas on the next flight, which seemed to help. I thought about Lucy less and less with every mile that passed below me, and I thought more and more about my final destination in life and those friendships I could still taste the ashes of in my mouth.

CHAPTER TWENTY-THREE

As Lucifer would have it, Lucy and I never met in person again—she came at a premium, whether I paid her with a major credit card or not. The airport wasn't done with me, though, and I had sixteen missed calls from the studio to remind me of that upon my return to my Manhattan Beach frat house.

The studio had begun to feature *Mexicali* all over the world and, as the mascot for the façade, I packed my bags again, anticipating a much longer trip away from L.A.—one that wouldn't be cut short by a porn audition.

Instead of some island in the sun, I found myself in New York, Berlin, Toronto, Melbourne, and a bunch of other random locations that I had never truly wanted to visit or re-visit. In reality, Berlin would have been great to see as someone who wasn't on a lame pseudo-magical mystery tour, but I was, and it made me sick to the point of drinking myself retarded day and night. I knew that my film sucked, but part of the agreement was to play the part, pose for photos, stand on red carpets with TV show hosts, and be barraged with the same questions over and over:

"Will there be a sequel?"

No, I fucking die in the end.

"Are you really dating Kyla Hemmings from the film?"

I don't date anymore, I just have meaningless sex.

"How was it to work with an all-Mexican cast?"

That's racist.

It really was just one expensive media push to try and build the film up at the box office. You see, there's this thing we talk about in Hollywood called the pre-screen factor. If a film doesn't screen well before its release —if the tomatoes are rotten, let's say—the factor is low, but if it's not *really* low, the studio will pump millions of dollars into the sort of shit that I was doing. It was all just a big business to squeeze every dollar, euro, or peso out of the general public that the studio could. Maybe this helps you understand that unsettled feeling you get when you leave a supposed blockbuster hit that felt like total trash—that's the system at work. And, hey, don't feel bad for spreading a good review of a film that you knew was total garbage. There are plenty of monkeys out there like me to ensure that you behave in this way.

So, there I was, stuck in the middle of it all, trying to convince you and everyone else that my film was hot when it was actually lukewarm, at best.

I couldn't afford my flat back home without the paychecks that these screenings provided, but I also couldn't ignore the sober urges to climb the Sydney Harbour Bridge and jump into the ocean during my time in Australia. In my mind, I stood there with the cool air blowing on my face, imagining what it would feel like to be half-paralyzed and then devoured by the sharks that everyone bitched and moaned about. I never climbed that bridge for good reason—I would have done it.

I wasn't sure why I had become depressed, it sort of just happened the more places that I visited alone. Call it loneliness, a lack of connection to something consistent, or perhaps I was already living out Jed's warnings of my unknown and fast-approaching irrelevance. I called my therapist, who told me that I had an "Adjustment Disorder with Depressed Mood"—I wasn't convinced, so I drank more tequila as an antidote.

Things finally began to turn around after a screening in Melbourne. The city was definitely more my scene, and the streets of St. Kilda were a welcomed reprieve from the Bangkok-style vibe that lined the avenues of Kings Cross in Sydney.

I had also managed to meet a few female surfers who doubled as models, who were visiting from the Sunshine Coast for a competition at Bells Beach. They didn't know who I was—or cared, for that matter—which provided me some relief from the monotonous everyday bullshit that my life had become. We spent a few nights out sharing the same hotel bed and exploring the various hotels (bars) in the city; we walked around with them hanging from my arms and I rented us Ferraris to race around St. Kilda in. We even made it onto the famous Instasham page @kookoftheday during a trip to the beach, where they taught me how to surf. I don't think that the foam boards sticking out of the back of the convertible helped our cause to avoid that spotlight.

On a Saturday night, we found ourselves at the Beach Hotel drinking expensive cocktails and rubbing shoulders with a bunch of Aussie politicians. I loved Aussie politicians because they weren't scared of the word "cunt." Every opponent was a "dumb cunt" and every good mate was also a "dumb cunt"—it was brilliant.

"So, you're that bloke from that new film that was being premiered the other night, hey mate? Bloody oath, that was an awful film, I was there with me girl," one of them laughed.

"Well, aren't you the direct cunt," his colleague had said.

"No, he's right, it's a pretty shit film. The best part about being in it is getting to chat with the likes of you—and, of course, getting to meet these lovely ladies here."

"Ah, good on ya, mate, we pitch shit policies all of the time. Brendo here is quite the environmentalist, but just last week he announced a bill to keep the bloody iron ore and coal mines open and booming—we all know it's totally fucked, but hey, that's politics. Look at em' here, this bloke is hanging out with a movie star now and a bunch of hot sheilas—comes with the territory, mate." They both laughed and ordered another single malt scotch to match their expensive Italian blazers.

"That your Ferrari I saw out front?" the one who went by the name of Peter asked. "Would look bloody good with my suit here. Business must be good, I don't think Brendo here will be driving a car like that despite selling his soul to the miners there—ha! Consider yourself one of the lucky cunts, you got a Ferrari and a round-the-world ticket to party; not everyone is so lucky, mate," he said.

"Yeah, I mean, I worked fucking hard in Hollywood, and I worked hard to get into Hollywood, so, yeah."

"We all worked hard to get to this moment, mate, don't fool yourself just because you're a yank movie star. I might be a no one politician, but I've got plenty a million in offshore investments that I worked bloody harder than you ever will to acquire." Their affects shifted rather suddenly and they grabbed their drinks from the bar and wandered off. Later, I would have the girls explain to me that Australians didn't give a shit what kind of a "yank" you were; they respected fame but they certainly didn't admire it.

We met more pseudo-famous Australian's that night to keep ourselves occupied and feeling important until eventually winding our way down a side street of St. Kilda, by the water. We shared the last of a bottle of Bundaberg and the three of us curled up in my blazer, wasted, and passed out waiting for the sunrise.

When the sun rose, I found myself sitting alone on a park bench with the empty bottle of Bundy at my feet. I tried to shrug the hangover off and walked for what seemed like hours, until I found myself back at the hotel with a stomach full of Tylenol and Gravol. I passed out under the silk sheets and slept like I hadn't slept since being in my own bed back in LA.

My last screening in Australia was in Brisbane, but I had stuck around for the girls' competition at Bells before I caught my plane up north. Luckily for me, I made @kookoftheday again just for showing up and giving the girls an Aussie kiss on one cheek when they came out of the cold water. Surfers were always the selfish, protective type—women, beaches, reefs; you flew there and they grew there, so you'd best "fuck off," according to them. I didn't care, I kissed every hot Aussie that I could find and pissed on the shoes of the guys who told me to "fuck off and go home." Cultural sensitivity was not in my nature and if I had been an avid surfer like the girls were, well, I may as well have taken up street fighting, because that's all that I would have ended up doing.

I eventually made it to Brisbane, which was a much lonelier experience to endure without the girls wrapped up, drunk, in my blazer with me every night. After my final premiere, I boarded yet another plane bound for France. I had finished with my promotional obligations for the film outside of one last screening in Cannes after a bit of a break in Paris. I boarded the plane alone and passed out almost immediately as we flew over Southeast Asia and the Middle East.

Paris was a place that I had stopped over in, but I'd never stayed there longer than a day or two. I had always considered the whole "from Paris with love" thing to be total bullshit, given my recurrent lack of appreciation for the concept of romanticism—you must remember that I never wrote that screenplay about a gay Russian in love with a politician, the one who would never be able to caress a dick with "Egyptian-twined silk in hand." I was a jaded motherfucker who drank pussy juice and OJ now instead of prosecco; the idea of love growing from the heart of any culture was all but lost on me. I was a raging boner in the middle of flaccid dicks looking for stimulation—nothing about love made sense to me at all.

I stepped out of the terminal at Charles de Gaulle and into a small taxi that was driven by a man who spoke zero English—I showed him the general area of where I was going on my phone and he hit the accelerator without responding.

Halfway through central Paris, I looked out of the taxi window and noticed chimneys spouting smoke from concrete dwellings, high up into the air. We didn't have that sort of thing in North America, and the realism of it all was refreshing. I imagined Nazis running through the streets in place of the mopeds and cars, artillery smoke instead of carbon emissions, and the yelling of dying soldiers instead of the laughter of children running by.

I had the taxi take me to my hotel and then to the nearest bar to order "whatever vintage was considered adequate this year by French standards."

He was a smart sommelier, smarter than my taxi driver, and perhaps even a Master, given his knowledge level. He poured me a glass that even I thought was overpriced at that stage in my life. I took a pull of the expensive Burgundian wine and looked over at a woman sitting by herself, staring at me with wonder.

Olivia was French; she wore a white French-looking hat and round, white sunglasses that covered her true beauty. Those sunglasses covered something more special than any thong bikini ever would. She smoked light, hand-rolled cigarettes indoors and was sipping on her own glass of overly-priced wine that she had selected herself instead of asking the Master to select for her. Her lips were luscious pink, juicy and full on the bottom and almost equally so on the top. Her arms were thin and her waist tight, with fashionable, loose black pants that were brought in tight around her ass. She had a tight, white spaghetti-string shirt on under her top shirt instead of a bra - you could almost make out the outlines of her nipples and the sides of her breasts from her profile.

She walked over to me with a confidence that would have stopped any soldier in their tracks in the middle of artillery fire. Those dying soldier's voices outside of the wine bar became those of laughing children for the first time since I had arrived; maybe that was the romance everyone was talking about in Paris.

She sat close to me at the bar, so close I could taste her skin and her fruity, youthful, yet elegant perfume. There was no sexual intention, or maybe there was, but either way she sat next to me and pressed her light brown arm hairs against mine. She put her hand on my glass, leaving fingerprints next to where mine had been placed—she observed this and smiled.

"I'm Oli. Nice choice of wine, but I think that you overpaid," she said in a French accent while taking a forty-euro pull of my juice into her mouth. She looked across the bar at the somm.

"Zachary Monte, actor from L.A." I had no idea what I was saying, and perhaps would have sounded more socialized if only I had remembered that I was actually Canadian and not an L.A. bullshitter.

"What brings you to Paris?"

"What brings most: love, distraction, work, hopelessness, a lack of love." Finally, something that might be worth writing down and using to bolster my status as an entertainer.

"Beautiful, are you having another glass? Perhaps I should order for you." She gulped down the remainder of my wine; roughly a 120-euro gulp at that point. "At least if I order for you, you won't have this look of poverty on your face when we share it." She laughed and smiled an honest smile, letting me know that if she had just wanted my money, she could have gotten it already.

We shared a bottle of Jura, on her, and then began to chat about the various things that I wanted to see while in Paris before I headed to

Cannes. We joked about my shitty Mexican movie, how my character died and how that was really my only claim to fame—I was being honest, almost vulnerable, for the first time in years.

She was so calm and assertive that I was convinced there was a ninety-nine percent chance that she was a con-woman. But she wasn't. After an hour of her providing me ideas of where to eat, where to watch people, and where to try and get laid, she made the bold suggestion that we should leave together so that she could show me a few things herself.

We left the *bar à vin* on her moped, myself on the back, with my arms wrapped around her. We dodged the traffic, weaving in and out of the metal bullets they called cars containing middle-aged Parisian women. No one seemed to give a shit about anything besides themselves, and it was infuriating to me because it was like seeing myself at every traffic circle and stop sign—and no one likes to be around themselves for too long, especially in traffic.

Despite having just met, we were holding hands and flirting at the next brasserie, already talking about which places to see *together* next—which vacant alleyways to explore, and which cafés to lose ourselves in. It was roughly 10 p.m. and the night was hot; too hot for Paris that time of year.

In Paris, your senses get tied up every minute in some new, minute detail that you would never notice back in America. The smoke from people's lungs that brushes past your nostrils but never makes you cough, the sweet smell of piss in the streets that evaporates in the warm air, and the seemingly endless noise of racing mopeds and motorbikes that fly through moving cars as if death were an inevitable annoyance to be given a "fuck you" to. I guess living through a few wars does that to a society.

"Where should we go? *Le Tour Eiffel?"* She laughed.

"Nah, maybe *Le Marais*, there are a few natural wine bars there that we can hit; it's a thing, my Italian buddy Tony told me about the area."

"Ah, look at you, *Le Marais*, natural wine. Okay, Mr. Parisian, let's go find some more of this overpriced wine for you to drink. I will pay the Paris price and you can keep paying the American price." She winked and then drifted behind me to squeeze my shoulders and whisper into my ear. "We will make you shed this American stress away before I am done with you."

We stepped out of the brasserie to light a hand-rolled cigarette each and began to walk down a sidewalk so narrow that the mirrors on the moving vehicles beside us became life-threatening hazards. I had expected most of the drivers to be steroid freaks, given the way they swerved, honked, and sped along the narrow avenues. Instead, they were dark-haired women, young and old, putting on their makeup, smoking cigarettes, and reading magazines while driving sixty miles per hour down the cobblestone roads.

We stood in a dimly lit *bar à vin* as there was no seating. I could hear American accents everywhere and barely any French voices.

"Lots of Americans here, fucking brutal."

"Yes, including you, Mr. Parisian, including you." She smirked a challenge at my self-centeredness. "So, where do you want to go to next, Mr. Parisian? Will you stay in Paris tomorrow, too?"

"I was thinking about wine country, spend some time away from the rush of it all. This is nice, but it reminds me of Brooklyn a lot. I think those guys stole a lot of this and ended up with something half as sophisticated."

"Okay, I will come, but first, we must ride the Metro for you to see what it feels like to be a real Mr. Parisian."

"Yeah, sure, why not," I offered. "But what about your moped?"

"This is fine, I live here."

We left our third *bar à vin* and headed down the street to a stairway that lead to the Metro. It was less chaotic than New York City's but had a similar warm-aired, slightly impoverished feel to it. The train was crowded, too crowded. We pushed our way on as the door slammed aggressively in my face. Somehow, behind us, music began to ring out; it was a clarinet player and a guitarist with a cheap portable amplifier attached to his backpack. The music was decent, but I didn't give them a cent—then again, no one did. They shoved a dirty old cup in my face filled with euros and I shoved it away. She laughed, I scoffed.

We got off of the Metro and, without any objection, headed into my hotel room.

So began my *Midnight in Paris.*

CHAPTER TWENTY-FOUR

I postponed my trek out to wine country and we decided to spend some time in Paris, waking up early every morning together and doing nothing. Coffee, light cigarettes for her, heavily carcinogenic American ones for me, French biscuits, and we were off to a casual start to our relationship. I eventually made my way down to Cannes, alone, and did a quick appearance at the film festival screening. Olivia had asked to come but understood that the media hype would surely surround and suffocate our time together in France if she were to show up on my arm. Really, I had just wanted one more night of philandering while on the road before I settled for a girl that wasn't rapidly becoming a familiar force in my life. The film got moderately positive reviews, which was surprising, and I was finally happy to be done with my commitment to the project.

After returning to Paris, I brought up a trip to wine country again, but Oli suggested that before heading off, we take the train to London to wander through the bogans and pubs just in case any media were still following me around France. I knew that the media didn't give a shit about what I was doing in Paris, but I pretended that she was right to make myself seem more important.

We took the train into central London and meandered through the markets, laughing in tune with each other about how seemingly uncultured the English were. She made jokes about their fashion, and I bought a bunch of new clothing just to keep up with it. We drank cider almost exclusively, which was a beverage that I wasn't used to. It was grippy, tannic, and warm but somehow managed to be one of the best-tasting things I had ever sipped on. It was nothing like the cheap shit I was used to back home; nothing in Europe was. A goddamn glass of cider had more authenticity in it than any single actor friend of mine across the Atlantic.

We returned to Paris and again put off a relaxing retreat. Instead, we went shopping in small boutique shops along *Rue de Rennes* and avoided the popular big ones. We sipped afternoon coffee at *Café de la Mairie* and watched the fashionable and urgent Parisians stroll by our window while preparing ourselves for the nights ahead. Most women those days were able to invite me into their lives fairly easily, given the right dimensions, but Oli was different; she was elegant and didn't smell like a gorgeous stripper, she smelled of class. She told me that she had found me in Napoleon's gutter and had made me a French peasant of status—at least, I think that's what it translated to in English.

"My Napoleon," she would say, "now come here and bone me, tear me apart." She had an uncanny ability to understand my need for vulgar humor, and she did love a good bone at any moment's notice. *America doesn't make women like her,* I constantly found myself thinking.

Oli introduced me to the lighter side of wine from Beaujolais, and we poured it down each other's bodies as if it were cocaine at an L.A. house party.

She mentioned that we should go to Burgundy, as it was one of her favorite regions outside of northern Italy, and, of course, Bordeaux. When the time was right, we finally left Paris and traveled east to do wine and cheese tours. I didn't oblige because I particularly enjoyed these things more than tequila and narcotics, but because I enjoyed that Oli enjoyed it, and that was a new sensation for me.

It was autumn and we had settled in a small cottage outside of Beaune, one that became our home for three weeks. We took trips back to Paris to meet her friends and sometimes they would come out to meet us—we never truly got away from the city, but that soon became a way of life that I grew accustomed to.

During our days in Beaune, we bought baguettes and wine and wandered to streams that crossed by our cottage and under cobblestone bridges. We would get drunk and throw rocks into the water together and talk about the state of our world—a world that was becoming smaller and smaller by the day. It reminded me of long-ago summers, the pleasant ones by memory that I had from my childhood.

A five-minute walk through a private vineyard led us to a seemingly enchanted, hidden park that we had begun to frequent to have sex in once a day, nearly every day. Our sex led to us becoming natural friends with the natural wine maker who owned the property that we were fornicating on. Our friendship was likely inspired by his fondness of our overt displays of public affection that we began to care less about as the days grew on. We began to drink his wines almost exclusively before, during, and after intercourse, day after day while we wandered the countryside in search of ancient romance.

We had been in Beaune only a few weeks when Oli told me that her best friends were coming to visit from Lyon. Although it should have had me excited to be introduced to people so close to her, if they were anything like her other highly sophisticated and opinionated friends from Paris, it was going to be an awful experience.

Pati and Sébastien were the artistic types—they were both musically and theatrically inclined, and when they had found out that a real Hollywood actor was spending a lot of time with their childhood friend in Burgundy, they had to come out and meet me for themselves.

Pati turned out to look like a sexy little French baker with bright green eyes, rich brown hair, and a skinny waistline with small breasts. Sébastien is how you would imagine a French guy who was into the arts—he wore baggy but fashionable brown trousers, a stained white v-neck, and loafers. Both of them smelled like cigarettes and aged wine. I could only imagine what their sex smelled like—probably musty rose petals mixed into a steamy bath of women in the 1800s.

We met them at a small wine-tasting bar in Meloisey. It was built into the side of a hill and housed several old barrels and bottles of aging wine —some bottles being much older than the country I was born in. Candles were the only means of light and everything smelled of French oak and damp, cool air; likely not dissimilar from Pati and Sébastien's bedroom.

"So, you are serious actor from America, yes?" Sébastien was the first to bring it up as he pulled a sip of wine into his mouth while simultaneously swirling it, shoving his nose deep into the glass, and smelling it. He proceeded to tilt his glass toward the light, appearing more interested in the hue of his wine than my answer.

"Yeah, I do some of that." My dickishness came out whenever I felt intimidated.

"So, you are Mr. Famous in America and you come to France to be with la Miss Olivia for some real experiences in romance?" His questions were intrusive, but I presumed that this was his way of being a better friend than I had ever been capable of being to someone like Mandy.

"Yessir, I think you got me all figured out, Sea Bass!" The joke appeared to be lost on him, but I had come to realize that indifference was the marker of beating most STIs and explosive verbal diarrhea. He looked back at the wine, took another pull, and set it down on the table, all the while not taking his eyes off of the Zalto glass.

At that moment, Olivia came to rescue me from the silence, resuscitating the conversation by talking about what a brilliant actor I was and how in touch I was with my feminine side; this and how much I understood the marginalization of homosexuals in Russia. *Perfect,* I thought, *I'm a millennial acting like a statue—nay, a global icon—for every goddamn anti-oppressive cause in Europe now.*

Oli's support bought me some points and the conversation shifted to other worldly progressive issues and liberal ideologies. I wasn't a conservative anything, hell, I fucking loved my life of liberty and freedom to fuck anything and anyone, but I felt like an imposter the entire conversation—likely because I *was* an imposter sitting next to two *real* struggling actors.

We continued to drink (too much) into the autumn night and Oli's friends eventually said goodbye and retired to their rented flat. After their long-overdue departure, Oli and I walked back along the dirt road to our cottage, where we eventually enjoyed a passionate session of sex next to the fire on the cold stone floor. We curled up in real animal fur, selectively ignoring *that* global issue, and half-passed out with my strong cigarette burning red in my hand next to her light one next to the wood fire.

"What are you thinking? Staring at that fire in the way that you do—so quiet, so empty and endless inside?" Olivia looked at me through a serious state of inquisition related to all things Zach Monte.

"I'm not thinking anything, I'm feeling."

"What do you mean by this?" she asked, taking a pull from her dying cigarette.

"I mean I have nothing on my mind, I mean that I'm just feeling this." I tried to answer her in a way that would fulfill her curiosity and stop her from talking.

"You are feeling what? Sad? Happy? Answer my question."

"Fuck's sake, I'm feeling good, I'm feeling this fire, it's warm, I'm feeling horny, still, I'm feeling slightly unfulfilled, yet fulfilled at the same time. I don't know. Just leave it alone, Oli, it's all good."

"You are, what they call, enigma. You are puzzle of a man that I am so curious and cannot understand for more than these thoughts and feelings that you describe."

"That's all there is to it. You're thinking too hard yourself, Oli, maybe doing enough—too much—feeling for the both of us, too." I took a pull of my own cigarette, burning the tips of my fingers as it ignited the last leaves of tobacco and my skin.

“One day, I will see you, one day.”

We finally both fully passed out, drunk, confused, and alive.

CHAPTER TWENTY-FIVE

"So what is it, you do not have any friends from Canada to come and visit? Or America? Are you actually a real loser with nobody? I cannot be with a loser who has nobody." Oli rolled over in bed and smiled at me as I put my hands into the air, taking a huge pull of a spliff.

I rolled my eyes to the sky and made my infamous smiling-jester face.

"I knew it! You are loser, but that is okay, I will be your somebody always. I love you, Zach Monte."

The funny jester turned into a shell-shocked world war veteran. "Shit, that's a pretty serious allegation there, Oli," I pointed out, pretending to be casual while putting out my spliff on the bedside table.

"That I am your only friend in this whole entire big round, or flat, world? Or that I love you?"

"Shit, well, it must be the second one, sweetheart, since I've got a friend coming to meet us tonight." French women didn't get overly hung up on the word love; she quickly deviated from it with ease.

"Oh! I am so excited, Zachary!"

She was. She got up from the bed with her robe half on and danced around like she was still half-drunk—she probably was.

“Yeah, my buddy from Canada is coming in, guess he’s a dermatologist now or something. Anyway, we have dinner at eight. I have to run around and take some calls from L.A. about something, meet me at *Le Gris Pigeon* a bit before and I'll see you there. And, hey, don’t fall for that fucker—he’s rich and handsome.”

She calmed herself and walked across the room, then poured herself a coffee and lit another cigarette.

“Oooh la la, beau!” She slapped my ass with cigarette ash brandishing it before I got a chance to pull on my pants.

I winked at her and went out into the day, already half-wasted on Moroccan hash and excited to see a familiar face for once.

CHAPTER TWENTY-SIX

There he was, sitting at the bar in a five-thousand-dollar suit, wearing that familiar face that part of me had longed to see while the other part had dreaded it. He liked to party and he liked to spend money. If it wasn't molly and expensive women, it was Grey Goose and soda for his perfectly sculpted physique.

Oli was already at the bar sipping a martini, dirty, having made herself known to him. I was late and had asked her to arrive early, which was typical of my behavior with anyone else besides Olivia.

"Excuse me, sir, I've got a rash on my dick. Can you get down on your knees and examine it?"

"Hey, buddy, that small bump between your legs is your cock. Now fuck off, I'm closing here." Steven turned to look at me and I at him, and then we both burst into laughter. Olivia looked perplexed and somewhat unamused at our tongues.

"The fuck's up, man?" he exclaimed.

"Just cruising, man, just cruising day by day."

"Fuck, how long has it been since I saw the old Zach Attack, anyway? No one back home has seen or heard from your ass in years, save for seeing your ugly mug in that shitty Mexican flick."

Olivia was really unamused now. She got up from the table without saying anything and wandered out the door and into the damp streets. I rolled my eyes, knowing that she was likely just going for a smoke to help digest the new-world garbage we were spewing out.

"Zach, for real, it's been a long time. I've seen your parents more than you, and they're always talking about you—er, talking about how they never see you. You remember Joe?" He took a long pull from his drink and a longer pull on a cigarette. "Fuckin' great, we can smoke inside, fuckin' love it. Fuckin' great country, bro," he added.

"Yeah, of course, I remember Joe, why the fuck wouldn't I?" I began to show my distaste for his nostalgia, smoking my cigarette like it was nothing.

"Just would mean a lot if you came back or called, man. His and Mandy's wedding was pretty special, everyone was there. Can you believe those two ended up together?"

"Fuck Joe."

"Fuck Joe? What the fuck?" He laughed, lifting his eyebrow and studying my body language for sincerity.

"Yeah, he was always chasing after my seconds, always bothered me."

"You know, Zach, you were always kind of a dick to that guy."

"Who is this? What guy?" Olivia sat back down with damp hair from the rain. "Who is my Zachary a dick to?"

"Woo hoo, you've got yourself a lively one here, brother, I'll give her that."

"You will give me nothing."

"Right, well, okay. Anyway, Zach, you should be happy that Joe settled down with his high school sweetheart." His words were beginning to sound more and more like home.

"The only thing sweet about those two is how they've managed to not change at all; actually, it's kind of pathetic. I saw Mandy in L.A. and she was totally stuck up and didn't even have time for me. Fuck 'em, man."

"Well, that's what happens when you don't attend someone's wedding and lie about fuckin' 'em," he laughed, a laugh he learned while attending medical school—bedside-manner-type laughter.

Olivia continued to look further and further disgusted, especially since I was now overtly jealous of another woman—she went back outside for another cigarette, rolling her eyes and appearing unsettled, upset.

"Man, you can't come in like that. She keeps fuckin' leaving because of you, I want you to meet her."

"What does she do, anyway? Trust fund kid?"

"She… she… Ha, fuck, I don't even really know, man. Something with fashion or something, online e-commerce, I don't fucking know," I laughed. I was getting drunk.

"She seems hot, man—like, obviously, looks-wise, but her personality, it's hot. Not many women like that back home, let me tell you, son." He seemed jealous, which I was enjoying.

"You got a girl or what? What are you doing here, anyway?"

"Derm conference, man, and no, I don't have a girl. I tried that sort of thing, got married, had a kid, lost the girl and the kid. Now I'm a bachelor with three houses across the world. Things are good despite the shit, man, things are lookin' up for old Steve-o".

"They fuckin' died?"

"No, you fucking idiot," he laughed. "Worse. Divorce." I laughed with him and we slammed back another shot of tequila.

We continued to order drinks and get drunk as the rain tapped on the french windowpanes. *Where the fuck was Oli now?* I thought to myself. She hadn't returned for thirty minutes.

We finished up with our nostalgia-bating and I wandered out into the street for some air and to look for Oli. I lit a cigarette that she had rolled for me earlier; she had sealed it with her lips so that I could taste her when I put the paper between mine. I looked around as if expecting to see Oli standing in the rain waiting for me. She wasn't there.

I went back inside.

"So, for real, Zach, you've found something in this girl, hey? She seems pretty legit French, you sure you can tolerate that sort of—"

"Sort of what… class? Dick."

"Ha ha! Well, you know, man, you were always more about blowjobs under the bleachers than being in a stable romantic relationship."

"People change, Steve, people change." I took a sip of my wine, swirled it, studied it, and ate some of the baguette that was on the table.

"Not you, dude, you're that same old savage fucker swinging his dick for the fences that I've always known. Just because you keep staring into that goddamn wine glass doesn't mean you've changed."

I began to become frustrated with his one-dimensional view of me.

"I don't think that someone of such limited mind could achieve what I have. Let me paint you a picture, bro," I continued. "There's a guy who works his ass off to be anything but a doctor, a teacher, a lawyer—

anything but a goddamn ghost in a small town that will matter nothing to no one, one day. That guy doesn't achieve greatness by traveling down the same goddamn road his entire life. He deviates, he experiences, but every once in a while, he finds a road—fuck that, a goddamn highway—that takes him somewhere so fast, he doesn't even give a damn about the destination or the speed he's going. That's Olivia, man, she's that highway. And apparently, she's left for the night because of this bullshit about Joe that you're on about."

"Woah, all right, all right, I was a bit unfair there. Don't have to call me a ghost, that's the shit talk that you gotta watch or you're going to find yourself slipping up. We're friends, bro, take it easy."

"I get you, man, but you don't seem to get me, not in the least. I wanted you to meet this chick because I'm thinking of marrying her."

"The fuck? Jesus, no wonder the average Hollywood marriage lasts three weeks."

"Fuck you!" I yelled, taking attention away from my wine glass and slamming my fist on the table.

"Dude, it's a joke. I'm happy for you, christ, take it easy. You're making a scene." He nervously pounded back his cocktail.

"Isn't that what us Hollywood fucks do? Make incredible scenes for the rest of you to gossip and jerk off to?" I smiled that jester smile that Olivia had so came to love.

"Ha! You salty dog, you're all right. Just don't forget me on the list for the bachelor party, and please forget me on the wedding invitation list—I fucking hate weddings. But you know what I do love?"

"What's that, fuck face?"

"Blowjobs under the bleachers."

We both began to laugh hysterically and I pounded his fist this time instead of the table.

We did a shot of tequila to wish Steven on his way before he left out the back door with the waitress he had been chatting with while I was outside. "So much for catching up and meeting my fucking friends," I said out loud as if speaking to Oli.

I walked for an hour back to our place in the light rain. The night was quiet and calm except for the odd moped ripping down the street. It had been good to catch up with Steven, but I truly wondered how much of my life back home Olivia could indulge, given that she couldn't even handle one evening of it.

I exiled myself to the dark cobblestone streets and entered a park that had a path leading through fresh, curated flowerbeds and green grass. I followed the trail until I found myself under a bridge that joined the two opposing streets, rising up and arching its way over the park. On the top of the bridge was a small film crew with a light setup, boom mic, and what appeared to be a few actors making out next to a gold-encrusted lion's head. I loved this city. It was a film set that you never had to actually build; you could shoot a scene anywhere, at any time, and walk away, avoiding a week-long teardown.

"You guys need a spare actor?" I shouted up during their scene. They followed by yelling something in French that I was sure was along the lines of telling me to piss off. I thought about Oli again and walked into a brasserie on the corner.

The inside was dimly lit and sparsely occupied, with only a few locals and tourists gathered around a table who were playing board games and speaking in poor English and French to one another.

"Just a cider," I requested.

"*Oui,*" he replied, pouring me a freshly tapped pint of golden, fermented juice. "This is from Normandy, you know of this cider?"

"Yeah, supposed to go there with my girl sometime, she likes it up there."

"It is very good cider, please enjoy."

I slammed the semi-sweet cider back in less than five minutes, in true American fashion—if they'd had a beer bong, I would have used it. I thanked the perplexed bartender for the juice and continued my walk home, hoping to find Oli in bed waiting for me.

I opened the big wooden door to our cottage, stepped inside, and realized that Oli hadn't returned. *I'll tell you what I'm thinking now,* I thought loudly. Exhausted, I crashed on the sofa, hoping to wake to some morning sex, assuming that Oli would arrive home at some point during the night.

To my unfortunate surprise, I awoke at 3 a.m. to find that Olivia hadn't returned home at all. *Could we have really been that offensive?* I thought to myself, half awake, half asleep. *Maybe I don't want to marry this chick; what the fuck was I thinking?* My decisions, my emotions seemed to change very rapidly. I passed out for three more hours and then awoke again from a terrible dream about losing Olivia to someone else.

I picked up my phone that was on the floor and hit her number on speed dial—no answer. I knew that my love had a pretty firm expiration date, but this felt like real loss, given her acceptance of me and her uncanny ability to see right through me.

I opened the heavy oak door, jerking the latch hard and pushing myself out into the street. It was cool, and I could sense the fall air creeping into the hallway behind me as leaves rushed in between my feet. I walked out in my briefs with no shirt on, half-drunk still and shaking slightly, given how much I had been drinking lately. Nothing.

I retired back inside the house and began to pace, throwing things, cursing, and then drinking what was left of a very expensive and now oxidized bottle of Burgundy pinot noir.

How could she do this to me? Was I really that much of a distasteful, uncultured asshole? I lit some Moroccan hash and sat down on the couch, thumbing through photos of her on my phone, repeatedly calling her over and over.

Twenty-four hours had passed since I had last seen Olivia and still nothing—no call, no text, no sign of my seemingly guileless lover; and then, the door opened.

"Where the *fuck* have you been?" I yelled, immediately regretting my tone of voice.

"Wow, what a reaction. Did you learn this from your friend Steven from back home, too?" She knew I was upset; she was treating her lack of presence as a lesson. "Have patience, my love. I had to leave last evening because, well, your friend is an asshole and he makes you an asshole. But then I was also called to meet a friend who was not doing well herself—it took some time to console her, her fiancé left her."

"What about a fucking—what about a courtesy call?"

"I wasn't aware that we were so married!" she explained in half French, half English.

"Whatever," I replied sharply, now more upset than ever with the mention of her mockery of us being married. The idea put the question of "will you marry me?" on some train destined for nowhere.

"Come here, my little Parisian. Let's go back to Paris for the day; I want to see the museums, the past again. There isn't much here for me today—other than you, of course."

"You're always so fixated on the past, on history. I swear, you never stay anywhere for one goddamn moment."

"Big words from an American who is always so concerned on the future. Perhaps you will learn something today, about respect for the history of things."

"You Europeans and your goddamn history lessons, it's like it's all you have to hang on to."

"And you Americans all want to make films about our history, our history and your little, insignificant part in it all."

"Good thing I'm Canadian," I said smartly, and we kissed.

We got into the car and drove the A6 back to Paris for the day. It was an easy three-hour drive, made two, given the speed limits in France. Things always slowed down once you got into Paris—we sat in every traffic circle for an hour trying to fight our way out in the right direction. It was worse than trying to get to Newport from L.A.

"I want to show you some of my favorite paintings in the Louvre," she said.

"The fucking Louvre? Talk about a lack of culture, there's way better shit in the other—"

"Yes, the Louvre, Steven," she interrupted.

"Okay, Oli, I'll give you this one."

"Yes, you will, it is my city."

We arrived after I cursed my way through Paris, all the while she did her makeup like every other attractive French woman during stressful traffic. We parked valet and approached the large, glass pyramid that stuck out between the old castle walls like a glass middle finger saying "fuck you" to the gothic era—it would be fitting in a place like Manhattan, but not here.

Olivia was focused on getting to the Napoleon paintings, so we pushed our way through the Airbnb tour guides and the annoying children and families stuffing up the air.

"This is my favorite; stop."

I paused and looked up at the wall into a large painting—a lot was going on so, naturally, Olivia began to explain.

"Look, here, this is the *Bonaparte visitant les pestiférés de Jaffa*, Napoleon Visiting the Plague Victims of Jaffa. Look, his hands, his face, he has no gloves. They say that he was either magnificent or suicidal for reaching out and touching the victims of the plague with his bare hands, but really, the bubonic plague was transmitted by fleas, so the soldiers next to him would have been all just as great as him for being there—but they did not know these things back then, when this was painted. You know, this is the royal touch that kings have, the touch that could cure those of any class of their ailments and diseases."

"Why do you like this painting so much? Why did we come all the way here for… this? I'm sure he didn't even really go there and touch those people—fuckin' Louvre." I was still angry at the traffic she had made us sit in—that and her absence.

"Ah, you see, but you don't. This one so reminds me of you."

"Of me?"

"Yes, this is why I call you my little Napoleon—*oui,* I wanted to show you and explain this to you."

"Wasn't this guy a total asshole who had paintings commissioned to make him look bigger and greater than he ever was?"

"Ah! Yes, you follow me," she laughed and began to kiss me in front of the painting. I wasn't sure if this was the biggest insult of my life or if it should have been the proudest moment—finally, someone calling me the great Napoleon, or finally someone calling me out on my shit. Maybe it was both.

We wandered past the long line to see the Mona Lisa, and then through some paintings done in the gothic era. Oli went on about the art, how the gothic era was a time before depth was incorporated into paintings and how most of the paintings were commissioned by the church at that time. She talked about the influence of religion in art and how modern contemporary art was completely missing the mark with its bruised bananas hanging on the wall and shitty street graffiti. I didn't care what she said; I couldn't, my house was covered in it.

I thought about taking her back to my house in Manhattan Beach for the first time, introducing her to my friends and maybe even my family one day. I thought of the gothic art and the Picassos that she would make me spend half of my net worth on just so they could hang above the bed while we fucked. Paris, likely the only place where I would be forced to think these ridiculous thoughts—I didn't even know if people bought Picassos or if that shit was just reserved for art galleries.

We exited the museum and had a coffee at the café while we watched the hordes of tourists pass by. The sun was shining through the grand hall windows and you could see through the famous *Arc de Triomphe du Carrousel* almost all the way to the arch itself. I had to give it to the French; their civil planning, for the time, was incredible—*what the fuck happened?*

"Let's go walk through Tuileries Garden. It is beautiful and always reminds me of the past, of history."

"So which ex-boyfriend did you *make love* to there?" I snarked.

"That's very unbecoming and American."

"Whatever, let's walk."

"Not if you are going to be that way. This is my special place in Paris, you are not welcome if you are going to be jealous of my fuck with Pierre in the Garden." She held a straight face and then smiled. "Come, come my Bone-a-part."

We held hands, and I held my triple espresso *alonge* in the other. I picked flowers and gave them to her, we bought a baguette and some cheese from the *fromagerie* and drank a bottle of wine. We began to get slightly day drunk on the wine and so we bought another bottle. It all went down like juice, staining our mouths as we pressed them together; purple lips and beating hearts, or some shit like that.

We laid on our backs in the grass, looking up at the clouds with the Louvre in the background and the birds singing around us. This was much better than Costa Rica and any webcam or porn star girl I had ever been with. Someone began to sing and play guitar off in the distance and I got a lump in my stomach, dreading the idea of the moment ever ending. Anxiety choked me like razor wire, just like in that *Alexisonfire* song I used to listen to when I was a kid; I finally understood the reference. Time bent on in all shapes and sizes in that park, on that day, and neither of us had any idea of how to grasp it; how to sit with it, nor how to be present. We were two comets racing through galaxies and universes, colliding with planets and just trying to hang on as time and future destinations folded into one another.

Once it got dark, we carried what remained of our second bottle of wine back into the heart of the city and checked into the closest five-star hotel, forgetting all about the car.

We drank each other in for the remainder of the night and Mr. Bone-a-part did his duty before we passed out on one another's naked bodies.

I awoke and Olivia was gone again, not to be found anywhere in the room. I drank some less oxidized wine this time and took a large bite out of a baguette, stuffing some prosciutto into my mouth with a slice of cheese—I really fucking loved that country after some time.

There was a letter beside the shower and evidence that Olivia had already gotten ready for the day. Steam still clung to the mirrors and the fresh smell of wet skin and perfume filled the air; an almost perfect morning.

My dearest Napoleon:

Meet me at the square out front when you wake, I will be drinking coffee and enjoying the view (and hopefully catching your naked body in the window).

Avec Amour,

Oli xo

I showered and threw on a pair of loose trousers and a collared shirt, relieved that my queen had taken the time to notify me of her whereabouts this time. *Maybe we will get married,* I thought as I smiled that jester smile of mine into the mirror. I stomped down the ancient, squeaky, wooden staircase to the lobby and headed out into the square.

Mopeds and cars were whizzing by as per usual, with no stop signs or right of way indicated, just chaos theory. I sat down at the café and ordered a long black coffee with a pastry. The sun was coming up over the buildings, cascading shadows and light through the cracks in the cobblestone streets—I had come to love this time of day in France and thought that nothing could ever ruin it; not even a great war.

Everything felt so perfect, and I hadn't even considered the need to look at my bank account statement or social media in order to receive affirmation that I was someone when the sun shone like that. I looked around the square; no sign of Oli.

"Here you go, *monsieur*, please, enjoy."

"*Merci,*" I replied and took a sip of my coffee. The strong, dark flavor coated my mouth and warmed me up from the inside out against the chilled fall air. I imagined the reprieve that this taste would have provided to those Allied soldiers who had stormed the beaches of Normandy. I became inspired and began to write out a poem on a napkin, comparing warm coffee to war. I looked up, and as the sun glossed over my sunglass lenses, I saw the most beautiful, miraculous woman appear across the square in front of me. She was dressed in all white with a baguette in her left hand and a leather-bound book in the other; I couldn't see the title from where I was seated. She smiled wide, lifted her left heel and posed as if being photographed for some 1920s Parisian fashion magazine—she was so fucking perfect.

I stayed seated and tilted my sunglasses down, lifting my eyebrow in her direction and then pretending to put my head back down into my business as if she hadn't flaunted her feathers wide enough to get a guy like me to notice. I looked back up and heard the dry screeching of rubber on old cobblestone.

SMACK!

It was the sound that a butcher's hook makes when slashing its way into the deep depths of a fresh, still bleeding piece of red meat. The only difference was, Olivia was still alive to vocalize the feeling of it all.

My face turned white as the sound of living, perspiring flesh smashed into the cold steel of a large bread delivery truck. In slow motion, the book Oli was holding flew into the air and landed seven feet from me, covered with the blood from the insides of her body. A piece of her small intestine, a splice of lung, a chunk of bitten lip that I had just tasted the night prior, the immediate stench of shit—it was all laid out there in front of me, for all of us to see.

It was the most intimate form of vulnerability that no one would ever want to experience in their lover.

Chaos erupted as pedestrians, shop keepers, drivers, and café-goers cursed aloud and rushed to the heart of the square to assist my queen. I sat there with hot espresso burning on the backs of my lips as if I were holding onto Olivia's kiss, not wanting her mouth to be pulled away from mine. I then realized that I was holding not only espresso crema in my mouth, but blood as well.

I sat there longer, and then noticed the title of the book in front of me: *Napoleon's Greatest Achievements.* I vomited blood and bile into the pastry basket. Now my insides were on display for everyone, as well—vulnerable myself, at last.

The crowd thickened like the blood curdling with the milk in my mouth; I found myself reeling in the fear of being recognized with her. The publicity, the interviews, the loss that I was going to be expected to experience by everyone who had never met me before—*she wouldn't want that,* I thought quickly.

I didn't stand up and run over to her, didn't tilt her bloodied head back and kiss what was left of her lips, one last time. No romantic Hollywood ending was to be found in the heart of that Paris square, only the bloody ending of every French revolution that involved the beheading of those more beautiful and elegant than those left standing around them. My thoughts raced as I imagined what it would be like to have your queen's head taken off by a baker during such a revolution.

This was the way of French history, and not even Napoleon's touch could heal what was transpiring right there in front of me. So, I ran.

CHAPTER TWENTY-SEVEN

Life happens quick, when it finally decides to happen, and after Olivia died I spent my nights in Paris getting drunk and trying to find any girl that I could use or get inside to avoid the pain and guilt that I was feeling.

I found myself praying for the first time since I was a child, and I lost myself inside old churches that I wasn't worthy of getting lost in. Some God found me just standing there, under great archways, with nothing to give—standing in the same space where so many others had wished for a miracle to happen, and it hadn't.

Every walk through the streets was a walk through a life that could have been. Every glass of wine, the taste of the blood in my mouth on that day Olivia's insides turned inside out—I had to stop drinking Burgundy wine. Every café seemed to serve up the same sounds and emotions that her loss had brought me. There was no reprieve. I tried lots of avenues to escape it all, including getting on the Eurotrain and visiting nearby countries, with little to no success.

I found myself in northern Italian castles, spending money that I wasn't quite sure I had. I searched far and wide for a famous wine that Oli had always talked about—a 1961 Giacomo Conterno Borolo Riserva Monfortino. Only later did I find out that this was one of the most expensive and prized wines in all of Italy. Everything felt impossible now, even trying to spend money on fine wine.

I left Italy and took a first-class coach up to northern France, where I checked into the small boutique bed and breakfast that Oli had always said she wanted to take me to. I got the key from an attractive middle-aged French woman, who I later ended up having sex with in the bed that Oli and I were supposed to share. She showed me around Normandy as well as the bedroom, but nothing felt the same save for her accent.

On the third day, we went to get sandwiches at a small shop in Juno beach—my companion had said that I should see the history of Canada at war, so we served up the war with some espresso and food. We wandered down the walkway past the now iron-sealed tiger tanks and monuments that stood on the same soil that was once covered in blood and munitions. I felt nothing until we got to the beach.

"The beach is cold this time of year, I will go back and wait here in the café if this is okay?" my companion had asked.

"Yeah, of course, sweetheart." I continued to walk down toward the beach.

On the beach was a long pier that was more like a boardwalk, made of old rickety wood and rusting, weathered nails. The wind was chilling to the soul and the brown, hard-packed sand stretched out for miles on either side of me. This wasn't a surf beach like I had in front of my house on Manhattan beach—this was a cold, unforgiving place. You could almost imagine the ships coming across the strait filled with soldiers just waiting to face their inevitable swim in an ocean filled with blood—my ocean. I floated over the failing wooden planks and tetanus-ridden nails to find myself at the end of the pier, looking out into gray oblivion.

I climbed onto the unstable wooden railing and flipped over the top of it. I held my body out over the ocean with my arms attached to the plank of wood behind me—I could feel the slivers cutting into my fingers as I leaned further and further forward. When I looked down, all I could see was swirling saltwater, and when I looked straight ahead, I saw nothing but gray skies and unsettled seas. Part of my mind told me to let go and give in to the same fate as those other Canadians who had been there before me. It was sad, really, everything those fucking guys fought for, and here I was contemplating the end of my life for no other reason than having lost one human life. I guess it's as they say; love and war are all the same. One loss invites another.

I let go with my hands and plunged deep into the freezing cold water at the end of the pier. The last thought that entered my mind before I met my icy demise was that I deserved and had earned the same type of admirable death that those soldiers had gotten to have on that fateful day on Normandy.

Under the water, there were no whizzing bullets flying by my head and there were no red stains when I opened my eyes, just peace. I was pushed and pulled by the currents, barely noticing the shock of the cold water until I was finally forced to the surface by the carbon dioxide in my lungs. When the shock began to set in, it pushed me to swim out from under the pier; to my surprise, the water became shallow quite quickly. I carried my intact limbs up the beach, dragging extra pounds of water with me, making myself look extra pathetic.

“Trying to act out old Juno?” I heard a man with an English accent say from atop the pier. “You wouldn’t be the first.”

“Yeah, something like that,” I replied.

“Honorable, I mean, maybe a bit more honorable if you were fighting for something and I was shooting shells and bullets at you, but I get it. It was an important event in history.”

“Boy, I am fighting. More than you know.”

The old man got back on his bicycle and shook his head as if now fully understanding the gravity of what had actually just happened.

I walked back up and passed by the café, looking in briefly to see my companion reading a book and eating a fresh croissant. I kept walking all the way back to the bed and breakfast, packed my bags, and took the first train back to Paris—I wasn’t in the space to be maintaining anything, especially a relationship beyond one fuck and a cup of coffee.

I sat on the train, watching orchards and rolling green hills pass by out the cabin window. I drank a cup of shitty public-tasting coffee to warm up my soul, but it didn’t work. I thought about those stupid *Chicken Soup for the (insert here) Soul* books that my mom used to read, which encouraged me to exchange my public coffee for something much stronger. I was offered a blanket and I took it in the same way that I had taken a blanket from my mother while staying home sick from school. As the countryside droned on outside the window, I continued to feel sorry for myself.

I got off of the train at Gare Saint-Lazare and took a taxi to the Eiffel Tower, where I had planned to stay in a very expensive loft that an actor friend of mine had said I could occupy if I had gotten tired of being a tourist while in France. Across the street from his loft was the Musee de l'Armée Invalides, which, of course, housed the tomb of Napoleon I and the graves of Napoleon II—some ironic, cosmic bullshit that I wanted no part of. I would later learn that it had also housed Allied pilots during the war; at least one historical fact that made me feel more comfortable in the area.

I pushed open a large oak door and made my way up a set of polished concrete stairs. The air was always cool and ancient in those types of buildings in France, regardless of the time of year. I opened up the door to his flat and dropped my bags next to a very expensive espresso setup in the corner of the room.

The room was dark with the curtains drawn, and small, much too small for a flat worth eight-million Euros. With the right light, the place could have been charming but it felt like a prison. I opened up the glass bathroom door and dropped my still-wet clothes from my body. I looked at myself in the mirror and noticed that I looked fucking dreadful. I traced the lines of the thinning muscles that covered my ribs and flexed my thinning biceps—my abs were showing, but in a bad way. I had been drinking alcohol and eating only baguette for over two weeks, and the French diet was not getting along with my body chemistry.

I stepped into the shower and let the hot water pour down my face as I scrubbed my bone-covered flesh raw with a bar of one-hundred-dollar soap. My hair still smelled of the ocean and my bones were still cold from it. I got out of the shower and felt my chest tighten up, my breathing become shallow, and my body start to sweat. I got back in the shower to clean the sweat off again and to try and calm the panic. I exited the shower again and was finally able to dry myself off. I went to the fridge, half-naked, and popped a bottle of French craft beer; I slammed it and then I slammed three more.

Slightly drunk again, I stepped back out and into the light of day. My swim at Juno had me thinking about what a waste it had all been. I looked up past the square apartments and office buildings and saw the Eiffel Tower looming against the gray sky, its lights only giving a dim sparkle as they flickered on in the daylight. I remembered the joke I had made about visiting the tower when I'd first met Olivia, over that first glass of wine we'd shared. The tower's lights began to flicker and mesmerize me into a trance that led me across the grand field to the famed piece of architecture's doorstep. I walked up to the gate, paid to skip the line, and rode the lift to the top in silence as those around me spoke with a joyfulness that I couldn't understand.

On the first balcony there were tourists, painters, and local families with their kids all hustling around, taking photos of themselves and the scenery around them. There was a small café where people sipped over-priced beers, and a series of locks with peoples engravings on them, hidden where only those looking for them could find them. Oli and I had once put a lock on the Pont des Arts and thrown our key into the Seine river like the cliché romantic tourists that we weren't—this reminded me of that and made me physically shake and become short of breath.

I ignored the static around me and walked up to peer over the edge of the tower, out and into the oblivion that was a cold Paris skyline. Everything had stopped. I put my hands on the railing and inched my body off of the ground like I had done on the bridge in Juno. I couldn't see, hear, or sense anything around me—just Olivia's last look into my eyes and the sound of her voice in my ear telling me to join her. I inched myself up higher and felt the cold, paint-faded railing press against my thighs as I began to slowly raise my legs from below me, up and above me. The wind caught my attention and I opened my eyes to see the gardens that surrounded the park below me. Everything had suddenly become vertical and upside-down when, in a blur, I noticed a fitting quote etched in the tower's copper skin: *"symbole d'amour."*

I threw my weight further forward and felt my body slip over the railing, rubbing more paint from the rails onto my thighs now. The last sensation I had was a tingle in my feet, that tingle that you might get when you're walking on a balance beam as a child or rock climbing up a mountain with your big toe holding all of your body weight.

"No! *Monsieur!*" Someone grabbed my ankles just in time and my shins pressed hard into the structure's frame. I felt the excruciating pain as my entire body was dragged back over the iron rail. I fell backward and found myself back on the cold floor of the tower. My view of the gardens below changed to the image of strange faces looking down at me as if I were some foreign creature pulled out of a deep lake. The couple who had been making out were now gasping for air and the family playing with their children now covered their eyes. I stood up, thanked the man calmly, and tried to head down the tower, rather than falling from it, before anyone could alert the authorities.

"See! I told you they put those nets there for the crazies, Jack!" I heard a young boy say to his brother as I passed them by.

I was stopped by an attendant who began to shout at me in French, telling me to stop and that I needed to be taken to the hospital. I tried to push past him politely; when that failed, I threw him to the ground and ran into the elevator and repeatedly smashed the “down” button. I successfully made it to the bottom of the tower as I began to hear the familiar wailings of French police sirens and an ambulance. I hurried through the park and onto a side street, where I took a seat at the closest café to watch the scene unfold. I began to act—I opened a newspaper, brought my heart rate down, opened my phone, and began to talk jovially into it to no one.

I watched through a crack in the old buildings as people gathered to give information at the base of the tower—likely providing my description and a recap of the scenario. I opened up my social media feeds to see if my name had shown up with any #suicideattemptinparis tags. Part of me wanted the world to realize what I was going through because I wanted people to see what she had meant to me—they needed to. Certainly my therapist would tell me later that a large part of my actions that day were based on my problematic personality structure, but that was all just bullshit in the wind. Olivia was gone, and if I didn’t act out my sorrow, what display was there for the world to know that it actually existed? I was an actor, and I truly believed that this was how actors showed pain. I recited in my head:

Without the drama, there is no scene; no witness to that last tree in the wood that falls at the hands of the antagonist. Such is the dilemma of an actors tortured life—we must show emotion for all the world to see, on-screen and in life. Otherwise, we are normal, and cease to exist in all realms of art and life. A ghost, just like the rest of them.

I finished my casual espresso as the scene and people around the tower began to dissipate. I returned to the flat to continue drinking and routinely checking social media for any semblance of a headline involving me. To my surprise, my frustration, there was nothing. I knew that I hadn't really wanted to kill myself, I just wanted the world to think that I had wanted to —that boy was right, those nets were there for a reason and I was well aware of them. Not attending to Olivia's dead, lifeless body on the ground that day was more problematic than I had anticipated.

I passed through the first two stages of grief and began to want the attention and the fame of being a famous man with a dead lover. I kept ruminating on the notion that her death was an opportunity missed, a headline that could have paved a road of sympathy leading toward my next role—at least then I would have been able to make something of the tragedy. I was broken to have lost someone that I had found love in, and I was angry because I hadn't done what I was trained to do—a failed lover and a failed artist. I switched back to tequila almost exclusively, and any desire to further my education in the world of wine dwindled with my disappointment in the mighty grape's poor alcohol potential.

-

When drinking tequila again and frequenting the red light district every evening had become enough of a problem, I figured that France had had enough of me and I packed what little clothing I had and bought a ticket for the next flight back to LAX. As I passed through customs, they took a double-take of my passport.

"Been here a while."

"Yeah, too long," I replied.

"Ah, yes, the tough love of Paris, like every other tourist."

Stamp.

I sat on the airplane in my first-class reclining seat and looked out the window as *The Album Leaf* played instrumental songs of loss in my ears. I watched as the clouds slowly passed by the aircraft, feeling myself losing more and more of Olivia by the mile. I opened my phone and began to delete all of the photos that I had filed away of her. Then, I opened my mind up enough to begin to delete the smells, tastes, and memories of her—one ounce of tequila more at a time.

The clouds below had seemed to be never-ending, a fluffy white apocalypse covering the death and chaos below them from those drifting above it all. I careened slowly through time zones, hardly taking notice of the day that turned to night and the night to day. I was sleeping but never really asleep, like the lonely ghost I had become. The airplane's landing gear struck warm concrete, jarring my mind into the present.

I exited the terminal at noon and despite the tortured, blood-stained guilt that I had harnessed inside me, it felt good to be back in the warm California sun.

I hired an Uber and departed on the twenty-minute drive from LAX to Manhattan Beach—a walk in the park compared to that Paris traffic—but despite this, I missed it. I found myself grabbing a handful of bills and mail from my mailbox once I arrived, but I threw most of it into the garbage as I walked between my house and my neighbor's.

I had paid a maid to look after the place while I was gone, and as a result, for once my house didn't look like a Mexican cartel's brothel. Really, you could have been convinced that a nice family and their golden retriever had lived there happily ever after, save for the half-drunk actor who had just stumbled in the door.

I switched my SIM card out and checked my voice messages, deleting all thirty of them before I had a chance to hear what they had to say. I strolled out onto the back patio and dipped my feet into the pool. I could hear the crashing waves in the background and the water felt cool in contrast to the warm Los Angeles air. I had been living the goddamn dream in France, but this city was the only place left in the world that could tolerate me. I had become like so many other L.A. plastic mannequins who had burned the rest of the world around them, making L.A. the last city to house their forsaken lives in its warm, aborted womb.

I passed out on the pool deck with my feet in the water and let the sun slowly introduce itself back to my skin. When I awoke, the sky was dark and there was nothing but loneliness for me to embrace. *Everyone says love hurts, but that's not true. Loneliness hurts. Rejection hurts. Losing someone hurts. Envy hurts. Everyone gets these things confused with love, but in reality, love is the only thing in this world that covers up all pain and makes someone feel wonderful again. Love is the only thing in this world that does not hurt.* Liam Neeson had said that, and I recited it to myself over and over as I looked up into the Californian night sky.

I got up, my wet feet tracking their way into the house as I wandered to the front room. dimming the lights as I went. I grabbed my L.A. Lakers jacket, which felt foreign to my body, and put it on to complement the cooling night air that was giving way to the final tears of France tracing their way down my face.

I put sneakers on my bare, wet feet and walked into the night with no intention or idea of where I wanted to go. Pushing my hands deep into my pockets, I found a small plastic capsule containing a tab of LSD—I took it like I was taking a Tic-Tac. Nothing truly mattered.

I found myself walking along the pacific coast highway, the lights of Audis, Jaguars, Porsches and Range Rovers flashing by my eyes as I followed the yellow lines of the roadside beneath my feet. My body felt good, nothing was intoxicating it yet, and my brain felt clear in a state of stale melancholy. I thought of where Olivia might be if she were still alive, what Joe and Mandy were doing and, despite everything I had accomplished, I wanted more, or less, depending on how you looked at it.

I kept walking as the lights flashed by; the traffic in the city never slept and there was always someone there to drive by you and your sorrow. The buzzing lives on the freeway were seemingly there to provide a sobering reminder of just how small and insignificant you were to the world. And if the traffic weren't enough of a reminder, there was always the vast ocean to your left or right, depending on your soul's compass for the evening.

I reached the outskirts of Malibu and began to walk up into the hills around Thousand Oaks. I found myself wandering off the cement and stumbling up a dry hill lined with black, charred trees from the forest fires two years prior. They lurked over me, forming a canopy, a black fence of scorched nothingness around me. Perhaps I was Lucifer himself, drifting about in the shadows, still holding onto the idea that I was the morning star; never fallen, never forgotten, and as dark and deserving as any sentient being on the earth.

I found myself atop one hill, and then another, hiking higher and higher into the night air, avoiding the real or imagined rattlesnakes in the grasses around me. I finally reached the crest of an even taller hill, where the lights of L.A. once again burnt holes in the night's dark blanket. This was heaven, or at least the one I had dreamed of for so long as a child. A place away from the small-minded, the insignificant, the powerless, the useless, the simple. I was beyond what anyone in Westfield could have ever imagined—everything and nothing at the same time.

I knew that I was carrying around the torch of thieves and liars, refusing to pass it off to the next one down the line—refusing to acknowledge that I had gotten to this heaven or hell on someone else's masterpiece. Most of me was okay with this, but a small part recognized that I would come to a crossroad someday where the masses would try to strike me down from the sky like Lucifer, the morning star himself—only to be replaced by none other than Jesus Christ. I was stuck with my soul in motion, sitting between the black scorched earth, blackened trees, and the darkness. I was able to ignore the green grass and flowers slowly making their way back through the burnt soil beneath me.

I took a breath in and felt the air spread out through my skin, then out and all around me. My black wings took flight, lifting up to tamper the brightness of the city skyline below. I rose up and into the air above the ground, my black feathers striking down the pacific and Santa Ana winds that resisted them. I floated higher above Hidden Hills; I was so high that nothing could ever touch me—this is what giving in to the darkness could provide, what so many people feared and resisted.

My satanic wings swept down again with a force that could cause tornados. My eyes began to glow, one red, one green, and my breath left my body entirely—I was now lifeless, floating, traveling, cosmically drifting beyond any schizotypal, pseudo-astral plane. My body became limp and I lay flat with only the air bracing my back and body up, my wings disintegrating into black dust, pouring down acid-black rain on the city beneath me. My eyes began to emit brighter and brighter lights that pierced pinholes in that star-studded canopy that seemed so impenetrable to those mere mortals who failed to do what was necessary to be great in this world. Ideas of viral population control, the benefits of war and famine, the power of Napoleon's conquests all crossed my mind like solar flares; the coronal mass ejections became the pieces of my soul, beaming out of my pineal body, permeating all time and space around me. *I am anti-matter, the bottom of a black hole, the indefinite, I am the sum and savior of all fears.* I exploded and the city remained at rest beneath me, despite my resurrection. "How the fuck could this be?!" I shouted out loud.

"He always wins. Every. Fucking. Time," Lucifer whispered through the Santa Ana winds into my ear.

The coming winter season was becoming heavier and there was no time to disintegrate into nothingness. I was destined to be more than that. I was destined to be more than Olivia, more than any fleeting loss of faith or famine of romance.

CHAPTER TWENTY-EIGHT

Christmas never really came in L.A., so after several months of living in solitude, I had decided that a quick trip to colder weather at my mother's request wouldn't be the worst idea. Most of my friends in L.A. were out of town at that time, be it in Hawai'i or New York, and I needed a break from the loneliness that continued to fill up my insides, without reprieve.

I awoke in the same fart-encrusted purple seat that had taken me to L.A. some five years prior, feeling highly undervalued by the stewardess and my in-flight companion that sat beside me. There was no option for first class on the route, so I was forced to settle in that gen-pop seat. When I first came down to L.A., it was all of the racing heart, testosterone firing, and dick deadlifting that any single stewardess could manage without jumping out of the emergency exit—now, it was a *Vogue* magazine because of its convenience and a mind filled with anxious thoughts.

We touched down in Westfield. As I walked through the terminal, out into the fresh, cold Canadian December air to gather my bags, I felt like this was a place that I could stay and visit for awhile. I walked through customs and was met by an officer who had a few questions about where I had been the last four years, yet as I started to rattle on about my fame, I was told to promptly collect my bags and get the fuck through. I hung a head that was heavy with five years of fame-induced exhaustion and the alcoholism that came with it.

There was no taxi, there was a goddamn fiesta waiting for me as I exited the international terminal—or so I had thought when I saw a large gathering of blurred faces beyond customs through the tinted windows. As I exited, happiness rolled over me for a brief moment before I realized that the gathering was for some Mexican family and not me. My welcoming committee was a dad who was late—no one was there to get me. There was no motorcade, no celebration, no signs to welcome my return, just a bunch of Mexicans excited about inviting their friends to Canada.

I sat on top of my bags, hunched over my iPhone, filing through various texts that I had missed during my three-and-a-half-hour flight. It was as cold as satan's locker room and my Californian skin burned from the midnight chill.

"It's cold as fuck and I don't know what I came here for," I posted on my social media. I took a photo of my breath and had 3,000 likes within thirty seconds. *Why the fuck did no one come and welcome me? 3,000 likes in 30 seconds, these people are fucked,* I thought to myself as my dad rolled up in his worn-out-of-luxury 1999 Lexus sedan.

"Zachary, good to see you, son. Apologies for the delay, I was tied up at the grocery store trying to get a few things for Christmas dinner this weekend… your mom, ya know."

Christmas dinner, I thought to myself. *When did Christ become more goddam important than me?* Olivia would have scorned me for thinking this, but she wasn't there.

She was dead.

My father took my bags and jimmied open the back trunk with some old-man strength.

"Nice car, what's with the trunk?"

"Well, you know, someone doesn't send us any of his glory money from the U.S., so I have to deal with a busted-ass trunk. Get in, hotshot." I had to laugh. My father had apparently developed a nice sprinkle of sarcasm in his old age; I liked it.

We drove down the highway past frozen tree branches on an icy-slick road. Los Angeles and Parisian drivers were intense, but none of those fuckers could drive 65 miles per hour on a Canadian road in the winter.

We passed houses lined with frozen electrical wires trimmed with icicles I had once known, and then my high school, which stood like a dark concrete mountain in the backdrop of a Soviet Union photo. It was nostalgic and sickening all at the same time. Part of me wanted to reach out to all of my old friends and part of me wanted my father to turn around and drive me back to the safety and comfort of narcotics and tanned, half-naked women.

We drove past a large tree that stood tall and alone in Fister Park, a tree that I used to take my first girlfriend to. It was the place where I got my first handy and the place where I began to learn the pains of love lost and how to avoid ever feeling that bullshit feeling again. Tanned, half-naked women with coke on their little bellies—that was a nice image.

CHAPTER TWENTY-NINE

I spent my first day back wandering around the neighborhood in a parka with my face fully covered to protect my fragile Californian skin from the bitter cold. I explored the field that I had been crowned Mr. November in under Friday night lights, and I wandered under the bleachers where Steve and I had preferred to engage in questionable behavior with women. The ground was entirely covered with snow that night after a day-long snowstorm had blown through, leaving the soundscape deafeningly quiet and the landscape bleak and beautiful.

I wandered around the neighborhood a little longer, lit a cigarette, and inhaled deep into the alveoli of my lungs. I pulled out a flask from my left breast jacket pocket and took a pull of Beefeater gin—it wasn't my favorite, but it was all my father ever had in his liquor cabinet. I took another hit of the cigarette and then another pull of the eater of beef.

I continued past the houses decorated in multicolored Christmas lights, jumping at the sudden sounds of slushing snow as cars whizzed by. I imagined where they were heading—to some amazing dinner with gifts and food. Everyone was heading home to some stable family system in my mind, and I was on my way back to a family who couldn't get past a hug without breaking into some egocentric diatribe.

My feet were getting wet as I noticed that my California designer sneakers were not cut out for the cold and wet Canadian winter climate. My damp feet reminded me of why I had wandered out to begin with. I walked another two blocks in search of the grocery store to pick up a few last-minute items that my mother had requested for Christmas dinner—bread, mint jelly spread, some weird Mediterranean spices that would likely take me ten fucking minutes to find before I gave up, and some bread crumbs.

I wandered across the deadening street toward the local grocery store that was garnished with festive decorations and white lights that shone against the backdrop of the dark night air. It was cold, but somehow it felt like a man's body should get used to that sort of thing at some point in his life.

I wandered the aisles, looked at the dairy section and recognized that the eggs were kept where they had always been kept; our ammunition on Halloween night for so many years as kids. There were a few changes in the bakery section and although the staff members had probably changed, they still all looked exactly the same: crusty, cardboard, cookie-cutter employees with no desire for greatness. I saw this everywhere as a kid, and I still saw it that day. I smiled to myself, knowing that that attitude and select form of narcissism had served me very well to get the fuck out of that town and its shitty paper-bag jobs.

"Evening and a Merry Christmas to you!" said the clerk from behind the desk. I didn't look up at her for fear of recognizing her.

"Merry Christmas" I said, in a tone all too guarded for those parts.

Beep, beep, beep, beep.

I could hear my items tallying up to a price that I once would have watched for on the screen above the till.

Beep, beep.

I was in a slight fog from the six ounces of Beefeater that I had already consumed.

Beep.

That noise was going to be the end of me. I grabbed my bags and pushed through the open gates that allowed the December air to flood in like an ocean's waves, right into the clerk's face. I wondered how she could sit there so calmly, so collected, with that ocean of ice pouring over her entire body every five minutes.

And then I stopped caring and stumbled home with everything but the spices.

CHAPTER THIRTY

Christmas dinner was always a fuck show, growing up. There were the cousins who we rarely saw from Europe and the wildcard distant relatives who came in from a place where God still encouraged moonshine and marriage at age twelve. The food was always home-cooked and decent, despite said distant relatives bringing their own versions of dinner, every goddamn time. This always resulted in an argument over which sweet potatoes we should eat and which ones we should save—everyone wanted to be at the center of attention in that family, even down to having their carrots in the middle of the dinner table instead of someone else's. Some might say that I simply stole this fight for attention and made it into something better than sweet potatoes and sticky pudding.

"Peter, pass the turkey, bro," I said to my cousin, who had been studying in Lisbon for the winter.

"Of course, Zacharias, happy to split bread with you, cousin!"

"I said turkey, not bread." I smirked; he didn't understand because he was European.

"I've got a great idea!" yelled Uncle Tito. "Let's all stand up and discuss what we're thankful for before we dig in." Everyone grumbled but complied.

“I, Uncle Tito, am grateful for this beautiful peach of a wife that I get to crawl into bed with every night… and crawl inside from time to time, god bless that peach!” I always liked Uncle Tito—fuckin’ guy; we spoke the same native tongue despite English being his third language.

“I'm grateful that Zach was able to find some time for his family in that busy L.A. life of his, and grateful that he is still alive and not dead from all of the drugs he looks like he’s been doing.” I didn’t like my cousin how I liked Uncle Tito.

“I'm grateful that we’re all here, just like old times.” My mother always was good at keeping the peace and being disgustingly traditional and nostalgic every year.

“Well, fuck”, I said, catching everyone by surprise. “I guess I'm grateful for getting out of this town when I had the chance!” I began to laugh, alone. Everyone sat back down and took a large drink of the wine that Uncle Tito had brought from ‘across the pond.’ Looking around at their faces buried in their alcohol, it was obvious where I had learned my coping strategies.

We continued to eat in relative silence as the snow began to fall again over the dead flowers and bushes in the garden.

The piano sat unused and unplayed in the corner, matching the paint on the walls of my bedroom upstairs that was beginning to peel with time. I could sense the loneliness in the house, despite having everyone in it. The truth was, my parents were fighting a lot, likely over stupid shit, and they both wanted to have retired long before I looked like I already did. I hadn’t given them a dime since I had stolen my way into Hollywood, and I realized while touching the surface of this thought that I hadn’t actually bought them any gifts for Christmas, either. I choked down some more wine and took a sip from my water glass, which was half-filled with tequila. I didn't swirl and stare into my wine glass anymore; maybe it's because it wasn't Zalto, or maybe it's because I had been lying to myself all along.

"So, Zach, we hear that you were spending some time on our side of the pond, there—France, was it?"

"Yeah, I was there for a bit." I choked down the throat lump of a twelve-year-old trying not to cry when telling his friends that his dog had just died.

"Why didn't you stop by? We could have shown you and that pretty girl we saw photos of in the tabloids around our neck of the woods."

"And by your neck of the woods, you mean the woodshed out back and the boring fucking library that makes this place look like London?" Again, no one laughed, but this time I didn't, either. He dropped the conversation and we all went back to our alcohol and food in silence. Forks scraped, throats gulped, and knives cut meat longer into the night.

Once everyone became marginally drunk, we finished dessert and my relatives walked out into the streets to greet neighbors and sing carols. I retired to the room in the basement, where the lights were still strung up on the ceiling above the couch. I turned on the TV and began to play an old video game, my cock slightly hard from the memory of the time that I'd had Mandy down there with me. This was the only nostalgia that I wanted to be involved in, the only activity under that roof of any purpose to me.

I lit a joint, something I would never have done in that house as a teenager, and blew smoke rings into the stars on the ceiling above me. Then, I paused my game and picked up my phone to call Joe. I was unsure if his number would still be the same, but from memory I dialed it, and sure enough, on the other end of the line, there was Joe.

“Joe, It’s Zach attack, I've got the old N64 queued up here. What do you say, come by and rip some mutha fuckas for old time’s sake?” It was a Christmas tradition for Joe and me where one of us would sneak over to the other’s and we would play some video games before the night ended.

“Fuck off.”

Click.

For the first time in his life, the guy wanted nothing to do with me—not even on Christmas fucking Eve. After all I had done for that ungrateful twat, and that was how he treated me on Christmas Eve. *At least he’s grown some balls—finally*, I laughed in my head as I blew another ring of smoke up into the neon twilight of my basement cave.

CHAPTER THIRTY-ONE

My trip home was quick, only two days, and my father dropped me off at the airport at six-thirty in the morning the day after Christmas—the first of two trips he had to make that day. The drive to the airport was mostly quiet except for the odd scolding from my father that I needed to be home more to see my mother.

“You know, Zach, it’s difficult on your mother, seeing all of this stuff on the social media about you—ya know, without you not being around to clear it up.”

“Jesus, it’s not called *the* social media, just social media.”

“Zach, you know what I’m saying.”

“Actually, no, Dad, I don’t, so why don’t you just fucking say it? Ha, you know, that’s always been your problem—you can’t just speak straight, it always has to be so… so filtered!”

“Are you using drugs? Is it true? Is that the reason for these emotional outbursts? You barely said anything to the family all Christmas dinner last night and then just took off to your cave in the basement.”

“No, Jesus, fuck. Okay, I'll call her more and keep my business private to her on *the* social media.”

“We just worry about you, kiddo. We’re very proud of you but, of course, we worry. You don’t seem happy—are you happy with this life you have created down there? Surely we feel guilty for all of the ways we pushed and drove you at times. Your mother and I, we argue a lot about you, about whether or not we should have pushed so hard, maybe it wasn’t —”

“I'm fine, I'm happy. This place, this place is what makes me unhappy. Seeing Mom unhappy, seeing you working still and grinding yourself to the bone and being worried about everything. Jesus, take another goddamn Xanax and retire for christ’s sake, Dad. What do you need? What do you want? Do you need money? Shit, I know that I’ve been an awful son who hasn’t provided you with anything—you gave me everything.”

“Zach, grow up, that’s what families are for. We build up the next generation so that the one after will be better off.”

“Well, the only one I'd ever have a family with is gone, so you can forget grandkids.” My eyes welled up right on cue as we approached the international departure drop-off zone.

Before my dad had a chance to open his inquiring mouth again, I said goodbye, grabbed my bags, and left him sitting worse off than he was when I had first arrived. *Story of my life,* I considered.

I headed straight for the bar after I checked in. Before the argument, I had surprised my dad in the car with a check for 25k and a membership to the local golf and country club—he had accepted it without hesitation, unlike most parents. The gift was an attempt to neutralize my guilt, and with one passing conversation, I had managed to build that guilt right back up again.

I sat down at some shitty craft beer bar and ordered a light beer and some breakfast when, finally, someone greeted me at the airport with the appropriate sense of notoriety that I had been expecting all weekend long.

"Hey, man, you're that guy from that Mexican movie, right?" It was some teenager who had gotten away from his parents while waiting for an early flight to Hawai'i that someone had gotten him as 'the big gift under the tree.'

"Yeah, you seen it, hey? Liked how I got those fuckers?" I was really enjoying myself for the first time since I had arrived in Canada.

"Man, when you were left for dead, that was fucked. I couldn't believe they killed you off, the main character; that's fucked man, they never do that! Anyway, nice to meet you, can I get a pic? It's my girlfriend's favorite movie."

"Yeah, sure, kid. Line it up." He took the photo. "Where you headed, anyway? That aloha shirt your pops is wearing looks like Hawai'i, hey?"

"Yeah, my dad is a kook. I can't wait to surf there, though, we go every winter for two weeks. Last year I got to surf on the North Shore, it was so gnarly and big, man. You ever surf down there in Hollywood?"

"Well, there's no surf in Hollywood, but yeah, I've gotten wet a few times at Malibu Pier and stuff. It's good times, for sure. I live on Manhattan Beach Pier, which can get good to epic."

"Nice, man, I'd be so fucking good if I lived by the ocean growing up; I'd be surfing all the time, probably wouldn't have graduated from grade six I'd be in the water so much. I can't wait to get the fuck out of this town, man. My parents are rich but, fuck, it's so lame here."

I smiled and my heart raced a bit.

"You know what, man? I was you once, wanting to get out of this place. And look at me, I did it. Don't let any of your whiny cunt friends or family drag you down; you deserve the ocean on your doorstep, you deserve to get out of here, you deserve it all." I felt like Gandhi.

"Oh, man, I've got the best friends, I would never go without them. This place is landlocked but the people are awesome."

I looked perplexed and had no words. "All right, kid, well, enjoy some waves on the North Shore for me. Aloha, bra!"

I boarded my plane and continued to drink myself into an afternoon hangover. *The main character never dies in the end, he's never killed off. What a little shit.*

CHAPTER THIRTY-TWO

I arrived back at LAX, grabbed an Uber, got home, and checked my mail. Along with the usual bills and bullshit, there was an invitation to a celebrity-only event out in the desert at Joshua Tree. It was an invitation that I had been waiting on for over two years, each year being more disappointing than the last. My mood finally improved for more than a brief moment and I tore open the envelope.

The event, over the years, had come to be known as the Deja Desert Festival, where a select few thousand celebrities were invited out for a weekend of debauchery and acid-tripping in the middle of nowhere. It advertised itself among the social-elite as an event that was so exclusive and so off of the grid that any attendee was allowed to bring whatever drugs, alcohol, sex toys, or animals that they so desired. There were stories of the most horrific and sexually satisfying kind, and counterstories that it was all just a massive publicity stunt. Either way, if you got the invite, it was known that you should most certainly attend.

It was early the next morning, when I had begun to pack my belongings, that I finally realized that there was evidence of some serious partying that had gone on in my absence. Beer bottles, bras, panties in the fishtanks—the place was a fucking mess and I hadn't even noticed. Now, back then, it wasn't uncommon for me to have invited a bunch of people over without my being there to party, especially over the holidays, but my cleaning lady usually made sure that shit was dealt with before I arrived back home. As much as I always liked to encourage people like the three jerk-offs to enjoy my lifestyle for a weekend, the mess was upsetting.

I called my cleaning lady and gave her an earful for not being on top of things and threw a bunch of clothing into a black gym bag in haste, looking forward to leaving the mess behind for someone else to manage. It's as if it were my cleaning lady who had made the irresponsible mess to begin with. That's how things operated back then. The poor were always at fault for not doing their jobs in cleaning up our messes; it never crossed my mind once to call out the people who had actually made the mess in the first place. It was all foreshadowing for the events that were about to transpire out at Joshua Tree—a bunch of dick-swingers expecting the world to clean up after their sexual warfare had commenced. It was just how things operated for those of us in Hollywood.

"Fuck's sake!" I yelled as I found a condom floating in the upper deck of my toilet, keeping it from flushing properly.

I couldn't wait for the festival's premium accommodations, expensive champagne, the even more expensive experimental hallucinogenic drugs that had not yet hit the streets, and the promise of absolutely zero press or ramifications for my actions. I left the toilet with a sticky note that stated:

Sticky domer cloggin' shit up—literally. Pls fix!

I had been given a plus-one to the festival and so, after doing enough of a clean to be able to make a cup of coffee, I had called up my friend Tony who worked at the 24/7 gym in Santa Monica.

Tony was a fitness coach for a few A-listers and had made his way into the peripheral limelight just enough to be invited to such an event one time before. In fact, Tony was the guy who originally had me checking my mail this time of year for such a letter for the past two years. As a result, it was only natural that I gave him a call to let him know that the day had come where he and I would be able to let loose and howl at the moon while tripping on LSD and pissing semen down our legs. Surely one of us, by the end of the weekend, would be telling a ghost that “daddy’s gift basket” had just been delivered while thrusting at the black night air into nothing. It was going to be a real treat, and Tony was as non-judgmental as they come when it came to anything but the shape of a human body.

I was miles away from where I had been the day before; it was as though I was living two lives, and one had no idea how to process the reality of the other. There’s nothing more surreal than air travel: being in one place, doing one thing at one moment, and then being in another world three hours later experiencing what you were born to do. The notion of departures and landings left me thinking about Olivia’s funeral and how I should have at least considered attending instead of just jumping on an airplane to avoid that teary, sunken gathering. I could have made an appearance and sat in the back row, but I couldn’t even stomach that.

The ability to live freely, to instantly leave any situation or relationship, is a valued gift for some. The ability to leave one moment to find another moment, one woman for another woman, one feeling for another feeling—simply following the expiration dates listed as any logical man would do. Be that not drinking from the curdled, expired milk carton or leaving a dead girlfriend in the middle of a populated square in

France, there is logic to it. Speaking of expiration dates and fleeting moments, that was exactly what the desert was all about.

It was a place where you could leave everything that had expired in life behind for a weekend. It was a place that reminded those who were rich and famous enough, that that was the best part about being who they were. Humans don't like to stick around in feelings too long, and we of the gifted celebrity echelon knew that all too well.

I know that you can all understand what I'm saying—you're just too deprived of choice to agree with me.

CHAPTER THIRTY-THREE

The warm winter sun covered the sky as it always does in L.A., and I tore between all of the cars on the 91 on my street bike, barely noticing the skyline, with Tony right on my heels on his less expensive red and black GSXR 1000. Everything was a blur of barely living streets and dead-standing cars until we reached the Morongo Valley, which opened up all around us with only the mountains and trees stretching up to the sky. We rode through wind farms that drifted in the wind, round and round, reaching high and up above the highway to display the fragile concept of human progression.

You know that you're getting closer to Joshua Tree when the trees begin to bend in shapes that no tree should bend, creating an out-of-this-world type vibe. We cruised past old coffee shops and climbing centers where the hardiest of Californians took to buy last-minute gear for a climb in the scorching sun. It was the southern sun-scorched climbing Mecca equivalent to Yosemite—but most big wall climbers would scoff at that sort of statement.

I wasn't a climber. I was here for the psychedelics, women, and maybe a fleeting solar flare of inspiration from the nature that surrounded me. We drove up to the gates of Joshua Tree and I handed my envelope to the gatekeeper. "Five miles in, hang a left at the big neon tree, you've got a yurt with all that you'll need for tonight's events inside your accommodations. Enjoy your experience."

And that was that—no waiting, no having to stop for food, no having to do anything. This is what being a celebrity was all about. You get to the point where people just throw you parties that you would have done very incriminating things to get into at any other point in your life before you obtained your status.

I hit the accelerator and tore past a group of what looked like one-hundred of California's finest non-important females, all lined up hoping that someone like me would throw them on the back of a bike. I left a cloud of red dust behind me and turned my headlights on, as did Tony, and the two of us rode with our helmets off to let the cooling desert air rejuvenate our recently manicured faces. From above, one would only see two buzzing lights dancing from left to right down the highway; two fireflies embracing the wind for all it was worth.

When we approached the bright, white neon Joshua Tree that was illuminated like a twisted, bent crucifix, the energy in the air changed from *tranquil night drive in the desert* to full-on *you might not make it out of this one alive*. Little did I know how much of an influence that very vibe was going to have on my life the second that I turned left at christ towards my fast approaching dance with the devil in the desert. There were rumors that Mike and Joe had brought their Bengal tigers and that a few ears might be lost before it was all said and done.

I was ready to fuck with some tigers.

CHAPTER THIRTY-FOUR

We drove through the entrance and all around us were the first 100 girls who had made it into the park, most of whom were already topless and covered in multicolored body paint, tripping on something and reaching out for anyone who could provide them love.

We arrived at our Yurt and turned off our bikes, immediately greeted by two female hosts who gave us glasses of Dom and lit us each a joint.

"Welcome to the desert, gentlemen. These are your phones for the evening. All numbers that you will need are programmed into them, including if you require more drinks, ice, marijuana, edibles, sex toys, or lube. Now, if we could please have your phones as per the guidelines, that would be greatly appreciated."

We handed over our personal phones and took the brand-new devices from our hosts.

"What's your number in here as, sweetheart?" Tony asked with a smirk.

"Just ask Siri for a good time." She smiled, knowing that he was not expecting that. "I looked you up before you arrived and liked what I saw, what can I say? That's what tonight is all about, gentlemen—pure, raw, and unfiltered humanity. The only rule is that if someone says 'no,' you respect that and don't let your emotions control your journey or anyone else's. Besides, we selected you two based on your previous female preferences—do you think it's a coincidence that you're both already half hard just by laying eyes on us?" She blew us a kiss and the two walked away, reminding us to call them whenever we wanted to deviate from whatever trip we were on to join theirs.

Once inside the Yurt, we finished our joints and had a cold beer from the fridge. We then noticed a handwritten letter posted on the wall from the director of the festival, Franz Lech, whose only request was that we put on the masks provided and enjoy the festivities.

To give you a bit of background, Franz was a German nightclub owner and legend who had been kicked out of his country just short of when the Berlin wall fell. He'd gravitated to L.A. at that time and began throwing exclusive parties for people like us. He knew that L.A. was craving the sort of novelty that only a post-war German elite could provide. I joked that perhaps we needed him even more than Germany had needed freedom of speech at the time. He had grown old, and most of the shit he threw was just in his name and signed off by his event planners, but Deja became almost more legendary as time went on. We clashed bottles and told each other "to each their own" and wandered out into the festival, Tony going left and I right.

The lights were spectacular, even before I had dropped any LSD. There were gymnasts and circus entertainers on trapezes strung below an arch that supported a live DJ who was spraying all sorts of foam and god knows what else on the festival guests below.

The EDM pulsed in my ears and I could feel the warm fuzz of the weed soaking into my bloodstream and brain. I took another sip of my cool beer and held it at my side as I walked through the crowd, kissing and hugging everyone who had gotten a step up on me already. Everyone was socially disinhibited and sexually open for exploration; a walk through the crowd at any point would provide a guided handful of breasts or ass, with a reciprocal gesture involving my leading a girl's hand down my pants for a quick feel of my size. It was a giant orgy waiting to happen, and some had already fully embraced the notion by taking advantage of the sex swings that hung from the red rock—fucking back and forth, strobe lights illuminating their actions as if it were some private show at The Box in Manhattan.

There were inflatable castles filled with bouncing titties and KY and objects that acted as perfect supporting actors to many a twisted and bent-over sexual act. For all anyone knew, they were inside a slim blonde blockbuster actress one minute and an orc from *Lord of The Rings* the next—zero inhibition.

The first level of the festival was as described; a portal into a carefree evening filled with overpaid actors engaged in anonymous moments of frowned-upon sexual deviance. One could stay happily engaged in this level of entertainment, but for myself, this was an average evening in my hot tub back in L.A. The real party began under the dim lights of the animal-hide tent that rested one mile out from the main festival, surrounded by candles that dimly lit a pathway into the middle of blackness. It was called 'the pilgrimage' and required one to walk in their bare feet on the cooling desert sand with only the support of burning wick and wax. The real treat once you arrived at the tent was the unknown revelations that one might find during a swift fifteen-minute interstellar drift on DMT. I wandered about looking for some semblance of the tent but found myself distracted at every step by groping hands, hard dicks that I didn't want to bump into, and tongues on the backs of my ears.

I made it out of a thick crowd of tits and dicks and into a clearing where to my left was an interesting ritual, if you could call it that. It was more like a bastardized prayer stolen from some ancient Norse clan, only to be made into fashionable spiritualism for rich cunts. There were a bunch of naked women with long hair—some dreaded, some golden and flowing—holding down the heads of men as they bathed in what looked to be a cesspool of mud, sweat, and likely semen. These men would roll around in an actual mud pit, some naked, some in briefs or boxers, all awaiting their turn to step up and into the once clear-blue water hole in the sand that was now murky and filthy-looking.

I watched on like some tourist, some voyeur, but knowing that we were all tourists there; especially the guys about to walk up to the pool in the sand next. One tall, athletic-looking guy walked up, covered head to toe in mud, and was greeted.

"Full disclosure, mask off. Are you a mermaid?" she asked seductively, taking his mask off.

"Yes, absolutely," he replied with unfounded confidence that was about to teach him a lesson. The girl smiled as his penis became slightly erect for all to see. He jumped in the pool and his head was held under the water for what seemed like an eternity. The girls watching from afar gasped, the ones doing the ritual rolled their eyes behind their masks. He raised his left hand and was let up.

"Ninety seconds," said a girl half-covered in blue body paint, looking unimpressed and somewhat scornful. She whispered in his ear, turning his smile and expanded chest to a cower. He walked my way, still naked, but surprisingly clean and re-masked.

"What did she say?" I asked curiously.

"She said I failed."

"Failed? At what? That was the longest time of anyone!"

"Exactly, brohem, exactly. This place always teaches me something, every year. This year, I'll be more modest, less elitist, and less confident that I am the best. Mermaids, brohem."

"Jesus, you got all that? A big hard boner is a boner, dude, and if any of those… mermaids? were straight, you'd have your pick." I laughed, amused at my uninvited defense of his masculinity.

"You'll learn, brohem, you'll learn. Mermaid!" He wandered off, clean, wet, and emasculated. I wasn't sure what the fuck had just happened, but it continued on; man after man trying his best to hold his breath under the power and pressure of some mermaid woman, only to be let up and shut down. "Fuckin' mermaids!" I yelled.

I lit a cigarette and asked a few people if they knew about the infamous tent and where it might be. Unsurprisingly, the response was, "It'll find you if it's meant to be, bro." I hated hipsters who thought they had to protect others from experiencing enlightenment; plastic gatekeepers for the pursuit of peace. I told them to all go fuck off and find the mermaids, and they did.

I flicked my half-smoked cigarette onto the sand, its sparks jumping into the air before extinguishing. I lit a joint, becoming somewhat unsettled and frustrated with all of the mysticism that was surrounding my half-enlightened mind. I wandered back to a small garden area that had several masked participants sitting around its ferns smoking weed out of hooka pipes. I sat down across from a masked man who had a hose stuck into his dark, black gaping smile. Smoke plumed out from what looked like a galaxy inside of his mouth and he grumbled with a raspy African-American voice.

"Looking for something?" His head tilted up as he blew more smoke out into the chilled desert air, covering the full moon above us.

"The journey tent, any ideas?" I replied.

"The gates to nirvana are faced with the red arched gates to hell," he uttered, and he blew more smoke in my direction as he spoke. He looked at my masked face, perhaps somehow able to understand my increasing frustration. "Look for the red arch and walk through it, man, it's about a mile into the desert from there. Shit, no fucking magic left in this world if people can't respect it here." I immediately recognized his voice and hand tattoos to be that of Inklined, a hip-hop artist from the East Coast.

"Thanks, Ink," I said with a smirk he couldn't see.

"Yeah, yeah, enjoy yourself, but not too much, know what I'm sayin'?" He laughed and I headed for the red arches, from atop of which the DJ was now spinning ambient experimental music.

There were a few people gathered around the base of the arch, some people sitting cross-legged on Moroccan rugs and some leaning up against the arch itself—you couldn't see their faces, but one could only assume they were enlightened by something. I walked past them, alone, and straight into the night.

It was astounding how dark and quiet it got almost immediately. The way the canyon walls erupted from the desert sand behind the archway perfectly blocked out any outside moonlight or sound pollution. I walked toward a large circle of lit candles, flames flickering in the wind that whistled through the old, red walls. I picked up a candle and continued further into the canyon, the air around me perfectly dark now, save for the small flame in my hand. I continued deeper and deeper, noticing the stars above the darkness of the rock to my left and right as the candlelight grew to have a sphere of electromagnetic light surrounding it.

I wandered, right foot forward, left foot, right foot, all the while wondering why no one was leaving, coming back down the canyon, knowing that DMT only lasted fifteen minutes on average. I considered what had happened to all of those who had dropped it already. It was dead, still, silent.

I could usually run an eight-minute mile in the gym, but it had taken me twenty minutes to reach the opening of the tent, which blocked one's ability to travel any further or see what was beyond the animal-hide flap that opened up into the pastures of Adam and Eve. There was a figure dressed only in a leather loincloth who had the build of a professional MMA fighter at the door; for some reason, I had been expecting a slim, female figure, but the man guided me forward into the tent with no vocal prompts. For a second, I had thought that I could see marked black drawings on his face, but if they were there, they blended in with the shadows dancing across it, adding to his intimidating energy.

Once inside, the tent was wide open and people were lying on their backs or curled up in fetal positions—some crying, some laughing, before it all ended and they moved out the back of the tent into an area that you couldn't see directly from inside. I found a space on a rug and sat there for five minutes—nothing happened, no one approached.

As roughly thirty more people filed into the tent, we were directed to take our masks off and "show our faces to the Gods of the universe" before we were given a small coconut bowl with the DMT inside. A man I had felt following me down the canyon sat extremely close to me and kept his mask on. He looked forward in total silence.

I tilted the coconut bowl and found a small, crystalline substance, roughly weighing maybe 25 milligrams. I was brought a small pipe by a man in a white cloak who stood next to me, gesturing toward the candle I had taken with me on my journey through hell's archway and canal. I watched as a girl beside me burned the crystal in her pipe, falling onto her back as the man took the candle and pipe from her hands and set them down beside her on a rock.

I held the pipe in my hand and began to saturate my lungs with oxygen by breathing heavily before finally exhaling one last, long breath—this wasn't my first rodeo. I held the pipe to my lips and it tasted somewhat metallic. I swirled the flame around in a circle as I began to inhale deeply into my belly. Once my lungs felt full, I kept sipping little amounts of smoke before taking one last big pull, consuming all of the crystal in the pipe. I began to count to five.

"One, two, three…"

From what I remember, I somersaulted forward, flipping several times, over and over, tumbling into oblivion. I felt my soul leave the husk that was my now old, crusted body, as I was thrust into a multi-dimensional reality made of color and light. I was on my back, flying over the Earth before the black sky broke open with a parade of colors and patterns that no words could describe. From the parting universe came a large, white hand that grasped onto my entire soul, propelling me up and into an inter-dimensional storm of patterns that collapsed into themselves. I could feel my identity being stripped away from me, having almost no sense of self left to hang on to. I was in the middle of what is often described as 'breaking through.'

It felt as though centuries and lifetimes had passed until I experienced a complete lack of the conventional notion of what time was. I was pulled up straight by a wire that was pinned to my pineal body and my eyes started to open. I could recognize the room around me, although it appeared hazy and vibrant, like a heavy trip of acid.

Without any notice, an entity that resembled a human appeared directly in front of my face; I couldn't tell if it was real or completely imagined, but it was menacing and had a thick, Russian accent.

"I know what you fuck-fucking did, I know what you stole, and I know that you are going fucking pay, guy. You are ruined, your legacy is false, in a world that you don't even belong to be in—we will find and we will strip person of everything that your pathetic, unartistic waste of skin thinks that it deserves."

The poorly-spoken words were unmistakable in what they represented. Suddenly, as if my DMT journey and my actual reality folded into one harmonious nightmare, I came back almost fully and saw only the back of a man being walked out of the room, escorted by the man who had greeted me at the main entrance earlier; all I could tell was that he was exerting some strength to remove him.

My reality was uncertain, and the only fact that I had to hold on to was that the man who had sat on my right side at the beginning was now gone. I felt panicked and, with my toes still dipped in one reality and my mind in another, I grabbed my candle from the ground and shoved it into my face, burning the flesh above my right eye. I then ran through the back door and out into the night, bleeding in a state of insanity, yelling, “Find the fucking Russian and kill him! Kill them all!”

CHAPTER THIRTY-FIVE

I awoke in the Hi-Desert Medical Centre with a large, Panamanian-looking male nurse standing over me, measuring my blood pressure.

"Where the fuck, what the fuck happened?"

"You're on psych watch, you tried to kill yourself last night—we think. We sedated you with Haldol and Ativan to restrain you from scratching a hole in your chest."

"Wait, what? The fuck?"

"You were saying that you needed to repent for your story and bare your heart to the world—by the looks of it, by literally trying to tear your heart out of your chest with your bare hands. Fucked up shit, man. You fucking rich-ass celebs, haha, searching in that desert and all you ever find is your own insanity. There were six of you admitted here last night, it's hilarious. Well, hope the stories about the sex are at least true. Heal up, Zach."

"Doesn't DMT only last, like what, fifteen minutes?" I asked anxiously.

"Yeah, I guess, but a substance-induced psychosis can last longer than that, my friend."

As he walked to check the monitors to my left, I felt the searing flames of pain burn across my chest, as if the act of trying to claw my heart out was happening all over again but this time during a state of sobriety. I looked down, my neck making rolls that I subliminally was disgusted by. My chest was covered in white bandages and reeked of antibiotic ointments.

"Hey, how the fuck can I get out of here? I want to go home!" I started to become increasingly irritable and then noticed that restraints were holding my arms down. I began to thrust in the bed and jerk around, despite the increasing pain on my chest.

"Give him another IM of Ativan to settle him down," I heard from the hallway. I was pushed onto my side before I felt a needle prick into my ass and, suddenly, my entire body relaxed. "Take it easy, Zach, you're in good hands, the doc will be by shortly."

CHAPTER THIRTY-SIX

I was discharged from the hospital after agreeing with the psychiatrist that I was suffering from an acute occurrence of substance-induced psychosis. I took an Uber—a large black Lincoln Navigator—from the desert back to my house in Manhattan Beach, sitting in the farthest seat from the driver with my head down, pretending like I didn't just get discharged from the psych ward after attempting to serve my heart to the Gods of the desert. I ruminated the entire drive on that voice, that man, those words, what I had done. *Was it all real? Did someone actually know? Was it all a hallucination?* I drove myself into fidgeting and slight agitation at the thought; I sweat through my clothing trying to avoid another full-blown panic attack.

"You doing all right back there?"

"Yeah, yeah, f-f-fine, man, just get me home."

"Let's stop and get you some Gatorade or something, man." He pulled over at a roadside gas station and I didn't resist.

I walked inside the store, still sweating and fumbling around, and then puked in the aisle between the chips and cigarettes. I bought a pack and returned to the car.

"You can't smoke those in here, buddy," he replied, noticing my entrance back into his car. Without debating, I got back out and leaned against the sedan, smoking a cigarette and appreciating the brief moment of relaxation provided by my addiction to the things. I got back in just as the owner of the store came out yelling at the car about paying to clean up my mess.

"Drive, bitch!" And he did.

We drove up the driveway, and I stumbled out of the SUV with shaking legs. The driver opened the trunk and gave me the one small bag that I had brought before he took off. I walked up to the door and punched in the alarm passcode, realizing that I hadn't turned it on when I left—this made me even more anxious.

My bike was sitting in the driveway; someone must have driven it back for me although I had no idea who that would have been. I walked into the bathroom and checked my eyes in the mirror, tracing my aging smile lines before splashing cold water onto them, hoping that this would help tighten up the lines as well as my mental state. I checked my phone and noticed that I had been hospitalized longer than I had thought—three days to be exact.

"FUCK!" I yelled in the mirror, punching it, still in a fit of agitation.

For the remainder of the night I sat in my bedroom, drinking, smoking cigarettes by the pack, and driving myself into misery. I called a few girls that I had slept with recently—no answers. I called a few other people and, again, no answers. I even called Joe and left him a lengthy voicemail about how I was looking forward to seeing him and reconciling our differences, as if we had shared the responsibility of destroying our friendship.

I paced around the house for one day, then two, and then an entire week on self-quarantine: ordering in pizza, peering out the window and becoming ever-more skeptical by the day of the pizza boy's intentions when he approached the door. I continued to drink and smoke, drink and smoke, and only obtained sleep at midday, when my mind became so fucked on weed that it had no choice but to pass out and reset itself—only it never really reset itself, which was a terrifying realization when I awoke.

I kept thinking over and over about that man's words, wondered again and again if it was all in my mind or if my world truly was about to come crashing down. I smoked more, I drank more, and thought more about it, coming to no conclusion. By the second week, I had gotten my drug dealer to drop off some Xanax, which allowed me to convince myself that it might be worthwhile to go out for a coffee.

I hadn't showered for two weeks and the prospect of going out did not create an exception. I put on a v-neck T-shirt, a pair of basketball training pants, and shoes, and walked out into the burning, dry L.A. sunshine. I put my sunglasses on so that the world couldn't see my bloodshot eyes nor any further into my self-doubt and anxieties. When I looked around, it felt like someone was watching me, talking about me, following me, reporting on me. The difficulty with being famous, let alone being famous and caught up in a scandal, is that there probably are people following you and monitoring you. It would be very difficult for a psychiatrist to determine if a celebrity such as myself was still experiencing ideas of reference from the psychosis or if these were normal reactions to the events actually transpiring.

I ordered a coffee with four shots of espresso, and the familiar taste of my favorite Santa Cruz roaster temporarily soothed my soul—my addictions were my best friends, at that point. I walked to the pier and took out a joint, not particularly caring about smoking weed in public. I smoked roughly half of it and felt somewhat at ease again. I finished my coffee, walked back and bought another, and began to walk back to my house.

The day was turning to dusk and the surfers were retreating from the ocean in front of my house just as the wind began to switch from a calm offshore breeze to an onshore clusterfuck, destroying any resemblance of a nice line to surf in the ocean. I thought of the kid in the airport who had gone off to Hawai'i to surf those perfect waves—I wished that I could take back the *wisdom* that I had offered him. I walked in through the back door and despite the eight shots of espresso in my system, for the first time in two weeks, at the right hour of the day, I passed out.

CHAPTER THIRTY-SEVEN

I awoke to a knock at the door. I looked at my bedside clock; *12:30,* it read. I was somewhat exhilarated and happy that someone had finally come to check in on me as I had been rather incommunicado for the better part of three weeks, feeling slightly abandoned and alone the entire time. I had made several, perhaps pathetic efforts to get people to reach out and care about me, all of which were in vain until that knock on the door.

I put on my red silk housecoat and made my way to the door. When I opened it, it wasn't a friend, a family member, or a reprieve from my lingering notion of abandonment—it was a lawyer.

"Zach Monte?" the suit asked.

"Um, yeah, what can I do for you?"

"Consider yourself served." He handed me a paper-sized brown envelope and then turned around, walking down the driveway as if this was his first of many life-sabotaging things that he had on his agenda for the day. I looked at the envelope and heard, in the back of my mind, that same song that had played as I'd collapsed in the dirt during my death in that shitty Mexican movie. As the steel guitar strings twanged in my mind, I collapsed to my knees and began to cry and curse the world. In my wallowing, I tore the portfolio open to read:

Mr. Monte,

Pursuant to The Copyright Act of 1976, you are hereby given notice that Vladimir Lebedev intends to commence a lawsuit against you for USD $8,000,000 due to the theft of the screenplay "A Struggle for Morning" written by Mr. Lebedev and then re-produced unlawfully by Filmcast Pictures under the assumption that this was the work of one Zach Monte and not the rightful owner of the works submitted and re-produced. We will file suit against you if you do not pay the damages within fifteen days after receiving this letter. Please contact me as soon as possible at 310.555.9623 to resolve this matter. The foregoing is not intended to be a complete recitation of all applicable law and/or facts, and shall not be deemed to constitute a waiver or relinquishment of any of Vladimir Lebedev's rights or remedies, whether legal or equitable, all of which are hereby expressly reserved, including Vladimir Lebedev's right to all available remedies against Zach Monte, including but not limited to the recovery of costs and attorneys' fees.

Sincerely,

Charles Leitz, Attorney At Law

$8,000,000, I thought. *Holy fuck, I didn't even make that on this shit script.* I buried my head in my hands and rolled over onto my side, gripping the paperwork in my fists, tearing them in a state of frustration and anger. I stood up feeling like I was floating, detached from my body, and began to pace around the house. First, I smashed a fist into a mirror, splitting my knuckles open. Second, I threw anything that was in sight, and third, I punched a hole in the drywall with my bloodied knuckles. In a storm of rage, I picked up my phone and dialed the number on the paper.

"Charles Leitz and partners, how can I direct your call?"

"Listen here, you fuck, put that Russian piece of shit on the phone."

"Excuse me, I will not tolerate that form of—"

"Bitch, you *will* tolerate me!" My blood was teeming with the devil's spirit, his sweet, seductive whispers filling my ears—it was as if I had prepared for this.

Click.

The phone went silent. I sat on my couch, staring at the phone screen, waiting for it to light up so that I could continue my tirade.

Ring!

"This fucking Charles?"

"Hello? Hi, this is Charles Leitz, I saw that you had called and recognized the number we have on file. Mr.—"

"Monte, you piece of shit, at least know whose life you're trying to ruin."

"Mr. Monte, brilliant mate, you're now known as the man who wants to take no responsibility for the laws he has broken; I see that you have found my letter well," he said in a calm English accent.

"Yeah, your fucking letter, you won't get away with this," I yelled with my ear off of the phone.

"Listen, mate, my client is a man of discretion. Perhaps we can meet for a coffee and discuss the terms; of course, you are welcome to have your lawyer contact me instead of this… whatever this is. You know, Mr. Monte, mate, it is quite strange and, well, perhaps not in your best interests to speak directly to me without your attorney present."

"I do my own talking, especially in matters involving Russian filth and lies".

"Right then," he said with a sigh, "so this leaves us with two options, you can get your somewhat more reasonable lawyer to call me and negotiate my client's terms, or we go to litigation in fifteen days—and, by the way, the last six presidents have had little luck using diplomacy and litigation with Russians. I doubt you will, either. Settle."

Click.

I hung up the phone and threw it into my seventy-inch television, smashing the LCD screen into more than the 4k pieces of resolution that it purportedly had.

Ring!

"What the fuck!" I yelled at myself. My second phone in the bedroom rang.

"Mate, I highly advise that you consult your lawyer or, at the very least, meet me; that's how these things are done. My client is reasonable, he just wants what is owed."

"He is owed nothing."

Click.

I threw my phone out the sliding window into the hot tub. I felt my heart sink and I suddenly vomited all over my feet, shaking with madness and fear all at the same time.

After an hour of shaking, my anxiety eventually propelled me to find my third phone, dial the office again, and schedule a meeting with the idea of doing what Zach Monte did best—being a famous motherfucker who can manipulate anyone into doing anything. *This Russian will suffer me.*

CHAPTER THIRTY-EIGHT

I walked in circles around the coffee shop, trying to imagine how the little Russian fuck might look. I paced for fifteen minutes in and out of the café until the majority of the patrons and servers likely began to wonder if I was about to detonate a bomb that I had on my chest—it felt like that's what was about to happen. I ordered a coffee, "Americano, no room, quad shot." I got the drink and drank it too fast, burning the insides of my throat, that part of the throat that actually has some feeling.

"Mr. Monte? Charles. Please, take a seat," he said in his recognizable English accent as he walked up to me.

He was a slim, short, blonde-haired man with no semblance of Russian in his blood at all, maybe German-English. He was dressed in a slim-fit suit and wore bright, shiny black shoes. His suit was certainly of Italian make, which forced some respect from me—respect that I could not afford to give.

"How about you tell me what you want to make this go away," I said, somewhat calmly (likely as a result of his suit).

"Where is your representation, Mr. Monte, I was under the impression that your—"

"No lawyer, just me. I am all you need to see."

"I don't recommend it, mate, but hey, it's your bloody social-media funeral. There is zero-confidentiality in this place, don't be a tosser. You should at least take me up on my offer to have this conversation in my office, in private." The guy spoke like a regular person; for some reason, I had expected, given his occupation, that he would mind his words better than he was doing.

"Fuck. That," I insisted.

He opened up his shiny brown briefcase and laid out several forms with sticker tabs on them, indicating the spots where signatures were required. He then proceeded to display the original script, which was time- and date-stamped by the Russian that was starting a cold war with my life. That sneaky fucking Russian had documented everything, almost anticipating that some American—or Canadian, for that matter—would steal his idea.

"This fucking guy wrote this anticipating that someone would steal it, is that not entrapment?"

"Again, Mr. Monte, Zach, I would recommend that you seek representation for this exact purpose. No, this is not entrapment, it is due diligence on behalf of the author."

I had no words, the Zach attack was on the defense, a role I didn't know how to act out.

"*Eight million U.S. dollars?* How the fuck am I supposed to come up with that sort of money?"

"It is roughly the amount that you have made off of this alleged copyright infringement, plus damages and legal fees. It's fair."

Jesus, I thought, *how the fuck have I made and spent eight million dollars?*

He continued calmly, "Listen, mate, I know this city and I know that this shit happens. Usually, it goes unnoticed because it is based on a stolen idea, which is very hard to try in a court of law in the state of California. But this, this is an entirely different case. You literally fucking—" He went from a loud tone to a softer one. "You literally submitted this script word for word and the only thing that's different is the return address and the name on the top—it's sloppy, at best."

Less formally, he went on, "I will be honest with you, this shit is bad for business in this town. I don't want this to go to court and I certainly don't want this going public. I'm technically a defense attorney who typically represents schmucks like you—I only took this case because it was for my cousin's friend back home, and it's a home run with a 30% payout. Do Hollywood a favor, do yourself a favor, and come back to me with a counter-offer worth my client's time. I can make sure that this doesn't see the light of day, and who knows? Maybe you'll be able to write about this and get it published and make some money back. This story, Mr. Monte, this story is not yours and it never was. Now, be a fucking right bloke and pay what is owed and get on with your life. And call your bloody lawyer!"

"Don't you idiots know Aaron fuckin' Sorkin?" I yelled in the fashion of a well-orchestrated crescendo of anger.

"I can't say that I know him personally, mate, but frankly, what the fuck does Aaron Sorkin have to do with—"

"I asked, don't you fucking know Sorkin?"

"Yeah, mate. Fuckin' hell, keep it down. What about it?"

"'Good writers borrow from other writers. Great writers steal from them outright.' He said that shit. This is show business, this is what happens in this town."

"I think you've lost it, mate," he said with a snide grin. "Entertained, I am, like really, you're good—applause and all, not a bad actor and such, but *fuckin'* hell."

"Do you NOT know those words?" I yelled now in orchestrated staccato.

"Jesus, mate, really lost it. Fuckin' right nutta, I think you had better check with your mate Aaron about what he really meant by that, and see a fuckin' shrink for christ's sake. This town is too much for you, it seems." He hit the nerve spot on.

"Fuck you," I grumbled. "You're a *bloody* fuckin' nobody Brit *cunt,* and I'll have you and your cunt Russian buried." I leaned in and tried to shove my forehead up against his, but he backed away from the table just in time.

"Careful, mate, I'll only tolerate that threat once," he responded.

Charles took the first sip of his latte and stood up, leaving it on the table for me to look at as he began to leave. I stared at the rim of his coffee cup and noticed the brown milk froth—I was frothing.

I sat there in a brief moment of silence, and then yelled at his back, "I want to meet this fucker who I have made famous!"

He turned around with a smug, English smirk on his face. "You will never meet him. You are not worthy of meeting a bloke of such creative capacity. And, hey, *cunt* is our word mate, that's not yours, either."

And with that, he left, after throwing fifty dollars on the table as a gesture of insult.

CHAPTER THIRTY-NINE

I spent the night in a state of total insomnia, drinking and smoking, drinking and smoking, smoking then vomiting and then passing out for four hours. My house was in total disarray, and the only form of sustenance that I had evidently consumed was Vector cereal and cookie dough protein bars. I sobered up enough for an hour to call my accountant and request a detailed statement of my estate and accounts, telling him only that I had run into some legal trouble while out in the desert.

Three-million-forty thousand in investments and four million in home equity, and that was to broke. My heart, for the first time, felt a slight reprieve from the 160 beats per minute that it had been pounding blood at for the past three days. There was at least a solution—it would leave me homeless, but it would also leave me intact from scrutiny. I repeated over and over out loud while I read over my financials: "I've made that fucker famous, he should accept knowing that his words are famous and fuck off and die by them. There is no fucking way he could achieve any of this without me."

I called up the slippery English fuck that went by the name of Charles and told him my offer of four million, hoping to retain my home.

“No dice, our counter-offer sits at seven-one.” Some cunt had done their homework—every goddamn dime in my possession.

“My client has lived a very marginalized life, and his desire is to make you feel a piece of what he has lived and nothing less.”

“How fucking poetic!” I yelled.

Click.

I was totally fucked and knew that calling my own lawyer would likely get me nothing but a bill and a scolding for doing what I had done. I knew that it was plain and simple—fucking stupid, even—to do it, but I still thought that my status and hard work was worth more to the situation. I was Zach Monte, famous from birth at all costs, and if I could hold onto that title, then perhaps I had a chance left in the world to hang onto that fame. I continued to consider the trade of wealth for status like a record skipping, repeating.

I sat on the boulders that made up the break wall behind my house, feeling the wrinkles on the backs of my hands. I noticed for the first time in years the sand between my toes, the fresh salt air against my skin, and witnessed the joy that the local Californians were having, riding waves off of the pier as they kicked out and above the crests. They wore smiles that no lawsuit could ever destroy, while mine was fleeting and now on the verge of total destruction.

I noticed the bikers on the boardwalk, the guitarists playing shitty variations of Led Zeppelin songs to tourists and locals alike, and I witnessed regular people doing regular things in a state of what appeared to be pure, ignorant happiness.

I had always wanted it all—the pussy, the champagne, the travel, the limelight, and the credit. Now, all I wanted was to be walking down the boardwalk with a Mandy and a dog, staring with pity at the rejected actors shooting fentanyl into their arms on the beach against the concrete break walls.

I thought for a long while until the sun began to set on what appeared to be a perfect California day to so many people other than myself. I had become used to that feeling in varying degrees over the previous few years. Still, for the first time, I began to consider what it might be like to go back to living a regular life in a shitty studio apartment, drinking shitty American beer and watching shitty American movies, pretending that I wasn't in Westfield.

CHAPTER FORTY

The phone rang. I tilted the blue light of the screen toward my face to see an unknown number on the caller ID. I hadn't slept at all and my head felt like it was being squeezed between two vises in a Mexican mechanics repair shop.

"H-Hello?"

"Zach," I heard over the sound of my throbbing head.

"What do you want?" I replied.

"Do you know who this is, Zach? These days, you should probably ask who it is when someone calls and doesn't introduce themselves—you know what I mean?"

"Who the fuck—"

"It's Benjamin Bellcheck. We have to talk."

My head became the least of my concerns as my throat began to tighten up like a knot in a shoelace, the kind that you have to cut to get out. I looked around the room in a daze, trying to find the words, but they escaped me. I felt like my father had just called me demanding that I come home immediately to talk about getting into his porn collection—except worse.

"What's this about?" I finally forced out.

"I think you know. I've left us an hour at 1 pm today, don't be late."

As a means to rectify my state of anxiety, I hastily threw on a dirty pair of purposefully-torn designer jeans and a UCLA sweater that were laying on the ground. I ran to the front door, slipped on my runners, and started the Porsche. Looking into the rearview mirror, I adjusted my hair, trying to comb it back to make it look somewhat presentable. It was 12 pm and I had one hour to make it across the city. I started the car and ripped out of the driveway in reverse, just missing my neighbor who was out walking a golden retriever. I didn't wave or apologize, I drove.

If you have ever been a tourist and wondered why people in L.A. fly by you in their expensive luxury cars in the middle of the day, thinking: "Who the fuck could ever be in that much of a rush to get anywhere?" Well, it's because people like me are entangled in things beyond your understanding, and that day, there was nothing more important happening on the streets of L.A. than me getting to that meeting.

I pulled into the parking lot with five minutes to spare, parking diagonally in a handicapped spot without realizing it. I ran up to Tammy, who was oblivious and joyful and totally unaware of why I was being called into the lion's den.

"Hey, Zachary! Fantastic to see you, head right up!" she said. I remember wishing that I could have bought into her positivity and enthusiasm.

"Yeah, hey, thanks, Tammy." She gave my disheveled look a second glance and then went back to her work.

I took the immaculate, arrogant elevator back up to Mr. Bellcheck's exclusive office above the clouds. When the bell rang to alert me of my exit, I almost vomited. I walked down the hallway and approached the big doors that had been so welcoming and exciting, back when I was a poor piece of shit. Part of me was wishing that it was all just a dream and that my fame had never happened—that I was back in Westfield, playing pool at The Den and sipping Pabst with anyone, even Rat Face.

Mr. Bellcheck was sitting behind his desk, talking on his phone in a tone that sounded more stern—more legitimate—than I had remembered. He waved me into his office and I pushed my way through the large glass doors, realizing that they weren't automated to reinforce the idea that you needed strength to get into an office of that prestige.

"Take a seat, Zachary," Benjamin said, getting up from his desk and walking over to his bar. "Drink?" he asked.

"Yeah, I guess."

He began to pour himself a single malt scotch.

"Tequila and soda, right? Jesus, you look like you've had a few already," he noted after finally taking a real look at me. He could tell from my face that I was perplexed that he knew what I liked to drink.

"I know a lot about you, Zach—even what you like to drink in that nice four-million-dollar home of yours in Manhattan Beach".

He sat down on the leather couch across from me and stared at me in silence, studying me like a lab specimen. Then he sighed, shaking his head.

"Zachary, Zach, because you look so confused and yet we both know why you shouldn't be, let me tell you a story—after all, that's what we do in this business, isn't it? Tell stories?" He took a sip of his scotch and set the clear rocks glass down on a round, crystal table with gold trim. He looked like he was about to read a bunch of children *The Night Before*

Christmas, given the flamboyant red silk shirt he was wearing; that, and his demanding posture that appeared to never stray far from perfect.

"Bear with me, it's an American classic that I think you might be familiar with—please, take a sip of your drink, you're going to need it." I drank my drink, half of the glass.

"I was five years old and I had this friend—he was a good friend, but not a great friend. We'll call him Ken. Now, Ken had a lot of money, his parents were very wealthy—and me? Well, my family was on food stamps, so I was lucky to even eat lunch at little Kenny's house. But one day, we were in his large sandbox—and I mean large, like this fucking thing was built for an elementary school, not just one kid," he laughed. I wasn't laughing.

"But there we were, in this massive sandbox big enough for a community of children, digging holes in the sand with a spade—you shouldn't dig a hole in a sandbox with a spade, you know that, right, Zach?"

I nodded and drank more.

"Well, it was the first time that I had seen a sandbox this big and all I wanted to do was fuck it up, like dig *really* deep down to the mud of the earth and fuck the thing up. Kenny, well, Kenny was a naive little boy who was easily coerced by a poor kid to fuck up the most expensive and cherished play toy that he had. So, Kenny began to dig deep into the earth and by the end of it, there were holes everywhere. Now, to be honest, Zach…" He took a sip of his scotch again.

"To be honest, I didn't know how to play in a sandbox at all, let alone a big one. I'd never been in one and I'd never played in one, so in all honesty, I was pretty naive myself. But do you know what I did know, Zach? I knew that what I was coercing this little shit into doing was destroying his favorite pastime—he really cried in the end when he realized what he had done. Little Kenny fucking loved that sandbox, he spent his entire life in it, and then big, beggar Benjamin comes along to fuck it all up for him."

I looked confused, I could feel it on my face.

"I've worked hard to have what Kenny had, Zach, but the personality and skills that I had developed growing up as a poor underprivileged child, well, Kenny will never have that and his parents could always afford to buy him a new favorite sandbox to play in." He paused for what seemed like an hour and then pulled another sip from his scotch glass. He began to stare at the glass with conviction.

"You're going to have to pay them off."

"What—"

"I'll spell this out nice and easy for your poor, underprivileged ears to hear, only because I know that this sort of thing would have been difficult for me to understand when I was a poor five year old, as well. I gave you something that wasn't yours, I put it in your trust and you weren't capable of handling it. I let you into my fucking sandbox and you turned it into a goddamn minefield! Do you see this stack of screenplays here, Zach? Right here on this desk, right where you took that script from and called it your own that day—do you see here, Zach?" He pointed and pressed his finger forcefully on a stack of letters that were neatly piled where I had gotten 'my' script from.

"I bet you were thinking you were pretty clever. Hell, I can only imagine the sensation; how great it must have felt to walk out of my office feeling like you had dug a hole in my sandbox without my knowing. I'm imagining what it was like to get that phone call from Benz, to sell some piece of shit car and buy that Porsche you like to roll around in—I bet it felt fucking orgasmic, like getting fucked and fucking someone at the same time. But the issue is, Zachary, the problem is, I don't like holes in my sandbox. I like sandcastles, big, fucking beautiful sandcastles. I like these because they don't remind me of Kenny, they don't remind me of poverty—your holes are reminding me of poverty, Zachary, and I don't like your fucking holes in my sandbox."

He began to walk across the room, massaging his finger where his old wedding ring used to be, until he stopped and began to massage the cock and testicles of his sculpture of a half-naked boy in the middle of the room.

"I like to give that to people, Zachary, I do. I'm a giver. I know that you've got talent kiddo, Sara told me so, and your determination to give up a fashion model for fame solidified that impression on me. I am always happy to reward talent with opportunity, it's the best part of my job."

He finally stopped caressing the young boy's balls, walked over to the floor to ceiling windows, and stared out at the L.A. skyline.

"You're going to accept the offer, Zach," he repeated.

I sat there, frozen, like the remains of a dead body under the weight of a million years of ice and stone.

"You're going to accept the offer because it's the only choice you have left—and because you didn't know how to capitalize on my generosity in a professional way. I gave you a nice, expensive sandbox of a life to play in and you brought in a fucking excavator. I've been successful in this business for many years and not once has anyone I've offered an opportunity to been so stupid and so bold."

"Wait a fucking second," I interjected, putting my tequila soda down, standing up for the first time. "To be clear, you knew that I had taken the idea off of your desk? How did you know that I—"

"It looks like you're dumber than I thought," he interrupted, then paused to finish his glass of scotch, telling me to keep my mouth shut with the finger that he pointed at me.

"Dumb, young kid like you comes into my office with my daughter, who is, let's face it, not the ex-girlfriend you were with at the yacht club. It's a bait-drop, plain and simple. I'm a realist; no one trades in the prom queen for the homely-looking housewife for no reason—your motives were painted all over you. You needed something from me, and I needed something from you."

I existed in utter disbelief, between universes.

"What do you know about American foreign policy, Zach? I know that you're Canadian and all, but take a guess at how that might apply to this situation we are in. Go ahead, take a guess". He moved closer to me until we were so close that we could touch. He took me by the shoulder and directed my gaze out at the L.A. skyline.

"I don't, I'm not sure what you're talking about," I said.

"Do you really think that Hollywood likes to pay Russians, or any foreigner for that matter, for something that could be fully produced by Americans? Do you really think that the United States wants to support the Russian Federation in any capacity, politically or artistically? It's all the same. Just like the government will not negotiate with terrorists, Hollywood will not negotiate with Russian scriptwriters. But, every once in a while, something fucks me so hard up the ass—in a good way, Zach—that I cannot ignore it. This synopsis fucked me nice and hard; it had the potential to be an incredible script. I needed my innocent little Kenny to come along to find a creative, artistic way to adapt it into a screenplay that would never stand up in court as full-on intellectual property theft."

He turned back to face the interior of the room and made himself another drink at the bar. I continued to look out the window, feeling slightly dizzy and exhausted as an airplane lifted up into the sky, taunting me, telling me that there was no way out.

"Do you know what happened to little Kenny?" he asked.

"I'm not sure that I want to know at this point," I replied.

"Kenny wasn't quite as dumb as you were, but close to it. When Kenny stepped out of his sandbox and looked around at all that he and I had done to destroy it, he took his spade and swung it at me, he struck me right here on my forehead." I began to stare at a scar that cut his left eyebrow in half on a slant.

"In hindsight, I couldn't fault old Kenny—he was just a kid, and that's how kids learn. But you, Zach, you are not a child. No, you are a pathetic excuse of an artist and you knew exactly what you were doing when you began to excavate in my sandbox. Now it's time for you to suffer the same consequence that I once did. It's your turn to be scarred."

"If you fuckin' knew, then why didn't you stop me?" I yelled. Benjamin remained calm.

"I had expected and thought that I was looking at a re-write, Zach, not total and utter plagiarism. For this reason, I never read entire foreign scripts—if the pitch sounds great, I get someone else to manipulate them and then I'll read it. Manipulate, not submit every original word, kiddo. As far as the State of California versus Zach Monte is concerned, I had never read the original pitch, and therefore I had no knowledge of its origin. All I had to tell Leitz—to satisfy his legal curiosities—was that I knew of a synopsis of a similar narrative, which could easily have been a coincidence. As far as any judge is concerned, I was approached by a young, struggling actor from a foreign country himself, desperate and eager to do anything to share in that piece of fame that surrounded him every day as a student actor. A man literally living inside of a dream that he could not touch, feel, fuck, or taste. No, Zach, I had no idea what you were up to—no idea at all."

Benjamin walked back behind his desk and sat down. "Now, if you don't mind, Zach, I have a phone call that cannot wait. Accept the offer, and maybe you'll have a second chance someday—just not with this studio."

As if I had already left the room, his attention immediately turned to his paperwork. I pulled the glass door open, feeling weak, struggling to do so. I had to take the deal.

CHAPTER FORTY-ONE

I never did get to meet that slippery fucking Russian again after he rolled into my DMT trip and forever changed the course of my life. His face still burnt a stale image in my mind that I couldn't shake from my dreams—*worst DMT trip ever.* I was broke, homeless, and unable to remain in L.A.

I had taken up shelter at my friend Benny's in Brooklyn, New York, in hopes that if there had been any social media leaks from my accountant's office, it would blow over as a bad investment scandal or cocaine habit that took control of me. Luckily, I had paid my accountants well, so my accounts were closed without any mention of a scandal.

In New York, Benny had acted on Broadway, which resulted in his having a great, charismatic personality; you would swear that he was gay for how flamboyant, caring, giving, and supportive he was.

He'd asked no questions of me when I'd met him at JFK unannounced asking for a place to crash. I had figured that his hospitality and lack of judgment resulted from his being a social, hard-to-stimulate guy who enjoyed the company; he had lots of friends and never said "no" to anything novel.

During periods of performing and rehearsal, Benny worked harder than anyone else on Broadway—and as a result, he was well talented enough for any script that might land in his lap. Yet, for some reason, he always stayed on stage in New York and turned down nearly every offer made to him to move out to L.A. to be in film. He was a man of strong values, the original hipster who made no allowances. I always joked with him that he was the Great Gatsby to all of the kids from around the block who wanted to be at his parties. The ones who always wanted to be staring out at that same green light that he did, flickering off somewhere in the distance across the East River. Everyone wanted his motivation, his drive, his lust for whatever he was lusting for—the guy was a fucking magnet.

After a week, Benny eventually got a break from rehearsal, so we spent some time going to small wine bars, the Comedy Cellar, and generally working at getting my head out of those vise grips that were twisting and turning, tighter and tighter by the day. I still had no money, but Benny didn't care at first—he pretended not to notice when he paid for whatever bills came our way, waving his Visa card at the server with ease.

He lived on the top floor of a ten-story building in a full-sized loft on the west side of Brooklyn. It overlooked Manhattan and had a hot tub on the roof that seemed to be constantly filled with actors, novelists, and chefs from famous restaurants that I could no longer afford. Benny's was the place to be if you were lucky enough to know someone on his contact list.

It was mid-summer and given the heat in New York that time of year, I slept on the roof in a hammock that he had strung up between two fake palm trees. It allowed me to stay out of the way, for the most part, and it also provided me the certain type of solitude that I was looking for.

Some nights, I pretended to be myself and got laid by average-looking Brooklyn hipster chicks in search of careers in the same field that I was no longer working in. Other nights, I lay speechless on Benny's deck chair staring up into the night sky, seriously contemplating the benefits of jumping from the roof as I had considered doing in Paris. I'm sure that having my insides turn up on the front page of *The New York Times* in the morning would have been a welcomed reprieve for most New Yorkers, given Donald Trump's non-stop campaigning and bullshit at the time.

I didn't jump from the roof, but what became more and more evident with every fuck and flee that I encountered, was that everyone was either chasing the L.A. dream or retiring from it back in New York City where they had come from. The notion of returning to one's roots became more and more of a mantra for me as the reality of my economic hardship became increasingly apparent to those around me. The only problem was that my Mecca was Westfield and not somewhere fucking cool like Brooklyn or Manhattan—hell, I would have taken Rhode Island over Westfield.

On my fourth week of living at Benny's, I had arrived back at the flat with a bag of fresh produce, some bread, and some spices that I had picked up on a credit card that was on its way to maxing out. I dropped the groceries on the counter with the intent to return to them and make dinner for Benny that night as a poor man's thank you for his hospitality.

I walked across the smoke-filled room to a silver-studded red leather chair in the corner next to a few guests who acted like they were more regular tenants than me. I sat down in the chair and struck up a conversation with a man in a 1990s multicolored sweater and torn-light blue jeans—jeans that spoke a little too clearly of his 1980s musical preferences.

"So, how are things in Brooklyn going for you? Any better than L.A.?" He noticed that I had been looking at his sweater up and down.

"Yeah, good, I guess. It's different than L.A. but, you know, you get a bit tired of that lifestyle after a while." I spoke with the pretend nature of a celebrity still.

"You don't need to pollute our air with that elitism, brother, I heard that some shit went down for you. You're in some deep *mierda,* boy, whatever, no need to impress." He took a long drag of his joint, making me wish that I could be as naturally chill as him. "What I can't understand is why you didn't just stick with acting."

I looked honest for the first time in months.

"What you mean?" I asked quietly as to avoid attention.

"Whatever, man, you stole some shit script; I heard it from an actor buddy in L.A. who knows things most don't. You gotta understand, man, us creative-minded beings, we fuckin' hate it when this goes down—better pray this keeps tight. Well, my buddy is tight-lipped. I mean, he wasn't with me, but that's me, ya know, brother?" He took an all-too-casual drag of indica.

"Not sure what you're on about, that's a pretty big allegation. What do you know, anyway? And, hey, pass that joint, will you?" I replied.

"Ha, bold, brother. Take it, you need all the inspiration you can get." Smoke spilled through his lips, getting tangled up in his thick, brown beard. "You know, there is a story here, I'm just not sure that you're artist enough to actually recognize what that story is. Best of luck, brother, feel for you. Sorta? Ha, fuck it, no, not really, not really at all."

The man I later came to know as Reese left the room with Benny's entrance, leaving for the upstairs balcony with a tall, thin model I had been stealing glances at when her side tit was showing. While I imagined it, he was likely fucking it.

"Zach! Hey, man, you want to go shopping? You've been in those clothes for weeks, man!" Benny laughed, ignoring the spices and groceries that I had placed on the marble countertops, under the commercial kitchen lights and stainless steel everything.

"I like them, fuck off," I said, still agitated by Reese.

"Listen, man, I don't know what's going on with you, and I totally don't mind your crashing here, but it's been a month and, I mean, I don't mind paying for stuff, but man, you gotta get your shit together." Benny looked concerned, as he would, but never mad—which was maddening.

"Look, I'm out, okay? I'll book a flight back to... fuck wherever I'm wanted." I was acting like the child I was beginning to accept that I was. With my pathetic outcry, a few of the girls in the room started to take notice. Looks of disgust were cast in my direction as if I were a supermodel eating a Krispy Kreme before a runway show.

"Listen, man, I know that you had a bit of a… like psychiatric break at Joshua Tree, but—"

I interjected, "The fuck did you say? What do you know about Joshua Tree? You don't know anything, dude, you're tied up in this loft with all of these wannabe celebrities who will never make L.A. Ha, it's obvious why you haven't made it out there yet—you're too scared of losing this little Gatsby circle jerk that you got going on here in Brooklyn."

"Listen, cool it, friend. I'm just saying that I'm here for you, but you also need to be here for yourself. Stop being so volatile, man. You drink and smoke too much, and you're a miserable asshole around all of my friends—you called Lisa a hipster barbie doll last night, one incapable of writing anything worthy of a grade school play, like, what the fuck? That's not the fuckin' Zach that I know."

"Well, fuck 'em, bro," I offered. I really had nothing to say.

"You've gotta move on, man, maybe you should go back to L.A., see a shrink, get some help, and get acting again. I loved that Russian script you did, it was incredible!"

I couldn't entertain his words any longer without giving way to a total meltdown involving my revealing the entire truth: that I had sold every asset I had owned to protect myself from the fortune of losing fame (though Reese was a good indicator that I had actually bought myself absolutely fuck all in the end).

For the second time in one month, I conceded to the facts.

"Thanks for the hospitality, dude, I'll be gone by morning. There are some spices and shit on the counter, I'm too fucked up to make anything creative with them anyway."

I'd developed the personality type where I had expected that Benny—or anyone, for that matter—would react positively to my strong emotional outbursts, but Benny just turned the other way, nodded and smelled my spices before throwing them into the empty crisper tray that was my life. Gone were the days where I could command a person's emotions to make them feel bad for me, let alone an entire crowd at a party—it was time to move on and find someone that still believed in my abilities.

After deciding I was going to leave that night, I looked around and realized that I had no clothing to pack, just my passport and a few hygiene products. I left Benny's spare key on the kitchen counter in a steel bowl that had been shaped by someone from the Bronx and opened his door to another batch of friends who were already spilling in for another evening of Benny's Broadway hospitality.

Once inside, they threw high-fives with the other guests that had already arrived and started in on the expensive Burgundy that reminded me all too much of the vacant, distant past that I had once shared with Olivia. I took a moment to look around the room, one foot in the hallway, one foot in the party. "Cold Little Heart" played in the background but I wasn't sure if the song was in my mind or on the speakers being broadcast through Benny's turntable and six-figure sound system. Either way, my next step was to enter the hallway entirely and leave Benny's party and lifestyle—my lifestyle—back in that loft apartment on that mid-summer evening. I grabbed a pen and wrote some words on an empty cigarette carton that I had in my breast pocket and pinned it to Benny's door:

Did you ever want it? Did you want it bad? Oh my, it tears me apart. Did you ever fight it? All of the pain. So much pride, running through my veins.

M. Kiwanuka—Stole that, too.

CHAPTER FORTY-TWO

I stood alone outside of The Great Benny's complex and hailed a cab, asking the driver to take me to a wine bar in East Village. I looked out over the trellises of the Williamsburg Bridge, out over the East River as the street lights that had shone on so many moments over the years appeared to fade in exhaustion as they cascaded their dimming beauty over the water below. There wasn't much traffic that time of night, so we took Delancey Street and I had the driver drop me at the corner of E 7th Street and Avenue A—adjacent to Tompkins Square Park.

I got out of the cab and wandered down the street past old record stores, coffee shops that were still bustling at eleven at night, barbershops still filled with smoking Mediterranean men, bistros that were just opening up, and a funeral home preparing itself for the next death to be had in the big apple.

The street, the city, had a buzz and noise all to its own. Even when you weren't riding the subway, you could hear it roaring beneath your feet and feel it rattling the aluminum trash cans that overflowed and flooded the side streets with garbage. I used to hate that sound when I visited New York; the noise always reminding me of a less fortunate way to live and the smell of the garbage always reminding me of the stale stench of impermanence. It was real, authentic, and contributed to the ambiance that was the streets of New York. Still, I couldn't help but see the parallels with Paris, and it made me sick.

I opened the door to *La Rébellion du Vin* and gazed around the room before entering. It was a small, intimate place that often hosted guests from all over the world, given its amazing selection of 'low intervention' wines. There was a long marble table with a sommelier behind it taking orders, and a cook cursing at a hot plate in a small kitchen off to the corner of the bar. I took a seat beside a skinny man dressed in a fashionable, slim-cut suit. He had a bottle in front of him and was mid-way through it when he called the somm by his first name.

"Pete, give me some of that charcuterie Tahir is laying out tonight, and maybe some of that Pan con tomate with the Garrotxa this time." He sounded proud that he was able to order and not care how it would show up on his bill at the end of it all. I was seated two chairs to the left of him and ordered the cheapest glass on the menu.

"Decent glass, but by far not the best," the man said to me.

"Yeah, it's good. I've had it before, thanks." He could sense my annoyance at the comment.

"What do you do?" he inquired.

"Actor, writer, I'm just visiting from L.A."

"Oh, yeah? Anything I'd recognize? I love L.A. but New York is home, gotta keep close to where the heart is, plus I'm a jew; what can ya do!" He chuckled in a fake Jewish accent.

Real profound, I thought to myself. "I wrote *A Struggle for Morning,*" I said with a level of enthusiasm that surely would have made anyone wonder if I actually had written it.

"That was a fantastic film; bravo, my friend, to you. Your drink is on me, and we shall toss this wine to the beggars in the streets and get you a proper glass." He pushed my wine glass in the direction of the somm and poured me a glass from his own bottle. It was incredible, and for the first time since Olivia, I shoved my nose deep into the glass and then watched it swirl in circles with the flick of my wrist.

"So, tell me, what's your next move? It has been some time since I've seen anything written by you, or there was that one movie about the Southern Californian kid who ended up dead and—"

"In the desert, I know," I finished.

"You ever thought about doing your own film? As in, directing something? I'm sure that you've got the budget and the talent. Seems to be the big thing these days. Sean Glenn just directed his own film with next to no budget and it came out fantastic, apparently. I'm sure like with most things, he invested a lot of his own money into it, but it actually screened quite well, I hear." His words were priming me for something.

"What do you do?"

"I've published a bunch of books and I lecture on the business of theater and entertainment at the *Academy of Performing Arts,"* he replied.

"No shit," I laughed.

"Ha, yes sir. Did you attend? I can't seem to remember you being on the roster there. Given your age, I should know—"

"I was rejected, believe it or not," I offered.

"No doubt, well, I'm sorry to hear that. It would have been a pleasure to teach and perhaps even work with someone like you. Alas, the faults of the education system are real."

With his ideas, I changed the topic back to my career.

"I'm actually thinking about moving back to my hometown in Canada to direct a movie," I replied, forecasting and planning my next career move as the words came out of my mouth.

"Now that is a grand fucking idea! I've been to Canada; Montreal was fantastic, incredible food, wine, and cider, a must-see." I remembered the ciders in England that I had forgotten about with time.

"Yeah, I'm from out west," I replied.

"Well, what's it about? Are you starring in it?"

"I can't say for certain yet, but I will be directing it. I want it to have a real organic feel, low budget, too. We'll see."

We continued to talk about Sean Glenn's film that was made with an iPhone, how to find investors, how to structure contracts, and what investors liked to hear when it came to putting their money into a production. I had made it into the *Academy* after all, if only for one night over multiple bottles of biodynamic wine in Manhattan.

Once class was finally in session, I had suddenly become ferociously convicted to direct my own film and make my way back into the spotlight. I wouldn't fuck it up, either, I knew I would build a goddamn sandcastle so big that Benjamin would regret ever having said those words to me. The trick would be using my new knowledge from my single-session with Professor Calvin at *La Rébellion du Vin* to recruit a bunch of Kennys to finance it.

CHAPTER FORTY-THREE

I found myself sitting in coach again, likely onboard that same metallic bird that had taken me from Canada to L.A. all those years ago. The seats still had the same stale, musty smell that they'd had when I was on my way to stardom. I pulled out a pen and paper and began to scribble out what I was going to tell everyone upon my return. I outlined a plot for a movie that I thought I might be able to pull off. It was something about a geriatric man with Korsakoff's who wound up in an old folks' home using the memories of those around him to make meaning of a life he had all but forgotten after drinking himself into oblivion.

It was a decent enough idea, but I didn't need decent—I needed marketable. Then again, I considered who my audience was and remembered that I wasn't about to walk into a pitch at a studio; I was about to pitch to a bunch of middle- and lower-class Westfield oil rig rats. All of these idiots would likely see a hero in anyone who said that they were from Hollywood, planning to film something in their shit-ass city. *I'm going to have extras lining up and paying me to be in it,* I thought confidently.

The stewardess was hot and had an ass that demanded the attention of both men and women. I sat back in my seat thinking that I was something more than her, even though she actually had a job and I was, well, broke and unemployed.

"Refreshment? Cookies?"

"Goddamn, tequila and soda please, double. And yeah, some of those cookies." My smile and confident tone of voice had no impact on her ass as she turned to her steel cart and began to ring up my fifteen-dollar drink.

"Cash or credit?"

"Credit, Black Card," I said.

She swiped it. "Sorry, it's declined," she replied.

I reached into my pocket and pulled out a wad of American dollar bills.

"How far will this get me?" I asked in defeat, though still slightly euphoric.

"Dollar is on par up here at 31,000 feet, so, fifteen dollars."

"Shit, fuck, make it a single," I coughed.

"I already poured it, just take the damn drink," she replied in frustration.

Getting handouts now, I thought to myself. *Hell, I deserve it.*

CHAPTER FORTY-FOUR

My father was at the airport on time this go-around and a few of my close family and friends were standing there beside him. They were smiling, waving at me as I stepped through the frosted security doors with my single rolling bag of luggage.

"So *now* I'm famous," I said audibly. "Hey, Dad, how's it going? Why did you bring all of these people?"

"Never enough, is it, Zach? Everyone here is excited about this new project you're here to work on."

I remembered that I had mentioned something on my social media about a project in Westfield between my third and fourth bottle of wine while drinking in Manhattan; apparently, I had a few followers in Westfield already.

"Everyone is excited about Mr. Hollywood coming to town to film his next masterpiece. To be honest, I'm not sure what they're all that excited about—your last Russian homo movie was… a little gay". He and I both broke our furrowed faces and began to laugh.

"The whole town is pretty excited, Zachary. It's good to have you home for more than two days. And, by the way, that golf membership is paying dividends for my backswing!" He was naturally very excited, how could I have blamed him?

We exited the airport and walked out into the summer night. The subtle chill in the air was a stark reminder that in that part of the world, summer only lasted six weeks. The season was on its way out along with my career—but no one there knew that, and that was the best facet of my charade.

CHAPTER FORTY-FIVE

NOT ALL STORMS ARE BUILT THE SAME
NOT ALL SHIPS ARE BUILT FOR THE SEA
NOT ALL SAILORS ARE WORTHY OF A SEARCH PARTY

ENTER: JOE. 27, bit of a ponce, married to a girl that is far too good-looking for him. Jealous of his famous friend, too insecure to do anything great with his own life besides brag about the hot wife he "stole" from said famous friend.

"Yeah, we had a bit of a blow out that never actually happened—to be honest, I considered us real buds for life up until our senior year, when he gradually became all about moving and getting the entire fucking town involved in his would be fame.

"I had gone on with my life, gotten an MBA and had married the girl of my dreams—a real sweetheart. So, when I heard that he was moving back to town to film and direct some movie, I wasn't amused or surprised that his ways would drag us all through his shit again; eight years had gone by and we had all just gotten over the first round of it.

"Mandy is my wife, but it took me a year to get over the school dances where she and Zach had close-gripped to every slow song that had come on them speakers; while I'd sat on them wooden benches that we used to practice our balancin' on during gym class. In hindsight, I was practicing my patience, waitin', balancin' my hope, hopin' for Zach to move away like he had promised just so that I could make my move on *my* girl."

"One thing you need to know about Zach is that he took himself so seriously that everyone either fell for his fame or dismissed it as his being one of them narcissists; I was the former in my junior high years, and the latter once I had graduated. The fuckin' guy probably still credits himself for my having married Mandy. I don't think he will ever understand her or the merit of stability in life.

"Zach was and always will be that Mr. November at school dances, break dancin' and getting quick blowjobs in the downstairs locker rooms, yet always falling short on the follow-up; likely because he thought it was beneath 'im. I'm sure that you've heard him refer to himself as that; Mr. November. It's a song by The National. Anyway, I traded all of them locker-room blowjobs in the world for years of blowjobs from a girl that had gotten out of the locker room business before it had exploded."

"Tell me about when you last heard from Zach."

"Well, Zach had reached out to me over the years during his visits, and when his voicemails didn't work, he started sendin' images of us in our junior years doing stupid shit. He also sent me pictures of Mandy and him—making jokes that we should all get together for a threesome to 'rekindle the movement,' whatever in the fuck that meant. Honestly, I hadn't responded to one phone calls, text messages, or emails because I couldn't stand the idea of his presence back in my life or Mandy's. He once called me on Christmas Eve totally wasted, wantin' to play kids' video games; well, that was fucked—I hung up."

“Mandy told me once that she run into Zack while she was down in Los Angeles for a friend's bachelorette party—it took me two weeks to get over my insecurities around the potential of them fucking on some beach or in some penthouse suite of his. You know what? I actually remember, I was driving to work when my phone rang. I had a call with Mandy and it went somethin’ like this:

‘Joe, it’s Mandy, never guess who I ran into in L.A.’

‘Oh, yeah, I can guess, How’s that fucking guy doing?’ I knew *exactly* who she was referrin’ to.

‘Harrison Ford, great guy,’ she had laughed.

‘Yeah, yeah, he wishes.’ I was super irritated, of course.

“And you know, she continued on, started talking about how he was looking ‘real good’ and how he was hanging out with some famous band—that we should go down there and visit him sometime. What really pissed me off was when she told me that he had offered up his place in Manhattan Beach to her when he was out of town. She’s still completely oblivious as to what kind of person he really is.

“So, I demanded to know when she was going to be back in town, like some grade-school asshat—you know, that’s what this guy did, does to me. He makes me jealous and full of rage. She hung up and probably went for more drinks thinking more about him than me, of course; no doubt. With that terminated call, my concern from years past came to blossom again like some poisonous plant coughing up sputum on those who walk by it—you can quote that, that’s good. So, when I heard that he was back in town and bringing his antics and fame with him, you can understand my concernin’ now.”

“Thanks for taking the time to give me some insight here, Joe, really appreciate it.”

“Yeah, whatever, just so long as people know the truth about what really happened here. I ain’t finished, though. As I was sayin’, I was real pissed about that whole thing, but to give you an example of what he’s doin right now, fuck me. This is what happened when he got back into town this time, before all this movie shit kicked off.

“It was a Saturday and I had just dropped Mandy off at a yoga class before heading into my office to tie up some loose ends; it had been a busy week consultin’ on a total corporate re-structure for a large energy company. I drove up to my favorite local espresso bar for my second dose of caffeine for the day before headin’ into the office. It was the kind of espresso bar that actors might go to if they were visitin’—which is exactly why I ended up having my first run-in with Zach on that fateful Saturday morning, when the sun was out and everythin’ else in the world seemed to be going smoothly except for his reemergence in my life. I’ll try to tell this story the best that I can.”

-

“Triple shot—and I mean three shots, not three pulls like last time, Tammy,” I joked, somewhat irritated still with her previous fuck up.

“Sure thing, sorry about that Joe, again”, she replied, somewhat irritated herself.

“And I'll have three *full* pulls, like a real man,” I heard from behind me. *Jesus* I thought. *It was Zach.*

I found myself responding in a friendly way; it had been so easy to ignore the bastard when he was in town calling and texting me incessantly, but in-person was a different story. “Jesus, if it isn’t the man himself,” I heard myself say over my left shoulder.

“Hey, bud, great to see you, back in town directing a new film. Have you decided if you’ll be in it?” The rumors were fucking true.

“Man, it’s been a long time, Yeah, I heard about that, not sure I'll have the time to commit to such a project, though. When are you filming and what’s it all about?” I was inquiring—I did not want to inquire.

“Triple shot with room!” I was momentarily saved by Tammy, who was looking shockingly sexy that day from behind her apron; I was glad that she was looking so good and that it appeared as though our banter made us seem familiar with one another. I grabbed my coffee and moved out of Zach’s way to the milk and sugar station.

“My brother, you will be involved. I want you in on this. I'm really looking forward to it, and you know, I'm really liking it back here, in this shit old town of ours. Who knows? Maybe I'll stick around a bit longer once the dust settles. Oh, bud, easy on the sugar, low carb that with Splenda, you could use a little less sugar for that freshly-married fifteen there.”

“Once the dust settles?” I said out loud by accident. “What storm are you on about now, Zach?”

“You know what I mean, these projects, man, Hollywood, goddamn! It is so good to see you. Well, anyway, Hollywood is such a desert storm, you wouldn’t believe my work life, I don’t even have a personal life, I just call it my life.”

I had no idea what the fuck he was talking about, so naturally, I just took it as his needing to be the center of attention, as always. I had begun to notice that almost everyone in the coffee shop had been listening in intently to our conversation—and that almost all of them couldn't wait until their turn to jump in and offer up their support as an extra or key grip on Zach's set. I put a non-recyclable lid on my coffee and told Zach to give me a call sometime. He had that effect, like static clinging to clothing hung in a closet for generations, never letting go.

"I'll send you details, I know you've got that finance background, would be an asset to see your name on the credits! For you and I both." And, with that, I continued on with my boring, small-town day, the one that seemed so much more important before Zach had ordered his goddam six shots of espresso—I bet he didn't even know what the fuck he was getting himself into. But that was Zach. As long as it kept him braver, stronger, and bigger than everyone else (at least in terms of public image), he would jump blindly.

I didn't tell Mandy about my encounter when she called later that day, I had elected to keep it to our dinner date that night. At that point in our relationship, we had already begun to need all of the material that we could get when it came to talking about things over hot wings and craft beers.

I remained distracted from my work and shuffled through my desk drawers, looking for a gift I had gotten for Mandy. I ignored the gorgeous view of the mountains that cascaded through my floor-to-ceiling glass windows—something a grateful man who didn't know Zach Monte would truly admire.

I found the gift that I had bought for her that week after I had found out that Zach might be coming home. It was a small necklace that I then stuffed into my blazer pocket, a token of my assurance that Mandy was still *mine*.

I had spent some years with a psychotherapist going over my 'insecurities and avoidance issues' that had resulted from the Stockholm syndrome that was my relationship with Zach. I had made good progress, too, though Mandy never seemed to notice or support me through it all. She considered Zach a celebrity like everyone else, but she had an eloquent way of compartmentalizing it all and pretending as if she had never been in his basement back in high school, on that couch, with those plastic stars glittering on the ceiling above her like fake symbols of destiny in the night sky.

To be truthful, my biggest insecurity when it came to Zach was that Mandy still wanted not just him, but all of what he stood for. His departure from that town, the warm California sun, the fame, the career, the benefits of fucking something on the silver screen—it always came between us. I packed my briefcase early that day and anxiously went home to wait for Mandy, hoping that she hadn't made her own plans to see Zach already without my knowledge.

That night at the restaurant, what started as a sober conversation about seeing Zach at the coffee shop ended up as a drunken argument over wasted good food and beers—a fight concerning how she still wanted his dick in her.

"Yeah, you asked how I felt about it all; well, he was back, and I was a lost teenager all over again—fuck me."

CHAPTER FORTY-SIX

NOT ALL LOVE IS AN EQUAL BALANCE OF LUST AND TRUST—
SOMETIMES, SACRIFICE GETS IN THE WAY

ENTER: MANDY, 28. Wife to Joe. Insecure and far too good-looking and smart to live the boring life that she does; she knows this. Cheated on Joe during their early courting years in college and now clings ever-so-tightly to him as a means to neutralize her guilt. A bit haughty, but in a small-town girl, attractive kinda way.

"Okay, can you turn on the camera? Yeah, thanks. Okay, go ahead, Mandy, we're listening."

"Well, what can I say about Zach Monte? He was a one-of-a-kind guy, the successful, well-rounded jock that all the guys wanted to be like—well, maybe. He was a seemingly complex person but, deep down, I knew that he wasn't."

"Did you have a thing? It says here that you had a thing."

"Well, I'm not sure what *a thing* is, you would have to define that—are you asking if we fucked? Because, if you are, the answer is no. But, somehow, it's as if we had, even though we didn't, ya know?"

"I don't. I hear a lot of that sort of shit in Hollywood, but no, I don't know what that means; fucking is, well, fucking."

"Ah, you've lost someone."

"This interview isn't about me, it's about you, and Zach."

"Right, well, where to begin, then? Zach almost had the hearts of more guys than girls growing up. That isn't to say that he didn't have his fair share of female hearts that he liked to drag behind his lust-filled carriage —he liked to drag us, women, behind that carriage by the ankles through all of his shit, ya know? Anyway, some of the girls fucked him, some just pretended, and some were lucky enough just to be had by him. But I knew that he was more than that, I was more of the type to see what the other guys seemed to see in him—Zach was going places, and in a small town like Westfield, that meant headlines for a guy like him nearly every day."

"Give me some anecdotes, some stuff that happened."

"Well, I would often go to the football games and celebrate the wins with the other girls. Jesus, it was so fucking long ago, but I would go with the girls and we would celebrate Zach for the win; not the team. We used to call him Mr. November, do you know that song by The National? 'Mr. November'?"

"Yeah, everyone keeps referencing this fucking song, blue blood, great white hope, and all that—it's good, I'll use it."

"Well, anyway, Zach *was* the blue blood, the great white hope, as you put it. We would go to these games, sneak in some flasks of Sour Puss, you know, the sour vodka shit? God, I can't believe we drank that. We would sneak in the Sour Puss, get nice and tipsy, and then meet up with the team after the games.

“I remember this one time—do you want to hear about the parties? Is that helpful?”

“Sure, I mean, I want to know what drove this guy to do what he did—so, if it helps…”

“Well, he would come to these parties after and always try to get a girl down to the water so that he could take them out on this rowboat—he wouldn’t fuck them or force them or anything like that, he was actually sweet and would talk about how he was going to make them famous someday, as well. Say what you want, but Zach was driven, and that was contagious enough that he didn’t have to force himself on anyone, ever.”

“Sounds very Harvey Weinstein—you know, there’s a lot of lawsuits out there right now about that sort of thing, promises of fame.”

“Right, well, I don’t know who that is, but there was Zach, with a different girl in this boat, telling them stories of Hollywood, Broadway, of his achievements and his time spent in exotic places singing, dancing, and acting—he was the great white hope for all of us, and I think that’s something you really need to appreciate here if you’re going to tell his story. Truth is, I went out on the boat a few times, had some chats, smoked some weed and drank my Sour Puss. Zach always liked to drink tequila, so he would have some of that, too. We would share stories about our shitty Mathematics teacher who used to get these white, gummy saliva-type things in the corners of his mouth; it was fucking gross, but hilarious at the same time. We had lots of inside jokes like that, not just about teachers but about other people we deemed losers at the time. Bullying wasn’t really bullying back then, it was just what people did to pass the time.”

"Did you ever get the feeling that Zach was full of shit? I mean, making some of this stuff up to get girls to sleep with him? To get teachers to adore him? To have his name put up on the wall in the drama department?"

"Well, that's a hard question. Yes and no. We all knew that some of it seemed a bit surreal but, as I said, this is Westfield. Nothing happens here, so when something does, you *want* to believe it so much that you just sort of, you just do."

"Huh, yeah, not too different than where I'm from."

"Well, I imagine Los Angeles is quite different."

"You'd be surprised."

"What else do you want to know?"

"Tell me about Zach's return to Westfield, tell me about this film project he was directing."

"Well, I ran into Zach in Hollywood when I was down there for a friend's bachelorette party, and when I saw him—I mean, I love my husband, but fuck. He was so hot, surrounded by those musicians; he had really done it! Anyway, I saw him and all of a sudden I was back in that boat again, except he had achieved what he had talked about all along and I was just a tourist in his life. So, when Zach came back to town, saying that he was working on directing this new film project, well, I don't think I was alone in that boat thinking that he had finally returned to give us all a shot at some fame. Truthfully, well, it sounds rather pathetic, but I thought that maybe his promises were all about to come true for us; for every girl and every guy he had encouraged over the years."

"Encouraged? It sounds like deceived might be a better word at this point. But I love it, this is great, keep going."

"Well, we didn't know any of this shit that you're doing your thing about when he first landed, we all were just transported—transported back to high school, back to simple times where budgeting, mortgages, family, relationships, responsibility, all that shit didn't matter. Zach had returned and it was a return that was welcomed by me, despite what my husband was feeling. You know, I personally think that he planned this all along, that it's like his lifelong project—sort of like that movie *I'm still here.*"

"The lukewarm film with the incredible actor, yeah, I know it. Tell me a bit about Joe and Zach's relationship, about your relationship."

"Well, Joe loved Zach, truth be told. He was always by his side, idolizing him, imagining that he could be like him, buying the same shirts, shoes, and workout gear. Hey, are you going to put exactly what I say in this thing, or is it somewhat confidential?"

"I just need an idea of who he was and is. You're going to be portrayed in a certain way, but no direct quotes."

"And this camera?"

"Don't worry about it, it's just for continuity and information gathering. I need to *see* how you experience him, for when I put this whole thing together."

"Okay, well, yeah, so I loved the idea of Zach but sometimes sacrifice gets in the way. Joe was, well, he's the mature form of Zach who never had the dream but lived big in other ways, the ways that he had access to. Joe looked up to Zach, which is why he was so crushed when Zach left and abandoned him—those are his words, not mine. He left for school,

Joe went off and was successful, we hooked up, and that was that. They had bad blood for a long time; they still do, even more so now.

"Isn't Joe helping Zach out with his current… how do I say this? *Situation*?"

"Well, yeah, I mean, that's Joe, he pretends like he is strong enough not to care until someone really needs him, and then he's there again. Joe could never really say 'no' to Zach; he loves him, and that's what brothers do. So, yeah, he's helped him out with understanding the financials and all that, but that's just Joe."

"And what impact does Zach have on your relationship with Joe?"

"Getting personal now, are we? All I'll say is that when he arrived back in town, it was bad for our intimacy and relationship, but good for his and Joe's. They hung out together, they did shit that they did as kids. I mean, Joe knew something was up, but he was like the rest of us and just assumed that Zach had fulfilled the dream he had promised us all—that he was back to produce his grand masterpiece in our little town."

"How did Joe know something was up? When did he realize that Zach was, well, this?"

"Well, he knew Zach maybe was in trouble, funding-wise, with the whole project. Joe had mentioned to me over the summer that Zach was asking around for funding from everyone in town, promising that they would have a brand placement in his film, that it would be an international success for everyone involved and their businesses. It made sense, ya know? Still does, it makes sense that that would be a good way to give back to Westfield."

“But what if it wasn’t? What if it was a racket, a scam, bordering on legally reprehensible?”

“That’s one way to look at it. I mean, I just see a guy trying to do what he can for the people he loves.”

“How do you explain his *fiasco* in L.A.? You obviously heard about the scandal he was involved in, the theft of intellectual property, the blatant ripping off of a brilliant screenwriter who lived in poverty while someone else—Zach—got rich and famous off of his life’s work and struggle? Honestly, I’m just trying to piece this whole thing together, myself. I have no fucking clue what went on here and I need to know if what I am producing is genuine, if this really is his idea of a masterpiece.”

“You need to know that Zach is a sensitive guy; he would never want to directly harm anyone. I mean, I think that his desire to be someone, anyone, was just larger than his sense of responsibility to those around him”.

“That’s well put, can I use that directly?”

“Yeah, sure. Hey, what’s the title of this thing, anyway?”

“It’s undecided. I want to talk to Zach myself before I get this thing off of the ground, the studio insists.”

“This is so crazy. It’s like, Zach is bringing Hollywood to Westfield like he always promised, just not in the way he had intended.”

“Yeah, certainly not in the way that he had intended—I don’t think, at least. I’m still trying to make sense of it all, maybe he is a genius.”

“I heard that some French girl almost died. Did you get that for your film? I don’t know much about it.”

EXIT: MANDY

CHAPTER FORTY-SEVEN

After I had gotten back into the swing of things in Westfield, I began to notice how different things were for me. Sure, I was broke, but that never stopped an actor from achieving greatness.

I was staying at my parents' place as a means to better submerge myself in my story, or so I told others. I sat up in bed in my old bedroom, staring out the window at the setting sun that was threatening to hide behind the cascading mountains not some fifteen miles away. I was in my old, wooden, single bed—a bed that I could still smell the remains of teen sex drive in, emanating from the mismatched sheets and pillows. There was a small early 2000s television on the dresser and a collection of DVDs ranging from rom-coms to old war movies. I had spent many a night playing that televisions audio very loud to drown out the moaning and creaking of that same teenage sex drive.

I reached over to a pillbox and grabbed a few Xanax like they were Chiclets and took a pull from a tequila bottle that was sitting next to my bed. I sparked a joint, opened the window to let the cool air in and blew the hot smoke back out of the window as a rebuttal, with force. I smirked and laughed to myself and closed my eyes for what felt like an eternity.

I awoke to my phone ringing; it was Reggie, aka 'Regular Reggie,' as he preferred. *Strange to be hearing from him*, I thought.

I had met Regular Reggie in New York one night at a party and had found his eccentricities amusing. Regular Reggie had the kind of attitude I had, except he was more likable. He knew what it took to be someone in the shit-mix of fame and he often found friends in those who liked to fuck the system around just as much as he did.

There was no politically-correct way to put Regular Reggie, he was a six-foot-six black dude with tattoos on his eyelids, sported thick dreads and the look of *hustle constantly* pasted on the parts of his face that weren't covered in ink. His dress was eccentric but suitable for his name. To be honest, within the groups of people I had hung with, he looked like a regular dude who was up on his fashion sense. We all dressed like our personalities; at least, we tried to, and Regular Reggie was no exception.

Regular Reggie had made his way through life enduring the tough reality that despite his family's wealth, his mother had died during his birth—something that his father had enjoyed reminding him of whenever the opportunity had presented itself.

"Hey, Reg, happy Mother's Day," "Hey, Reg, too bad your mom isn't here to see what a Hollywood fuck-up you've become," or "Would you look at that son over there? He's behaving so well, he must have had a good mother." He was relentless, apparently.

Reg Reggie often joked that it would have been easier to grow up in the Bronx with no father at all than to endure the life with his father had offered him in a penthouse high-rise. I mean, the guy was literally fucked from the day he stepped into this world; no amount of psychotherapy can reverse a father's loss like that, nor a son's suffering at the hands of such a fate. Reg Reggie dealt with it as it came, and if it wasn't a 'Mom' face tattoo, it was a 'fuck the world' creative outlook that was destined to inspire some group of hipsters somewhere.

In fact, after the *Ghostship* fire in Oakland, Reggie had become somewhat of an icon for the outspoken street art he had done all over the central business district in San Francisco. The guy was everywhere anarchy decided to show its postmodernist, non-binary, anti-racial face, and he was typically behind bars as a result for a few days thereafter. He used his family's wealth and status to create radical change, and for that I admired the fuck out of him.

I answered the phone.

"How's it, my main grandmother-fucking shifty sailor?"

"Regular Reggie, what's going on, man"?

"I followed you, on that Instasham app you still use, all the motherfucking way to these erect mounds of rock that protrude into the cold Canadian skyline. Like hills of Greek-god phallic members of glory; I'm in Westfield! I got bored in NYC, what can I say?"

I sat up again, slightly dizzy from the pills, booze, and weed, and took another buzz off of the joint, this time not bothering to open my parents' window—I was all grown up.

"Shit, yes, where are you staying?"

"Fairfield downtown, if you can call it that. Where are you?"

"Uh, at my parents', you know, garnering that artist—"

"Poor bastard, just tell me that you need me to buy you drinks and girls all night. Yo! Consider it done, poor bastard, consider it done."

It was a welcome reprieve to confide my bullshit in someone who loved to see right through it—he was perfect for that chapter in my life.

We met at the strip club and had some tequila shots from a bottle that Reggie had brought with him from his recent trip to Mexico. We did some cocaine, licked some girl's asses over a lap dance, and found ourselves out back in the alley laughing by 1 am. Reggie stood out on a good day in a place like Westfield; hell, even in the back alley of a strip club, the guy stood out.

"Woooe WEEE, what a fucking town, Zach Monte. Now I know where you got your grit from, these bitches know how to treat a man. Goddamn, fuck L.A., my man, let's set up in WF and make it the fucking Vegas of the cold and wild north!"

We grabbed an Uber and drove around to a few bars that wouldn't let us in despite my best efforts of reminding them that I used to bounce there when I was underage. "I was the best and biggest sixteen-year-old bouncer you've ever seen!"

"Get the fuck out, buddy." The town had grown to accept outsiders, and these outsiders landed jobs as bouncers who didn't give a fuck about the locals.

"Let's go shit on the steps of your high school." Regular Reggie grinned. "Just a little shit, like, a high school-sized shit."

"My shits were huge in high school, like, protein, man." I laughed, showing him the size of my high school shits with my hands.

We took an M3 BMW Uber to the steps of my old high school and began to take pulls of a shitty bottle of tequila that we had grabbed from the store along the way. Regular Reggie ran over to the steps and literally took a shit at the door, then came back and lit a joint with his shit fingers.

“You know what, old Zach, man, you’re all right. I gotta go, but you’re all right. I know why you stole that Russian Fed fucker’s script, I get it, man.” His speech was sped up from the cocaine and I was speechless, I didn’t know that he knew. “Haha! Everyone knows, bro, I'm just cool as fuck enough to say it to your face. Your old buddy in NYC didn’t take to it; he fucking told half of Brooklyn and Manhattan. Listen, you gotta keep your bearings, man, keep your ship straight. This is Hollywood, this is the bare fucking bones of the industry; it’s built on people like you.” He took a long drag and spoke through the smoke as he exhaled.

“You were smart, man, steal from some Russian gay kid who likely would be imprisoned and murdered if it came out that he actually wrote that shit—come on, bro, that fucking guy, you did his Russian Fed ass a favor! No one would have ever seen that script if it weren’t for you, and now he’s rich and probably living in a massive house in Malibu where he can be as gay as a rainbow-colored leprechaun. I'm happy for him, really. It’s you who is suffering here, and that ain’t right by me. Everyone wins in H-Wood, man, everyone’s gotta win.” He took another pull of Canadian weed with total ease.

“Fuck me, bruh, this shit’s good up here. I’m rolling out tomorrow, man, back to NYC to make some coin.” He could see that I didn’t know what to make of it all. “If you ask me, dude, go overdose *lite*—take some pills and pop yourself into a nice day coma, just for a day or two, and make sure your agent gets your publicist behind it. All will be well, bruh.”

I couldn’t tell if he was being serious or not, or if he was staying or going. It didn’t matter. We smoked and drank and looked up into the stars as if we were back in high school, though I wasn't sure at all what his high school years had been like.

A slow, melodic, melancholy, 80s synth cover of "Come As You Are" came out from my phone speaker as I drifted through space and time under weather so warm that homelessness could be in fashion. As a saxophone rang through the air and the artist began to sing, "Well, I swear that I don't have a gun," I dumped a bunch of pills into myself that I had stowed in my pocket, drank some more tequila, and watched as the night sky above me spun like a turntable.

I was in Jerusalem, looking through a kaleidoscope at God's universe. The last thing I remembered was hearing a car roll up and then reaching over to find that Regular Reggie had left in typical Regular Reggie fashion. The man dropped in on the anecdotes of people's lives and left as fast as he had arrived—that was his luxury in life that he never fully appreciated.

At that point, I had taken his advice, whether he had been serious or not, and the headlines the next day in the small, insignificant town of Westfield would surely read:

School's out forever—Local L.A. actor and Westfield High graduate found unresponsive.

Zach Manuel Monte had been in town garnering serious interest and financial support for his latest film, which remains heavily secretive in title and theme. Monte had been working on enlisting as much local talent as he could to put Westfield on the board of places to visit and see. A true believer in the local arts community, Monte had made several presentations to local schools, media, and production companies in an effort to rally all the resources this town has to offer. Perhaps the project had proven too difficult to entertain? Too large in scope? Or perhaps it was the hardships Monte faced in his closed-door legal battles in Los Angeles that had followed him home?

Well, that was how I figured it would have read. But I woke up at 6 am to a teacher shaking my shoulder and offering me a shitty cup of coffee from the local 7-Eleven instead. I took the coffee and began to walk back to my bed, in my parents' home.

Just like the old days, I thought. *Took a shit on the doorstep and this place still believes in me; why shouldn't I?*

CHAPTER FORTY-EIGHT

I spent the next two weeks drumming up interest in my film, like my yet-to-be-written *Westfield Weekly* headline might soon profess. I spoke with local art studios; inquired to the local college about borrowing GoPros, red cameras, lighting, boom mics; and tried to gain volunteers from just about anyone in the city who had an ounce of film or audio talent in them—or, more importantly, money. It was helpful that I was regarded by these people as "one of the lucky ones" who had made it in the *real* world of film and that my mother was a dean at the college. I even had someone say that they had loved *Mexicali*—it was hardly a cult classic, but I owned it to get what I needed from them. I could feel the advice of Professor Calvin running through my veins; I had dragon's blood.

I managed meetings with a few local businesses who had reached out with an interest in investing in the project. I spoke with old friends and family members, promising them roles and stardom—any affiliation with Zach Monte was sure to promote some sex appeal for the men; importance for the women.

Shit was on the up until those local businesses began to do a bit of their own digging into Hollywood and how funding film projects actually worked. I lost a lot of potential capital when they had found out that it was an independent film with no storyboard yet.

Yet, despite their skepticism, I still had access to all of the pseudo-talent and camera gear in the city, so I didn't care. "You'll be sorry," I said, "you're missing out on making yourself a *real* name," I said, "you'll regret never working on the only important thing to ever happen in this shit town," I said. Westfield money men don't appreciate nor understand that sort of value or fame.

I released a formal casting call on the local news and announced that filming would commence in a few weeks—I still had no idea what the fuck I was doing, other than keeping myself afloat above the plebs that surrounded me. I was propped up high in the clouds, looking down on the rest of them as if I could never fall. There was no consideration in my mind that my bullshit would ever catch up to me; again.

All I needed was a story, any story, and that would surely keep my project moving forward. As *Jimmy* had said atop those Westfield hills, I was always destined to be so much more than this—I just had to sit and watch the fireworks. I *was* a story, so there had to *be* a story somewhere in it all.

After a few nights of heavy drinking and pot-smoking, I had decided that all I had to do was come up with a bizarre enough storyline that people would just assume that the creativity and talent that had gotten me into the movies in the first place would get me through the details of the project. I wasn't actually sure why I was pursuing the whole thing, but if Olivia had been there to ask me at that point, I would have told her (and only her) that it was to remain relevant and to finance one last flee from Westfield for good.

Certainly I knew that I wasn't going to be able to create something that would make any money. My plan was to make a shit film and write off the invested capital to myself as the writer, taking off to L.A. to restart my career. I had initially figured that there was enough free talent and equipment that I could film the project, make it seem legit, and get away with a new life. I had no idea what I was doing, I just kept doing it until the call came.

"Zach, this is Joel Perkins. I own a large oil and gas company; well, small in the big picture, but I've got a budget that might work for you—I love your movies."

Thank you, Prof. Calvin.

I met with Joel Perkins for the first time over a scotch and some appetizers at the restaurant of the hotel where Regular Reggie had stayed when he'd visited. It was a swank place that overcharged for just about everything, even the secret blowjobs that were on offer if you knew to request some lipstick from Jackie in the laundry room.

Joel and I chatted; well, I bullshitted for a few hours and convinced him that the secret plot and storyline were all part of the hype surrounding the project—I had never intended to be a con artist, I still don't like that term. Joel was reluctant, but he had so much goddamn *childhood me* in him that he finally trusted the Hollywood star sitting in front of him with one million dollars.

What Joel Perkins didn't know was that one million dollars was nothing in film and it sure as hell wouldn't float any real production for more than a few weeks. But I was "using local talent and production methods," which helped quash any questions Joel Perkins had around budgets and the film industry. With any luck, I would at least be able to bag 750k and restart my career with another *Mexicali* of sorts once I relocated back to L.A.

By the end of our meeting, Joel was so fucking thrilled to be talking to me that he cut me a check right there, drank his rye, and left for another meeting before I could tell him about the services Jackie from laundry provided—Joel Perkins seemed like that kinda guy.

-

It all comes so easy when you're famous, when you're what mountains were once considered to be back in the ancient days of old. I was a towering mound of rock spending time in the clouds among the Gods, while those humans below me looked up in fear and amazement from the bases of my rocky ridges and icy crevasses. For many years, people just survived and cowered to mountains like me; that being adventure enough. Take the Nepalese, for example, enduring the weather, the constant states of change and lack of food presumably caused by those Gods up in the mountains, always fearing the climb up to meet them.

In a town like Westfield, where surviving the mundane was adventure enough, it was going to take someone from afar who had become bored with looking up at Gods and mountains to see my holiness for what it truly was. I wasn't living in Nepal, there was no vast view to personify and deify, just a mountain of oozing, stinking shit that had the potential to erupt like Mount St. Helens at any moment's notice—all over the town of Westfield below it.

CHAPTER FORTY-NINE

THE NAKED TRUTH IS:
FUCK ZACH MONTE

ENTER: CREATIVE ARTS TEACHER, 32. Alcoholic (whiskey), emotionally unstable, divorced due to his inability to separate the acting-self from the actual-self. Spiteful and easily swayed by the powers of fame.

"Yeah, we can roll it."

"Jesus, Zach Monte. Working with him on this project, this fucking film. What a goddamn shit mix."

"Tell me a bit about your role in all of this."

"Zach approached the drama department at the high school, all joyful that he had received a million bucks to fund this film project; he wanted me to produce the goddamn thing with him. What was I to say? Sure, I know that movies cost more than a million bucks, but hey, the guy is from Hollywood, he knows things that a high school drama teacher doesn't."

"Well, he's actually from here, from Westfield."

"You know what I mean. He was the promised one, the talent, the real deal. Anyway, I took him up on it and, Jesus, was it a ride, or rip on my time, however you want to look at it.

"Listen, the guy is like Christianity, or the meth them riggers can't get enough of on their days off—a guy gets glued, stuck to a guy like him. Like he's gonna be your savior, take you away from this place. Every show tune on dem lips he taught me and every piece of bullshit spewed—if it was about him and me goin' somewheres, fuck it, I believed it all and ya best believe I went along. When we's was kids, we even went around with our girls together, hangin' out by the river, real good memories and all with that cat. True-blue kinda character but a no-bullshit-gunner, gonna-get-shit-done kinda attitude. I loved 'im man, fucken' eh. Gonna miss those theatrics and dreams of ours."

"Tell me about the craziest part of it all."

"Ha! Well, fuck, where do I start? Okay. Ha! I know. So, old Zach Monte comes to me one day with a handful of GoPro cameras and says that he wants to put these on… Wait, no… ha! I've got a doozy. So, the guy, everyone is wondering if he's actually kinda, ya know, fucked up in the head, mental-wise, you know?"

"What do you mean?"

"Well, the guy comes into the school one day babbling on all fast and such that he can see the faces of people in their youth when he looks at 'em—like he can see them as like, 20, 30 or something, even though they're in their eighties, nineties."

"He actually believed this?"

"Well. I dunno, that's the thing, right? No one knew with that guy, but he sure seemed to believe that all those old folks he rounded up were young-looking or something."

"Old folks?"

"Ha! You don't know half the story, do you, Cheech? The guy goes on roundin' up all these old decrepit types from the under-funded old folks' homes and tells 'em he needs 'em, that they got this great purpose before death in his movie, that he can see them for their life stories and all that shit."

"Ya know, they all thought he was just being kind and obliged, but Jesus, when I came to that first day on set and there was all one hundred of 'em standing there with their catheter bags in hand, Zach zippin' around taking video of them touching each other's faces, shaking hands, fuckin' what a disaster."

"I think I did hear about this."

"Well, you oughta! To be honest, it's the only goddamn funny thing that came of this. Bunch of old people for actors with no acting experience shitting themselves after standing around for hours enduring Zach Monte's diatribes and directions. He was yellin' at 'em, 'Dance here, touch her tits, grab his dick'—ha, goddamn, what a mess that was."

"He was telling them to grope each other forcibly? Fuckin' worse than Weinstein."

"Well, no, I mean, he suggested that they oughta give in to their primal urges as they were all about to die in a few years, anyway—believe it or not, they all started trying to fuck in the streets! It was all consensual and stuff, I think. He had two that he really liked, one he kept calling Olivia, she kept kissing the younger and older guys and girls, everyone was kissing, grabbing, all the shop keepers and neighbors got real upset. But old Zach, I gotta give it to him, he just kept on filming and directing."

"Sounds like quite the scene."

"Goddamn right, shame the fuckin' guy got busted and didn't know what he was actually doing. I always knew it, I always knew even when he was young and all them teachers praised him; he's just a pretender like the rest of us who watch those big Hollywood movies and pretend that we could be in them—important, worthy of film."

"But you got involved, you bought in, you *loved* him."

"Hell ya! Come on, you're what, an actor or something, right? You oughta know that we artists love this kinda shit—I don't think he knew it, but the real story is him. Shame he couldn't see that."

"You know, it is funny how you, the high school drama teacher, can see the story in this nightmare; it sounds like he never really listened to you as a friend."

"Zach? Oh, he was the best—you're getting this all wrong, Cheech. He was the best goddamn actor in town, still is. Look at all he orchestrated, do *you* know any actor who could have pulled all of this off? The guy is fucking brilliant! You asked me why I joined on, that's why I joined on—because I believe in the art and I believe that this is what Zach was doing all along."

"That's not the first time I've heard reference that he knew what he was doing all along, as if he was involving everyone in some grand meta-focused film that was his life. But I will be honest with you, the guy lost over ten million in the U.S. after stealing some script—he isn't who you think he is. Coming up here was not something he ever wanted to do, the guy fuckin' loathes this town; he told me so."

"Whatever, man, this shit over? He's the one in jail, not me."

"Do you know what, exactly, he was charged with?"

"Fraud, manipulation, stealing from others."

"So, he's a con artist."

"Man… confidence-*man*, not artist—I won't give him the satisfaction of that title until I see the fuckin' thing… but, hey, could be. I get to decide that title now."

"Let me fill you in a bit more here, *Cheech*, I'm curious what you think. Some are saying that this is the greatest living acting job ever pulled, that he is actually brilliant beyond anyone's initial perception of his actions. They're saying that he actually played the long game and that he had planned all of this out from when he was a teenager—that he really committed to this role. Some are saying that there's another director in town already poking around, interested in producing the *real* story here."

"Ha! Next thing you're going to tell me is that someone is you, there, Cheech."

"Yeah, *Cheech*, I am, and fuck, stop calling me that—what is it, fuckin' 1980? What is it with this town and the eighties, I know they sucked and I wasn't even around to see them. Jesus, what I was saying, what I'm telling you, is that Zach either grew this project from its infancy, or he's the dumbest motherfucker ever to have stepped onto Hollywood Boulevard. I'm going to make the art and the story that he's never been able to see: him."

"See, poor son-of-a-bitch, you're just like the rest of us—stuck in Zach's kaleidoscope as he turns it round n' round, watching us all for his entertainment."

"Whatever. Try having 150k in student debt; we all need a way out. I have no idea if his calling me was his plan all along, or if he's simply trying to get himself off and back into fame, but honestly, I don't give a shit either way. I've been paying down student loans for far too long. If Zach can be my big break, then, hey, man, I'm like you—I'll fucking take it! Shit, turn that camera off, fuck. Yeah, delete that bit."

CHAPTER FIFTY

THE NAKED TRUTH IS:
MY BOY'S A GENIUS

ENTER: THE MONTE FAMILY. Supportive parents, stern but loving. Father is an aloof alcoholic with a prescription pill addiction, mother is more insightful than she lets on. Unwilling to acknowledge having made the classic mistake of forcing their child into doing something that they actually wanted to do themselves–disappointed, but won't admit it.

"I'm recording, go ahead."

"He's my son."

"Yeah, I know, that's why I'm speaking with you. You're the perfect person to provide me some insight into this whole… thing."

"What do you want to know? And who exactly are you? What agency do you represent?"

"I'm an old friend of Zach's, from L.A. We go back, he wants me to help him out with this other project, which is related to the failed project."

"So, you want to interview me about Zach and his issues with the authorities—Do I need my lawyer?"

"Jesus, no. I just want to get an idea of who Zach was as a kid, what could have driven him to this end."

"To what end?"

"Are we going to do this all day, Mr. Monte? Or are you going to help your son out?"

"I just have a hard time seeing how this is going to help my son and his… his situation."

"Listen, I've got it on good authority that you and your wife curated Zach to be some famous actor from a young age—that you both invested not only your retirement plans in him, but literally your entire adult lives."

"I don't think you understand how these things work in our culture,"

"Well, then, explain it, please."

"We look after our family—family is first, and our role as parents is to get our kids as far up the curve as possible so that he can do the same one day for those in his life."

"You hear that he had a girlfriend he was going to marry in Paris? I heard that she died."

"You're being inflammatory, son. You want to call yourself a professional? Act like it."

"Did you hear about her?"

"Next question."

"Listen, I'm making a film here—love interests; there isn't a goddamn movie without one."

"I heard that he had some girl in France, yes; Zach was a popular guy. I mean, he's a popular guy with the girls, just like his old man was."

"I see."

"How is this going to help his legal situation?"

"My theory? Zach planned this all along. What do you think of that?"

"Well, if you mean he planned to be at the top of the game and a magnificent actor someday, I would say that he accomplished that at a young age—he's a great actor."

"No, I mean that this whole 'failed actor returns to his small town to launch an obscure indie movie' thing is his true masterpiece, the one he had been planning since he was a kid."

"You're telling yourself what you need to hear to make this thing, this thing that you're doing, I see. But hey, my Zach, I wouldn't put it past him. The guy *is* a genius on stage, have you seen him? I mean, he really shines in theater."

"Yeah, I've seen his movie. My theory, again, is that he knows his weaknesses and is incapable of actually writing anything, so he decided to have the story write itself by returning here and lighting the entire fucking city up in a blaze. But what I can't understand is the risk—I want to understand the mindset that someone must have to want to take that risk of swindling someone out of a million dollars and doing jail time just to make a goddamn film! It's pure madness!"

"Well, I don't know about this theory of yours. Zach is a good actor, but this seems a bit farfetched. He's always made some questionable decisions in life, at times."

"So, you think that he's a criminal?"

"I didn't say that, I said—"

"Right, well, what would you say if I told you that he actually reached out to me several months ago and pitched this idea?"

"He reached out to you several months ago and told you that he was going to try and get arrested? Why didn't you stop him?"

"Not exactly, he reached out and asked me to do one simple thing: show up to this town, on this date, and start asking questions and creating a narrative. I think that he *wanted* this to happen. Did you know that I studied screenwriting? That's no coincidence."

"Well, that might be good for his lawyers to know."

"This isn't about the crown, man! This is about the art! The drama!"

"You really do sound like him, you know."

"I think that he knew some shit was going to go down in this town, and that he was smart enough to maintain a backup story if it did."

"Might I interject, gentlemen?"

"Oh, hi, Mrs. Monte, glad you could join us on the call."

"I've been on the call all along, young man. You both need to pull your heads out of each other's asses—Zachary has been using both of you, all of us, all along."

CHAPTER FIFTY-ONE

THE NAKED TRUTH IS:
DESPITE ALL THE RAGE
ZACH IS A RAT IN A CAGE

ENTER: SGT. RAT FACE, 27. Steroid user, antisocial personality traits. One of those guys who looks muscular, can lift heavy weight but is actually just fat as fuck and out of shape. Arrogant, though doesn't have the social status to really pull that kind of thing off.

"I'm here at the Westfield PD office, recording with Sgt.—"

"So, what is this? How'd you get in here? I don't know what you fairies down in tinsel-town call this sort of a thing, a deposition? But up here in Canada, this sort of a thing is a formalized process."

"This isn't a deposition and I'm not a lawyer. I'm a screenwriter and a director."

"Jesus Mary fuck, Bill? Get this clown out of here, who let him in?"

"It's about Zach, Zach Monte? I think you knew him."

"Ho, lee, shit. That name has been ringing from the fucking church bells, ain't it, Bill? What the fuck does a big shot from L.A. want to do with that skid on my underpants?"

“Tell me about what happened here.”

“He’s fuckin’ right where he oughta be after all them years, is what’s up! Guy was a philanderer and a fuckin’ criminal from the start—cheatin’ his way through life like he was some important piece of meat.”

“It sounds like you have a history, the two of you.”

“History? Hell, we were friends at one time, but out of convenience, you know? Everyone pretended to be that guy’s friend, but everyone really hated ‘im. Just takin advantage of those old people like he did—classic Monte, classic asshole.”

“So, you know a bit about the case?”

“Know it? I fucking arrested the guy—happy to do it, as well. Really sweet victory for me. I got a girl now, a good mortgage on a nice place, good job, new Dodge Ram Quad Cab—I’m a made man! And where did all that schmoozin’ get that cocksucker? A ticket to lockup, with me as his gatekeeper. I love having him in the back there, to be honest, right where I can keep my thumb on ‘im.”

“You sound… vindicated, almost.”

“Vindictive? The fuck you sayin’, boy?”

“Vin-di-ca-ted—like you got your chance to get back.”

“Well, that I did, hey, Bill?”

“Who is Bill? You keep shouting for Bill.”

“Oh, old Billy? He’s in the back there, workin’ away on processing. He fuckin’ hated Monte, too. Didn’t ya, Bill? Ya old teabaggin' son of a bitch.”

“Tell me about his charges.”

"The guy stole a million dollars and got a bunch of old people to fuck in the streets, what can I say? Twisted, he was a twisted guy. Ya know what, though, he always did that sorta shit to get a rise outta the common people here. He was a real self-centered kinda guy. He'll rot now."

"You seem sure about that."

"I know for goddamn sure, because I'm his gatekeeper."

"Well, money talks. I heard someone is in town looking to bail him out of all this."

"Ha, would take goddamn God himself comin' down here for that to happen—and God ain't around, is he, Bill?"

"I think we're in for something special here. Zach Monte is no ordinary guy, there's people from my studio who would see him released to film my movie, and petitions from fans to have him released. Some of the footage from that film he was making has actually gone viral—he might have planned all of this and it could be big, real big."

"Is that your role, boy? Writing some movie about this shithead? Fact is, he's a goddamn criminal who belongs in that cage back there, surrounded by four concrete walls for eternity."

"Some would say that despite the cell he's in, he's still only surrounded by three."

"The fuck is that mumbo-jumbo tinsel-town metaphorical crap mean to a guy in a prison cell?"

"All the world might just be his stage, after all."

"Don't patronize me with your misinterpretation of first-year sociology concepts, boy—I took those same courses. That guy, whatever his name was, he wasn't talkin' about fairy-drama fucks like the two of you; he was talkin' about real men, with real hard-workin' jobs, and how we all come to be real men. I may be from a small town, but I ain't no fool. Now, get out of my office before I throw you between them four walls, too."

"Not four, three."

CHAPTER FIFTY-TWO

Aaron Sorkin really did famously once say: "Good writers borrow from other writers. Great writers steal from them outright."

At the end of all this, you might find yourself asking what this really means—and if it's really true. Is the world of entertainment really devoid of artistic integrity? Are we free to steal, plunder, and re-write any script or idea that we please?

To be honest, I knew what I was doing all along—and Aaron's words were a paint-by-numbers of my life since I first laid eyes on Sara. People will say that I was a criminal, or perhaps insane, and maybe that's the angle my lawyers should take when they represent me.

I'm now sitting in a jail cell keeping company with three men who probably don't know who Aaron Sorkin is, nor give a shit, and one girl who is pretending like she still doesn't belong here, but she does. No one is saying anything to one another—no one cares enough about life to bother.

While my companions are an unlikely gang of fuck-ups, surely here on charges related to domestic violence and solicitation, I'm someone that no prosecutor in this town knows what to do with. I stare into the eyes of these fellow inmates behind the cold, locked iron bars and all I find are the vacant glares of every Westfield life that was born to die.

On the wall, there is a date carved into it: 1988. That's the year I was born. It's crossing my mind now that I was raised inside this prison cell and that I never actually got out of it. Born into a cell in a small town, and no matter how hard I tried—no matter who I pretended to be, no matter how many old people I got to fuck in front of a camera or how many girls I slept with, myself—I've always been in this small, single-cell block of purgatory with no key.

I am Prisoner 1713, the illiterate-turned-literate man who wrote all of those books between his own four walls of insanity. I achieved, but I achieved it all while living with chains on my wrists and a cast-iron neck cuff around my throat. It's apparent to me now that Prisoner 1713 found his way to salvation through the ideas given to him by the pages that he taught himself from—and that I had lost my entire fortune for doing that very same thing. It isn't fair. Just imagine what that man could have accomplished if he'd had the same access to the world that I did for those brief eight years—maybe I would be quoting him instead of Mr. Sorkin.

My lawyers told me today that if I don't release half of the money that I (allegedly) stole, I'm stuck here for five years. The ironic thing about all of this is that I am the only person in this town who *had* that type of money to lose and not stress over—keyword being *had*. I'm fucking broke after my international relations flop with the Russian, and I'm still bitter at how he got paid for my hard work.

I placed a call out to an old friend who might be able to make all of this go away. I bet he's just dumb enough to think that this was my master plan all along—fucking hipster-artsy idiot. He isn't a lawyer or anything, but it might actually work if he's able to write something out of all this. There's a movie or a screenplay in here, maybe.

I'm looking around the cell now and tracing my fingers along the brick walls, trying to remember the feeling of Parisian stone, the history, the life of the walls in France. I'm getting a searing fire of pain through my heart as I'm now thinking that the only key to this prison died right in front of me and I did nothing to help stop it.

What if I hang myself? Fuck, that's an option, but not really—that didn't work in Paris, no one important had noticed or cared. What if I had stayed that day? Fuck, is it possible that she survived? What if what we wish into reality really does come true? I'm thinking now that she for sure was the only key to my release from this cell. I'm realizing that money is not a key; it's a coffin. It's Rat Face as a cell guard who promises you release if you give him enough dough week after week—but the truth is, he will never release you, no matter how much you give him. That fucking gatekeeper will just make your life worse off than it was before you started trying to sell him your soul; the parallels with fame are beginning to make me feel nauseous.

I'm thinking about my family and what they must think of their son, who ended up in a literal prison cell. I'm thinking of Joe and Mandy—why couldn't I just have recognized that no one ever leaves their cell when they come from a place like this? Why couldn't I have just found a cellmate like Mandy to die slowly with?

I could use that sheet over there to hang myself—fuck, I could do it, but I won't. *Your luck has run out, Zach Monte, no one to bail you out now*; that's what I'm thinking. I'm thinking that maybe there is a lesson here—not that I could learn from, but that I could teach others.

"You have a visitor."

Who the fuck could this be? I wonder. *Joe.*

"Zach, Jesus, bud."

Should I even speak to this asshole?

"What do you want, Joseph?"

"Fuck, it's really true. Look at ya now, sitting in this place."

"Yeah, you want to join me? This hooker over here looks pleasant enough."

Joe continues into what he came here to say to me, "I've watched you, bud, over the years. I've seen you struggle and suffer, and go through all of this alone. I wanted to drop in and at least see how an old mate was doing."

Mate? You're not a fucking Brit or Aussie—cunt. Joe's pretending like he found some culture over the years.

"I've seen your need for more, your desire and greed get the better of ya, bud. Look at you, look at what you've become. We were supposed to grow old, mate, hike those hills, do shit. I don't know what I'm sayin'."

He's weeping now.

"It's all right, Joe, be the little bitch you've always been."

"Is it? You're not all right, buddy. Mandy is a mess worrying about ya, and her grandmother." He pauses to cry. "Her grandmother, you made her make out with some old Polish veteran. Is it true? Are you actually, like, mentally sick? Is that your defense here? Because I don't buy it—*should* I?"

We should both be laughing at this point, I'm thinking.

"You've ruined it all. Mandy and I were fighting and she wants space. Space? I don't even know what that shit means! I didn't know what it meant when I last heard it in high school, and I don't know what it means right now."

"Are you here for relationship advice again, Joseph? I let you have her; if you can't handle her, that's your own fault."

"This is what you do, Zach. You fucking ruin everyone, everythin', all at the cost of your needin' a bigger, more accomplished, better, more worthy-than-everybody-else kinda life. But look at ya, you're a pathetic… motherfucker! Sitting there behind them iron bars, wondering what the fuck happened, where it all went wrong."

No, that isn't what I am thinking; I know what went wrong—

"I had hoped that you would grow up, finally, once you had all of this fucking fame and fortune. That you would grow up and finally stop trying to fuck over the world to get yourself a larger piece of it. Then I hear this news that you didn't even make your way in Hollywood, that you're a fucking fraud, that you stole to get yourself known—that movie you were in *did* fucking suck. It doesn't surprise me, though, Zach, that you came back here and tried to swindle all of us good people after swindling your way through Hollywood. A million dollars? Seriously? That guy has kids and a sick wife. Honestly, someone wants to do a movie about ya—I was interviewed, everyone was, some fancy guy named Jeff. I can't believe I fell for your shit again."

Jeff, jerk off number three came through. Smart man, he is, I'm thinking to myself. *That's one friendship that I'm glad to have maintained, unlike this babbling idiot in front of me.*

"You'll get your goddamn fame in the end, it's so fucking unfair. You're like the criminal who gets a goddamn Netflix special, except you'll probably be out of this cell to act in it—you goddamn asshole, you'll get your way as always and I'll be left in second place with a broken family."

"Thank you."

"Thank you for what? What the fuck does that even mean, *thank you*?" Joe asks, clueless, unsettled.

"Thank you for the inspiration."

"You're impossible Zach. Fuck off and die."

"Take it easy, Joe. Enjoy your wife, and your life—it's all part of the script. And not just my script, but your script, too."

I slink back into the darkness of the cell and push my back against the non-Parisian brick wall. And, with that, I just performed the greatest final act in the greatest living feature film of all time. Perhaps I was always a little bit too hard on the guy, but if I hadn't been, he never would have been the man that he was that day, speaking to someone like me in the tone that he did. I felt proud.

Lights, camera, purgatory; for now. I really need to chat with Jeff.

CHAPTER FIFTY-THREE

THE NAKED TRUTH IS:
GREAT FORTUNE *DOES* FAVOR THE FAMOUS

ENTER: OLIVIA, 32. Businesswoman but Parisian first, wealthy, cultured, but bored by French men. Secretly obsessed with celebrities. Aspired to be an American beauty pageant winner as a child (preferably from New York state). Strong ability to manipulate and control people, though mindful of when these tactics are employed. Despite her intelligence, still mistakes emotional train wrecks for a potential fairytale ending.

"My Napoleon, open your eyes. You need to get up, off of this floor and out of this place, you don't belong hidden away," says Olivia, whispering in my ear.

"It's not so easy. These bars that they've got me behind—well, they're not figurative like the way you and I used to talk. I've really done it now. I think of you, all the time. I always wonder what it would be like if we had made it together. Now I'm just here—alone, afraid, and useless."

"Do not speak to me as if I am dead and don't feed me your self-pity. Start behaving like yourself. You were born between the walls of a theater, do not shatter the fourth and break character now. You need to use him like you used me—you need to find Jeff and produce the masterpiece you were born to do. These people will never understand people like you and me. I can hear your thoughts whispering to you in the cold of night, telling you that you were born in a cell and that you will die of the same fate, alone. You are lying to yourself, Zachary—you escaped with me, I gave that to you and I am *still* giving it to you. Call for him, before time runs away on us again. You know what you need to do. You need to do what you have always done—perform.

"This is your opening act, your stand to greatness, not your curtain call. Now get up from this floor and dance in the flames of our slowly burning world; turn to ashes with me, Zachary. It is your destiny."

CHAPTER FIFTY-FOUR

Westfield Weekly

Artistic genius or con artist?

The verdict is out for former Westfield resident and movie star Zach Manuel Monte, who was found innocent on two counts of fraud this past week after his lawyers argued that the entire situation was actually part of a larger theatrical performance for his new feature film ***Bonaparte****, written and directed by Jeff Stephens.*

There was speculation that the one million dollars Mr. Monte received from a local businessman to produce the film was never going to be used for the project some were calling "despicable, offensive, and a sham." The prosecutors argued that he was going to write the film off as a loss, use minimal funds to produce it, and pay himself the one million dollars for his role as the screenwriter.

Monte's lawyers argued that writers receiving funds prior to production is typical in the budgeting for a film and certainly not out of the ordinary. They further defended that anyone who invests in a film is taking a risk and that although people might be "star-struck" by the idea of funding a major motion picture, they should not neglect their processes of due-diligence when vetting the legitimacy of their investments.

Nonetheless, the question of embezzlement was at the forefront of the case as Monte had transferred the full amount into an offshore bank account, which certainly did not work in his favor during the trial. This action is what initially prompted the local business owner's inquiry and the interest of local authorities to investigate and eventually charge Monte in the late summer of last year.

With Monte's agreement to release half of the funds back into the project "in an effort to make the masterpiece a reality," the film gained further attention by H4 productions in Los Angeles, California, which allowed for the film to continue production while Monte was out on bail.

For some background, the film follows a once-successful Zach Monte through France, where he allegedly lost his mind while on a film tour, having had tried to kill himself—twice. There is some speculation as to whether the events are true, as the woman Monte had spent much of his time with while in France is unavailable for comment and cannot be located.

The film then follows an older Monte through his process of being arrested and the subsequent court trial, where he defends that he was adding a theatrical edge to the project by actually living out the role as a mentally unwell writer, unable to come to terms with a failed acting career. He apparently asks us in his film, is it fact, or is it fiction?—a compelling proposition from a very controversial project.

To some, Zach is a true believer in the local arts community, and there is evidence that he has been since he was a child. Monte made several presentations to area schools, media, and production companies in an effort to rally all the resources that he could—an attempt to support local arts? Or an attempt to con? Some residents still question his motives.

The controversial film will premiere in Los Angeles next week and is expected to receive very positive reviews. It's not every day that Hollywood comes to Westfield, so get your tickets before the curtain drops locally—our very own Westfield premiere is bound to sell out fast.

CHAPTER FIFTY-FIVE

It's late spring and I've found my way back to Paris. I arrived in a G4 after successfully convincing the entire world that my poor attempt at fraud was the greatest feature film idea of all time. I feel no guilt; I act like I've just received an Oscar for my performance. I am Whitley, but I made it the Wilcox way.

Olivia's voice haunts me still, like it did for those entire two months that I spent in that prison cell—but she also has led me to my vision, to my salvation at this end. Now I'm here, standing in front of this same café that played stage to the start of the toppling of my empire.

EXT. PARIS CAFÉ - MORNING

ENTER: ZACH MONTE, 27, exits a small café to sit at a table set for two, alone. He looks around the square, feeling the cool fall air as he takes comfort in the warm espresso he holds in his hands. He takes a bite of a chocolate-covered croissant and puts it down on the plate across from him; Olivia's plate. He pulls a book from a brown leather Gucci satchel. He studies the book's binding and opens it to the cover page, only to quickly close it again as the waiter approaches.

WAITER

Anything else that I can get you, monsieur? Will you be eating alone today or should I prepare a café for—

ZACH

I'm alone.

(ignores waiter's exit)

Zach places Olivia's book on the table—*the* book from the day she died. He notices her blood still splattered on the cover and traces his fingers across it.

My therapist had warned me before I left L.A. that I would experience a heightened degree of sensory awareness and anxiety, should I decide to return. Now, sitting here in this café, the mopeds and laughter are almost too much to take in, but I continue with my scene.

He then slowly opens the book again and feels the parchment pages of the book—his book. As if he can smell her scent in the ink, he closes his eyes like a man reading braille and traces the outlines of the words until—A LETTER falls out of the book and into his lap. The book lies open on the table with the painting of Napoleon at Jaffa staring back up at him. His hands begin to shake as he unfolds the yellowing paper to read what it says:

OLIVIA (V.O.)

Napoleon, my dear Napoleon the conqueror. You have found me in this book next to a spitting image of yourself! Alas, I am glad that you have decided to actually read it, I know that you prefer writing life more than reading about it. I do know that you understand greatness, just not the toll it takes on others, which is why this book will find you well. I will always forgive you, though I worry more often than not that one day, this world may not be so forgiving to you. I can tell that something weighs heavily on your heart, but I also trust that your actions have always been for a greater purpose all along.

Zach looks at the vacant seat across from him with his half-eaten croissant in place of his guileless lover. He looks genuinely sad, as if displaying a real emotional response for the first time in his life.

OLIVIA (V.O.) (CONT'D)

Now read my words and envision the wine that we share swirling in our glasses, round and round till eternity comes to greet us—I am here to be with you and to drink down all of the entire, big, round, and flat world. Drink it in, mon amour—the nature of greatness always lies within the spirit of one's muse, and I am here, I have found you. With me in your world, there is no need to worry or rest uneasy—I am yours, forever.

ZOOM OUT TO SEE: ENTIRE SQUARE FROM ABOVE-CENTER

Zach sits at the table reading the letter as the crowds of people continue on with their obviously less-important days around him—no one is as still as Zach.

OLIVIA (V.O.) (CONT'D)

If you ever should need me and I am not around, you can always find me in that small café where I first gave you this book. You may order your favorite long espresso and chocolate croissant so that I can recognize the smells and tastes of you when my eyes can no longer find you in the dark. The day will come when there will only be one of us sitting at that table, and then another day more when there will be none. When that day comes, end this scene, and fade to black with me.

I push my hand deep into my pocket and feel the cold steel that I'd picked up from an old friend in that part of Paris that tourists don't visit. I take one last dramatic sip of my cooling espresso and wipe my hands of sticky crumbs, leaving the half-eaten pastry on the small table.

I stand up and walk slowly into the center of the square as the camera hangs above me—getting its all-so-critical final angle of the wreck of Zach Monte.

Finally, I am in perfect frame for all to see. I can't hear the sounds of the mopeds or their horns any longer. Clutching the steel in my hand, I pull the revolver out of my pocket, pushing the gun's cold metal hard against my temple. I can feel my heartbeat pulsating onto the muzzle of the gun as it wrinkles my skin upward and into my hairline. I act like I'm in distress, but I'm not; I feel redemption. I can't see the people running up to me to try and stop me—but I can feel them.

ZACH (V.O.)

A tragic ending in the only city capable of calling such a scene home—the guillotine rises. I will spill my final blood on this stage in the same way as Molière spilled his own. Yet, unlike Molière, there will be no widow to beg nor throw herself at the feet of a king—no mercy of a sacred burial on consecrated ground. I will go underground at midnight without pomp. Until then, I am the dark morning star that rises for all angles of light to cascade against, for all cameras to see.

My eyes look effortlessly up and into the sky. Entirely out of my control, the surrounding Parisian building walls are guiding my peripheral vision into the natural limelight of the sun. I gaze with burning retinas until they finally focus tightly onto my fame. Everything goes white, as Olivia and I fade to black.

CLICK, BANG.

FADE OUT.

About the Author

Brendan Alexander Kearns: A guy who apparently can't pick a single profession. He is a Canadian author, psychotherapist, commercial hard cider manufacturer, former professional chart-topping musician, avid traveller, surfer and climber. *Raconteur* was written during his time in Lyon, Paris, Southern California, New York and in his home in Canada.

www.ingramcontent.com/pod-product-compliance
Lightning Source LLC
LaVergne TN
LVHW091024080826
845145LV00002B/347

9780994937520